T0373916

WELSH FOLK TALES

Mae hi'n bwrw hen wragedd a ffyn.
(It's raining old ladies with sticks)

Diolch o galon
Three songbirds who trod these paths before:
Maria Jane Williams, Glynneath;
Marie Trevelyan, Llantwit Major;
Myra Evans, Ceinewydd.

WELSH FOLK TALES

PETER STEVENSON

The History Press

For my son, Tom,
and my mam and dad,
Edna and Steve

First published 2017
Reprinted 2018, 2019

The History Press
97 St George's Place,
Cheltenham, Gloucestershire, GL50 3QB
www.thehistorypress.co.uk

British Library Cataloguing in Publication Data.
A catalogue record for this book is available from the British Library.

ISBN 978 0 7509 6604 7

Typesetting and origination by The History Press
Printed and bound in Great Britain by TJ Books Ltd

CONTENTS

INTRODUCTION: CHWEDLAU

There is a Welsh word, 'Chwedlau', which means myths, legends, folk tales and fables, and also sayings, speech, chat and gossip. If someone says, 'chwedl Cymraeg?', they are asking, 'Do you speak Welsh?' and 'Do you tell a tale in Welsh?' Here is the root of storytelling, or 'chwedleua', in Wales. It is part of conversation.

The writer Alwyn D. Rees explains that when you meet someone in the street, you don't ask how they are, you tell them a story, and they will tell you one in return. Only after three days do you earn the right to ask, 'How are you?'

One afternoon, I was talking to a friend in a shop when a 'storiwr' spotted us through the window, did a double take, came in, and without pausing for breath, began. 'You know my next door neighbour? Miserable old boy, never had a good word for anyone, how his wife put up with him. Well ...' Twenty minutes passed. He finished his tall tale, said, 'There we are', and left the shop. He had spotted a performance space and an audience, and he had a story stirring in his mind. There was no way of telling whether it was true or invented, and its likely he didn't know either. This happens all the time in the west. Takes forever to do your shopping.

The Welsh story writer, quarryman and curate, Owen Wynne-Jones, known as Glasynys, told of a tradition of storytelling when he was a child in Rhostryfan in Snowdonia in the 1830s, and of his mother telling fairy tales in front of the fire. Sixty years later, the writer Kate Roberts, from nearby Rhosgadfan, thought Glasynys's recollection might well have been true of the people in the big houses, but there was no tradition of telling fairy tales amongst the cottagers. She added:

> But there was a tradition of story-telling in spite of that, quarrymen going to each other's houses in the winter evenings, popping in uninvited, and without exception there was story-telling. But these were just amusing stories, a kind of anecdote, and fellow quarrymen describing their escapades ... the skill was to make these amusing stories seem significant. I remember literary judgements being passed by the hearth in my old home: if anyone laughed at the end of his own story, or if he told the story portentously and nothing happened in it. Indeed, the way we listened to story-tellers like that was enough to make them stop half way, if they had enough sense to notice. But anyway, the tradition ... could have come indirectly to the quarrymen of my district, because many of them originated from Llŷn, where I believe traditional story-telling took place.

Kate Roberts

Pen Llŷn was renowned for its storytellers. They were farmers, poets, sea captains, garage mechanics, artists, mothers, quarry workers, crafts folk, preachers and teachers, and they moved effortlessly between gossip, fairy tale, politics, songs and criticism. Their fuel was humour.

They would tell you, 'When the gorse is in bloom, it is kissing time'. There are three species of gorse, their flowering times overlap, so it's always kissing time in Wales. When the pair of ceramic dogs in the window faced away from each other, it was a message from the lady of the house to the gentlemen of the village that her husband was away. And the tylwyth teg, the 'fair folk', were everywhere, small and otherworldly, tall and human, inhabiting the margins of our dreamworld, that space between awake and asleep, where time passes in the blink of a crow's eye or freezes in an endless fatal heartbeat. Elis Bach lived at Nant Gwrtheyrn in the mid-1800s, and frightened anyone who met him. He was a farmer, a dwarf, a mother's son, and everyone agreed he was 'tylwyth teg'.

The storytellers spoke for their communities. Eirwyn Jones worked in a carpenter's shop in Talgarreg, and was known after his home village, 'Pontshan'. His stories were often scurrilous and hilarious. 'Gwell llaeth Cymru, na chwrw Lloegr,' he said, 'Better Welsh milk than English beer'. He once walked to an Eisteddfod in Pwllheli where he and a friend slept the night on a rowing boat in the harbour, only to find the morning tide had washed them out to sea. There they stayed, telling tales to the mackerel, till

Eirwyn Pontshan

the tide flowed in again. At least he had time to wash his socks. 'Hyfryd iawn,' he said, 'very lovely'.

Old Shemi Wâd sat outside the Rose & Crown in Goodwick spinning yarns to the children about how the seagulls had carried him over the sea to America.

Twm o'r Nant from Denbigh travelled from village to village performing 'interludes' from the back of his cart. Myra Evans collected fairy tales and gossip from her family and neighbours in Ceinewydd, filled sketchbooks with drawings of local characters, and documented a way of life rooted in 'chwedlau'.

Shemi Wâd

Myra Evans

In lime-washed farmhouses in the hills, conjurers recited charms from spell books and kept potions in misty brown bottles. Harpers disappeared into swamps, dreamers vanished into holes in the ground, drowned sailors called to long-lost lovers and castles were preserved as bees in amber. Stories, history and dreams entwined as memory.

Into this land came travelling people. The Romani arrived in the mid-1700s, with tales of Cinder-girl and Fallen Snow, ladies darker by far than Cinderella and Snow White. Somali sailors came to work in Cardiff docks in the 1800s and stayed, saying, 'A person who has not travelled does not have eyes'. Refugees fled Poland after the Second World War and settled on Penrhos Airfield near Pwllheli, where their families still live in 'the Polish Village'. The Cornish traded with Gower and worked in the lead mines, Italian POWs became farmhands and married local girls, and Breton men cycled the lanes selling onions. All the while, the Welsh emigrated, fleeing poverty and loss of land, becoming miners and missionaries, searching for new hope in the Americas, Australia and Asia. Their stories travelled with them. There are echoes of old Shemi's tall tales in the Appalachian Liar's Competitions. Honest, there are.

No amount of caravan sites, bypasses and barbed-wire fences can hide an ancient enchanted land with tales to tell. Standing stones double as gateposts. A Lady of the Lake lives beneath a pond in the midst of a Merthyr council estate. An old church in Ynys Môn was converted into a mosque that now overlooks a nuclear power station. Wind farms have grown amongst the ruins of peat cutters' cottages on Mynydd Bach. You can trampoline in the depths of a disused slate mine in Snowdonia. Red kites wheel in the air over the National Library of Wales where twenty years ago they were near extinct. Trees once pulled their roots from the ground and marched into battle, where spruce and fir now grow. And a woman was conjured out of flowers to satisfy the whims of a man.

Kate Roberts said, 'I'm a thin-skinned woman, easily hurt, and by nature a terrible pacifist. My bristles are raised at once against anything I consider an injustice, be it against an individual or a society or a nation.

Indeed, I'd like to have some great stage to stand on, facing Pumlumon, to be able to shout against every injustice.'

Storytelling has always offered an ear to those who feel their voices are lost in the wind, or caught in an electronic spider's web. It draws upon an archive of folk tales, memories of times of upheaval, personal philosophies, revolutionary ideals and the comfort that we are not alone in our dreams. Storytelling is the theatre of the unheard.

There is an old story of a Welshman who was bursting with a secret, so he told it to the reeds that grew by a pond. A piper cut the reeds to make a pipe, and when he blew, he played the secret for everyone to hear. You could whisper a message to a songbird, who would fly to your lover and sing to them of your heart's desires. The lakes and streams are looking glasses into this world. There are no secrets here. Listen. You will hear stories. Hush, now.

BRANWEN, RED AND WHITE BOOKS

Charlotte and *The Mabinogion*

Around 1350, the 'White Book of Rhydderch' was thought to have been copied out by five monks at Ystrad Fflur in Ceredigion for the library of Rhydderch ab Ieuan Llwyd, a literary patron from Llangeitho. A few years later, Hywel Fychan fab Hywel Goch of Buellt wrote out the 'Red Book of Hergest' for Hopcyn ap Tomas ab Einion of Ystradforgan. These two books contain the earliest versions of 'Y Pedair Cainc Y Mabinogi [the Four Branches of the Mabinogi]', the ancient myths and legends of Wales. They are written in an old form of Welsh, and lay largely unknown to the wider world until William Owen Pughe translated the story of Pwyll into English in 1795 under the title, *The Mabinogion, or Juvenile Amusements, being Ancient Welsh Romances*, while leaving out the sexual shenanigans. In 1828, the Irish antiquarian Thomas Crofton Croker published Pughe's translation of *Branwen*, which caught the attention of the sixteen-year-old daughter of the Ninth Earl of Lindsey.

Charlotte Guest

Charlotte Bertie was a free-thinker, a rebel and a Chartist, who disapproved of her aristocratic parents' politics. Aged twenty-one, she married John Guest, manager of Dowlais Ironworks, and moved from Lincolnshire to Wales. On her husband's death she took over as manager, created a cradle-to-grave education system, built progressive schools, supported Turkish refugees, learned Persian and Welsh, brought up ten children and read them fairy tales. When Pughe died in 1835, she completed his translations of the Red and White Books into English, and published them three years later as *The Mabinogion*.

Within Guest's book are the Four Branches of the Mabinogi. They have a narrative structure very different to literature, a sense of tales for telling. They sketch only the bare bones of characters, moving through time and space as if they were mist, and make little attempt to be moralising or didactic. They are tales of the tribe, snapshots of moments of upheaval in the history of the land.

The first branch tells of friendships and relationships, the meeting of Pwyll and Rhiannon, and the birth of Pryderi, the only character to feature in all four branches. The second concerns the avoidance and aftermath of war between Bendigeidfran of Wales and Matholwch of Ireland, and Branwen's doomed arranged marriage. The third tells of the human cost of immigration, settlers and craftsmen forced to move on, and Manawydan's frustrated attempts to hang a mouse who has stolen his corn. The fourth describes the pain of desire, the rape of Goewin, Arianrhod's virgin births, her sibling rivalry with Gwydion, and the objectification of Blodeuwedd.

Guest's politics influenced her passion for the female characters, and through her translation the myth of Branwen became known far beyond Wales.

Branwen Ferch Llŷr

Bendigeidfran fab Llŷr, the giant King of the Island of the Mighty, sat by the sea at Harlech in Ardudwy, with his brother Manawydan and his two half-brothers, Nysien, who could make peace between two armies, and Efnysien, who could cause war between two brothers.

Bendigeidfran saw thirteen ships approaching from the south of Ireland, sailing swiftly with the wind behind them, flying pennants of silk brocade. One ship drew ahead, a shield raised with its tip pointing upwards as a sign of peace. A voice cried out, 'Lord, this is Matholwch, King of Ireland, seeking to unite his land with yours by taking your sister Branwen ferch Llŷr, one of the Three Chief Maidens of the Island of the Mighty, as his wife.'

A council was held at Aberffraw. Great tents were erected, for Bendigeidfran was far too big to fit in a house, and a feast was prepared. Bendigeidfran sat in the middle, Matholwch next to him and Branwen by his side. They ate and drank, and when everyone thought it would be better to sleep than feast, they slept. That night Branwen slept with Matholwch.

Efnysien had not been told of his sister Branwen's marriage, and he was furious. He went to the stables and took hold of Matholwch's horses, cut off their lips to the teeth, their ears flush to their heads, their tails down to their crops, and where he could get hold of their eyelids he cut them to the bone. He maimed those horses till they were worthless. When news reached Matholwch, he was insulted and humiliated, and prepared his ships to sail. Bendigeidfran sent a messenger to explain that he had known nothing of this and he offered gifts as compensation, a new horse for every one maimed, a gold plate as wide as his face, and a silver staff as thick as his little finger and as tall as himself.

Matholwch returned to Bendigeidfran's court. A council was held, tents were erected, and they feasted, though Matholwch's conversation seemed touched with sadness. Bendigeidfran offered him another gift, a Pair Dadeni, a Cauldron of Rebirth, saying, 'If one of your men is killed in battle, throw him in the cauldron and the following day he will be alive, though unable to speak'.

Matholwch asked where the cauldron came from. Bendigeidfran explained it had been given to him by an Irishman, Llasar Llais Gyfnewid. Matholwch knew Llasar. 'I was hunting in Ireland, when this huge red-haired man walked out of a lake with a cauldron strapped to his back. A woman and children followed him, and if he was big, well, she was enormous, as if she was about to give birth to a baby the size of an armed warrior. They stayed at my court, grumbled about everything, and upset everyone. After four months, my people told me to get rid of them, or else they would get rid of me. So I employed every blacksmith in Ireland to build a hall of iron and fill it with charcoal and beer. Llasar and his family followed the smell of the beer. Once they were inside, I locked the door, set fire to the charcoal, and the blacksmiths blew on the bellows till the house was white hot. Llasar drank all the beer, punched a hole through the molten wall and they escaped, taking the cauldron with them.'

After a night of singing and feasting, Matholwch set sail in thirteen ships for home, taking Branwen and the cauldron with him. In Ireland, Branwen was embraced and offered brooches, rings and jewels. In nine months she gave birth to a son, Gwern, who was taken from his mother and given to foster parents, the finest in Ireland for rearing warriors.

When Matholwch's people learned of the cruelty inflicted on his horses, they mocked him, and he knew he would get no peace until he took revenge on the Welsh. So he threw Branwen from his bed, sent her to work in the kitchens, and ordered the butcher to slap her face each day with his bloodied hands. For three years, her only conversation was with a starling who sang to her from the kitchen windowsill. She poured out her heart and wrote a letter to her brother Bendigeidfran telling him of her woes, tied it to the bird's wing and sent it flying towards Wales.

The starling found Bendigeidfran at Caer Saint in Arfon. It sat on his shoulders, ruffled its feathers, and sang. When Bendigeidfran heard of his sister's punishment, he called a council of the warriors of the Island of the Mighty. They came from all one hundred and fifty-four regions, and after feasting, they set sail in ships bound for Ireland. Bendigeidfran, with his harpers at his shoulders, waded through the water, for the sea was not deep and only the width of two rivers, the Lli and Archan.

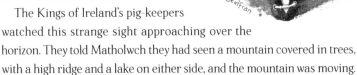

Bendigeidfran

The Kings of Ireland's pig-keepers watched this strange sight approaching over the horizon. They told Matholwch they had seen a mountain covered in trees, with a high ridge and a lake on either side, and the mountain was moving.

'Lady, what is this?' asked Matholwch.

'I am no Lady,' said Branwen, 'but these are the men of the Island of the Mighty. They have heard of my punishment.'

'What are the trees?'

'Masts of ships.'

'What is the mountain?'

'My brother Bendigeidfran, wading through the shallows, for no ship is big enough to hold him.'

'And the ridge and the lake?'

'The ridge is his nose and the lakes are his eyes.'

Matholwch and the warriors of Ireland retreated over the Shannon, and burned the bridge behind them. When Bendigeidfran and his army reached this strange river, he made a bridge with his own body and his warriors crossed over.

Matholwch sent a messenger to Bendigeidfran offering compensation for Branwen's punishment. He offered to make her son, Gwern, King of

Ireland. Branwen advised Bendigeidfran to accept, for she had no wish to see her two countries ravaged by war. A council was held, Matholwch built a house bigger than a tent, big enough to hold Bendigeidfran and the men of the Island of the Mighty, and peace broke out.

But the Irish played a trick. They hammered long nails into every one of the hundred pillars that held up the house, hung a skin bag, a belly, on every nail, and in every belly they hid an armed warrior, two hundred in all. Efnysien entered the house, smelled the air and looked around with eyes blazing. He asked what was in the bellies, and was told, 'Flour, friend'. He prodded the 'flour' until he felt a warrior's head, and he squeezed it until his fingers cracked the skull into the man's brains. He placed his hand on another belly, asked what was inside, and the answer came, 'Flour, friend'. Efnysien squeezed every bag until there was not a man alive. Then he sang in praise of himself.

Matholwch entered the house, seated himself opposite the men of the Island of the Mighty, and crowned Gwern King of Ireland. Bendigeidfran called the boy to him and mussed his hair, then passed him to Manawydan, until everyone had fussed him. All except Efnysien. Bendigeidfran told the boy to go to his uncle, but Gwern took one look at Efnysien and refused. Efnysien cursed, stood up, took hold of the boy by his feet, and hurled him head first into the fire. Branwen saw her child being burned alive, and leapt towards the fire, but Bendigeidfran held her between his shield and shoulder. All the warriors rose to their feet, drew their weapons, and there was a most terrible slaughter.

The hall was strewn with the bodies of the Irish dead. They were stripped to the waist and tossed into the Pair Dadeni until the cauldron overflowed. The following morning they crawled out alive, scarred and mute. Soon the hall was strewn with the corpses of the men of the Island of the Mighty. Efnysien saw that he had caused this, and would be shamed if he were not to save his comrades. So he buried himself with the Irish dead, was stripped to the waist, and thrown into the cauldron. He stretched himself across the rim, and pushed until the cauldron shattered into four pieces. Efnysien's heart shattered too, but his redemption spurred the men of the Island of the Mighty to victory, if victory it was.

Bendigeidfran was wounded in the foot with a poisoned spear, and only Branwen and seven men escaped, Pryderi, Manawydan, Glifiau, Taliesin, Ynog, Gruddieu and Heilyn. Bendigeidfran ordered his men, 'Cut off my head, take it to the White Hill in London, and bury it facing France. But first, go to Harlech and feast for seven years. The birds of Rhiannon will sing to you, and my head will keep you entertained as if I was alive. Then go to Gwales in Pembrokeshire, and look towards Aber Henfelen in Cornwall. Stay for eighty years, I will be with you, then open the door, and bury my weary head in London.'

So the seven men cut off Bendigeidfran's head, and sailed with Branwen to the Island of the Mighty. They rested at Aber Alaw on Ynys Môn, and Branwen turned and looked back at Ireland, and cursed the day she had been born. 'These two good islands destroyed because of me,' and her heart broke in two, and she was buried there, in a four-sided grave on the banks of the Alaw.

And the Second Branch of Y Mabinogi nears an end.

Branwen

LADIES, LAKES AND LOOKING GLASSES

The Lady of Llyn y Fan Fach

On the Black Mountain lived a dreamer, a poet and a romantic named Rhiwallon, whose job was to look after his mother's cows. One day, he saw a herd of small milk-white cattle grazing on the meadowsweet that grew round the edge of Llyn y Fan Fach, and standing in the water was a girl, plaiting her red hair. He felt an urge to give her a gift, but all he had was his lunch. So he offered her some stale bread. She took one look at the bread, grinned like a Cheshire cat, told him he'd have to try a lot harder than that, rounded up her cows and vanished beneath the water.

Rhiwallon was entranced. He decided to impress her with softer bread, so he asked his mother for some unbaked dough, and he sat by the lake and waited. The milk-white cattle appeared, followed by the girl, who was nibbling water-cress. He offered her the dough, it squelched between her fingers. She stared at him, shook her red head, laughed like a donkey and vanished, cows and all.

Llyn y Fan Fach

Rhiwallon was entirely enchanted. All he needed was bread that was neither hard nor soft, and she would be his. His mother made him some lightly baked muffins and he sat by the lake and waited. When she appeared he offered her a muffin, which she sniffed, nibbled a little and then gobbled it down. He begged her to be his wife. She looked bemused, wiped the crumbs from her mouth, pulled the pondweed from her hair, and said if she ever received three unfortunate blows in any way other than love, she would leave him forever. He said he would rather sever his hand than strike her, so the marriage was agreed.

She brought a dowry of milk-white cattle, and counted them out of the water in the old way: 'un, dau, tri, pedwar, pump', remove a stone from one pocket and place it in another, 'un, dau, tri, pedwar, pump', over and over.

Time passed. She raised three fine sons, and taught them about the medicinal properties of water and the curative nature of herbs. But she rarely smiled and never laughed; there was a melancholy in her.

At a christening, she told the mother that the child would die before his fifth birthday. Rhiwallon gripped her arm and told her not to be so miserable, for this was a celebration. She freed herself and told him that was the first unfortunate blow.

At a wedding, she burst into tears, for she thought the couple were doomed to unhappiness. Rhiwallon held her by the shoulders and told her this was a time to smile. That was the second unfortunate blow.

At a funeral, she burst out laughing, for her friend was now free of worldly cares. Rhiwallon pushed her out of the church and told her to pull herself together. The third, and final, unfortunate blow.

She whistled her cattle, the brindled, bold-freckled, spotted, white-speckled, four mottled, the old white faced, the grey Geigen, the white bull, the little black calf suspended on the hook. They followed her over Mynydd Myddfai, even the slaughtered little black calf came alive and galloped after them, and they all leapt into Llyn y Fan Fach and vanished.

Rhiwallon raised his three sons alone, and they grew into fine young men. One day their mother appeared, and told them they were to use their knowledge of herbs and water to care for others. They developed cures for aches and pains, charms for melancholy and miseries, potions for gloom and despondency, and they became the most famous healers in Wales – the Three Physicians of Myddfai.

But they never cured their mother, for there was nothing wrong with her.

The Lady of Llyn y Forwyn

A farmer from Ferndale fell in love with a young woman who lived beneath Llyn y Forwyn, where she tended her herd of milk-white cattle. He courted her, they were married and lived happily at Rhondda Fechan, and each morning she was heard singing to her cows. A girl at Ysgol Llyn y Forwyn, when asked if she knew the story, said, 'Yeah, saw her this mornin' on me way to school. She was singin'.' The lake is now surrounded by a housing estate, and a wooden statue of the lady was charred by fire a few years ago, when arson was popular with the valley boys.

Ladies, Lakes and Looking Glasses

The Fairy Cattle of Llyn Barfog

Llyn Barfog

One morning in late summer, a cattle farmer from Cwm Dyffryn Gwyn was standing on the hill above Llyn Barfog when he saw a gwraig annwn, a lady of the Otherworld. She was dressed in green, with ivy and holly berries in her hair, and rouge smeared on her lips. She was tending a herd of small milk-white cattle who were grazing on the meadowsweet that grew by the side of the lake. The farmer desired one of these milk-whites, so he caught a small one and tethered it in his farmyard. He barely noticed the lady.

The little cow was eager to please, and gave the finest, foamiest, frothiest milk, cream and cheese. She flirted with the Welsh Blacks and soon the farmer had the sturdiest herd of breeding cattle, and he became the richest man in Meirionnydd. But his wealth drove him mad. As the fairy cow grew old, instead of putting her out to pasture, he fattened her for slaughter. Killing Day came and the butcher raised his knife. There was a shriek and the butcher's arm froze in mid-air. The lady appeared from the lake, dripping with slime and pondweed, and whistled for her little cow to come home.

The cow ran to her mistress, leapt into Llyn Barfog, and where she touched the water, a white water lily grew. All her children, Welsh Blacks and milk-whites alike, followed their mother into the depths and soon the whole lake was covered in white water lilies, as it is to this very day.

And the rich farmer was a poorer man for the rest of his days.

The Red-Haired Lady of Llyn Eiddwen

Llyn Eiddwen

There I was, sat drawing by Llyn Eiddwen on Mynydd Bach, when a farmer with short bottle-red hair, a ruddy outdoor face, big smile and an even bigger baggy multi-coloured jumper and little black leggings, sat down next to me, and asked, 'What you doin', love?' and offered me a fairy cake.

Now, I had been warned not to speak to any strange red-haired women on Mynydd Bach, as one is known to live in the lake where she tends her herd of snow-white cattle who paddle in the shallows at dusk. The lake was the site of rave parties in the late 1800s when a wealthy young man, Mark Tredwell, built a castle on the island, and kept a private army of boys mounted on Shetland ponies. In 1819, Augustus Brackenbury, a gentleman from Lincolnshire, bought the commons around Llyn Eiddwen to build another castle. The boys of Trefenter, thinking Brackenbury had no right to buy the commonly owned land where they dug their peat, dressed themselves as women and demolished the castle in one night. The battle over land rights and enclosures lasted ten years, and is known as the War of the Little Englishman.

Another Lady lived just down the valley in Llyn Fanod, and a beautiful creature once walked out of nearby Llyn Farch, only to be shot for the pot by a local farmer. There were more Ladies at Llyn Syfaddan, Llyn y Morwynion, Felin Wern Millpond, Llyn Du'r Ardu, Llyn Dwythwch, Llyn Corwrion, Llyn Coch, the Pool of Avarice at Twmbarlwm, the Taff Whirlpool, and more. They are voices from the past, visible in the reflections in the water, memories of those who lived there before valleys flooded.

I told these stories to the red-haired farmer and asked if she had ever seen the red-haired Lady of the Lake. She bellowed with laughter, and said that no lady could ever live in Llyn Eiddwen. 'It's full of leeches. She'd be eaten alive.' Then she told me tales of encounters she had when she was a girl with the tylwyth teg, corpse candles, and fairy funerals. And off she went down the lane, singing.

Well, I reckon I met the red-haired lady that day. And I have a stale fairy cake to prove it.

Dreams and Memories

A young servant from Nannau was in love with the dairymaid at Dol-y-Clochydd. One dark night, he was on his way to propose to her when he fell into Llyn Cynwch near Dolgellau and sank to the bottom. He found himself in a beautiful garden full of flowers and herbs that surrounded a marble palace. He knocked on the door and was greeted by the King of the Fairies. The King recognised him as a lost lover, so he led the servant along a tunnel to a slate door. The servant stepped through the door and found himself in the kitchen at Dol-y-clochydd, where the dairymaid was sat by the hearth weeping because her lover had been missing for months and she thought him drowned. They embraced, she kissed him on the lips, and the King closed the door.

In 1936, the writer T.P. Ellis, who told this story, wrote, 'I asked one of the shareholders of the local water company if he knew what was at the bottom of Llyn Cynwch, and with a brain-wave of super-realistic rationalism, he said, "Yes, mud".'

SUBMERGED CITIES, LOST WORLDS AND UTOPIAS

Plant Rhys Ddwfn

In Cardigan Bay, between Pen Llŷn and Pembroke, was once a fabled land of forests and villages. The people were fair and handsome, though small. They cared for the land as if it was their own, but never once believed they owned it. They planted forests where they hunted and foraged, and always left offerings in exchange for anything they took. This was the land of Plant Rhys Ddwfn, the Children of Rhys the Deep – not deep below the sea, Rhys was a thinker, a philosopher. He planted herbs that hid his land from the prying eyes of the mainlanders. Only if you

Plant Rhys Ddwfn

stood on the one small clump of this herb that grew on the mainland would you see Rhys's world, and if you stepped away you would forget how to see it again. No one on the mainland knew where this piece of turf grew, so no one saw Rhys' land. All they saw was rain.

The Rhysians had children, their numbers grew, they built more homes, and soon there was barely enough land to grow food. The mainlanders heard the distant rumble of empty bellies, although they mistook it for the anger of the Gods. The Rhysians took to crafts, they became quilt makers, wood carvers, and iron smelters, famed for their black cauldrons. They traded by sea like the Phoenicians before them, and visited the markets of Ceredigion where they traded their goods for corn. As soon as they were seen at the markets, prices went up. The poor folk of the mainland said the Rhysians were friends of Siôn Phil Hywel the farmer, but not friends of Dafydd the labourer.

They traded with a man named Gruffydd ap Einion, as his corn was fresh and his prices fair. Gruffydd was a libertarian, a free-thinker, intrigued by the stories of their idyllic life. As years passed, the Rhysians honoured Gruffydd by taking him to the clump of herbs, and in that moment he saw all the knowledge and wisdom in the world, kept safely in forests and books. Preachers and politicians were few. Sheep were plentiful. Choughs wheeled and kestrels hung in the air. The land was rich beyond dreams. It was the Utopia he had dreamed of.

Gruffydd asked how they kept themselves safe from crime, and they told him that Rhys's herbs hid them behind a veil of watery mist and the rain kept the mainlanders away. Rhys had rid their world of those who lived only for personal gain in the same way St Patrick had ejected snakes from Ireland. The only memory they had was a curious drawing of a creature with horns, a bosom of snakes, the legs of an ass, holding a great knife, with bodies lying all around. No one wished to meet that creature.

When Gruffydd stepped away from the patch of herbs, he forgot how to see the land of Plant Rhys Ddwfn, though he still had his memory and dreams. The Rhysians never forgot their friend and traded with him all his life, until one day they came to the market to find Gruffydd had passed over to the Otherworld and the traders had increased their prices. The Rhysians walked away and never returned.

The land of Rhys the Deep, the Welsh Utopia, is still there, glimpsed from the window of the train as it trundles past Cors Fochno, hidden behind sea defences designed to prevent flooding, heard in the ringing of the bells of Aberdyfi, written in the storybooks about Cantre'r Gwaelod, the Welsh Atlantis. The sea keeps no secrets.

Oh, and Plant Rhys Ddwfn, in West Wales, is a colloquial name for those who lived here before, the marginalised, the dispossessed, the fairies.

The Ghost Island

Gruffydd ap Einion was visiting St David's churchyard when he looked out to sea and saw a ghost island. Before he could reach his boat, the island vanished. An old woman who lived on the mountainside told him he had found the herb that allowed him to see the land of Plant Rhys Ddwfn. The next day he went to the churchyard, and as soon as he saw the island, he dug up the herb with a ball of soil round its roots, and placed it in his boat. With the island visible, he rowed towards it, and landed in a cove where he was welcomed by Rhys. He visited every evening until, one day, he never returned. Everyone agreed he had gone to live with the fairies, where he belonged.

Rhys Ddwfn

The writer Jan Morris saw Rhys's land from the doorstep of Llanon Post Office. As a child, I saw it from the shoulder of Yr Eifl on Pen Llŷn.

I still see it. No matter where I stand.

The Curse of the Verry Volk

The Norman Lord of Pennard Castle on Gower was celebrating his daughter's marriage with feasting and orgy, when a guard reported seeing strange lights in the woods. The Lord, fearing the Welsh were attacking, gathered his soldiers and went to investigate. In a clearing, they found the Verry Volk, dancing in celebration of the marriage. The drunken Lord, thinking he was being mocked, ordered his soldiers to charge. The slaughter was unexpected and terrible. Standing amidst the carved bodies of her dancers, the Verry Queen pointed at the Lord and called him, 'Coward'. She cursed him for his cruelty and stupidity, wailed into the wind, and vanished.

The following day the wind blew and the sea stirred, and sand poured over the land. For hours the storm screamed, until the castle and its people drowned in sand.

A wailing was heard in the wind, which was said to be a gwrach-y-rhibyn, a death witch, although a golf course has been built next to the castle's remains so the wailing is more likely to be a frustrated golfer trying to chip out of a bunker.

The old town of Kenfig was also submerged by a sandstorm after the indulgences of the Normans; excessive feasting and indulgent orgies accounted for the flooding of old Tregaron which lies beneath Maes Llyn. Tegid's palace is at the bottom of Bala Lake; Llys Helig was flooded by the sea off the Great Orme; King Benlli's court was swallowed by Llynclys; and it is still a mystery how old Swansea came to disappear below Crumlyn Lake.

Queen of the Verry Volk

The Reservoir Builders

In 1881, work began constructing a dam across the Vyrnwy Valley to create an artificial lake to supply Liverpool with clean drinking water. The village of Llanwddyn was evacuated and demolished, and more than four hundred people were moved to a new village built by Liverpool Corporation further down the valley. Even the ancestors in the churchyard were exhumed and reburied. The dignitaries of the Vyrnwy Water Works Project were so pleased with their dam they erected a public monument to themselves.

In a peaceful place amongst the trees, there is another memorial. The Obelisk was paid for and built by the workers who constructed the dam, and lists the names of forty-four men who died. One of those men lodged with his family in the upstairs room at the Green Inn in Llangedwyn. His little daughter liked to sit in the front window and watch for her father walking home along the road from Vyrnwy. One day, he never returned, and for many years, a little girl was seen in the upstairs window, staring down the road, endlessly waiting for her father to come home.

A few years later, Birmingham Corporation began constructing six reservoirs in the Elan and Claerwen Valleys in Powys. Such was the scale of this project that they built a new village for the two-thousand-strong Midlands workforce, and a railway to connect the reservoirs and take the children to school. Eustace Tickell, the civil engineer on the Pen-y-garreg Dam, fell in love with the beauty of the valley and spent his leisure time drawing the villages before they were flooded. In 1894, he wrote and illustrated a book about the Vale of Nantgwyllt, which he described as 'one of the most charming valleys in Great Britain. Scenes which are soon to be lost forever, submerged beneath the waters.'

This beauty also attracted the poet, idealist and revolutionary Percy Bysshe Shelley, who in 1811 as a nineteen year old walked from Sussex to visit his uncle Thomas at his mansion at Cwm Elan. Shelley had a small wooden boat with five-pound notes for sails, which he launched in the fast-flowing mountain streams, often with a cat on board, while he ran along the bank, guiding it through the rapids with a long pole.

He spent the summer of 1812 at Nantgwyllt with his sixteen-year-old wife, Harriet Westbrook. Within two years Shelley left her for Mary Godwin and *Frankenstein*. Harriet threw herself in the Serpentine, and in 1822 Shelley drowned while sailing off Tuscany. His home at Nantgwyllt was submerged during the building of the Caban Coch Reservoir. In 1937, the water level dropped by over fifty feet during a drought, and the ruins of Nantgwyllt reappeared, a ghostly reminder of Shelley's watery life and death.

The *Dambusters* was filmed at Caban Coch in 1955, just as plans were afoot to build another reservoir to provide drinking water for Liverpool. In 1965, the Tryweryn Valley was flooded and the village of Capel Celyn near Bala was evacuated and submerged, causing a tidal wave that changed Welsh politics forever. During droughts, the spire of Eglwys Capel Celyn reappears from beneath the reservoir, another reminder that water, like languages and people, never keeps a secret. There is no word for 'reservoir' in Welsh.

The Lost Land Below Wylfa Nuclear Power Station

Wylfa Head on the west of Cemaes Bay, Ynys Môn, was once known as Millionaire's Row, due to all its grandiose holiday homes. One was Glan Dŵr, bought in the 1930s by New Zealand opera singer Rosina Buckman, who worked with Thomas Beecham at the Royal Opera House. Rosina turned Glan Dŵr into a musician's summer retreat for her students, and gave recitals at Cemaes Village Hall to support war charities. She was often seen rehearsing on a rock overlooking the bay, wearing flowing white gowns, long golden hair over her shoulders, and a Pekinese tucked beneath her arm.

During the Second World War, the house was requisitioned as a radio location station and Rosina was evicted. She died in 1948 and the house fell derelict, until the Central Electricity Generating Board (CEGB) bought it, demolished it, and began to build Wylfa Nuclear Power Station Reactor Two on top of the ruins. The ashes of Rosina's mother-in-law, Emma D'Oisley, had been buried in the garden, and her urn was removed and reburied in Llanbadrig churchyard. The fury of the two ladies was soon evident.

In 1964, four workers on the night shift saw a woman dressed in a white evening gown, walking towards and over the cliff before fading away. A local electrician working on the building of Reactor Two heard melodic operatic singing. As he moved closer, the singing became louder, the temperature dropped, and she was standing next to him. He dropped his tools and ran. More and more workers saw her, and soon they were convinced Rosina Buckman had returned.

Volunteers for the night shift became scarce. Four Irishmen known as the Black Gang agreed to do the job, providing Father Taff, the local priest, carried out an exorcism. This done, they set off down the tunnel. As they walked along, they heard what sounded like 'Red Sails in the Sunset', and in the lamp-light they saw a figure dressed in white. They dropped their tools, screamed with terror, and ran away as fast as their legs would carry them. They refused to return to work until investigations proved the singing had come from a reel-to-reel recorder, and the ghost was the tea boy, a mischievous local lad who had wrapped himself in a white sheet to play a joke on the laggardly Irishmen. The lad was sacked for wasting company time.

A woman in white with long blonde hair over one shoulder continued to be seen. Lights in Reactor Two switched themselves on after being switched off, there were cold spots and the sound of singing. Some said the ghost was not Rosina but her mother-in-law, old Emma D'Oisley, furious at being forced to leave her final resting place.

There is another restless spirit at Wylfa, a tall dark-haired man dressed in a white shirt and black waistcoat, buff-coloured breeches and riding boots, always accompanied by the sound of a cracking riding whip. A receptionist said it followed her home to Porth Amlwch, where she heard the cracking of his whip as she lay in bed. The Reception Centre at Wylfa was built over the stable block of a farmhouse called Simdda Wen, owned in the 1860s by a wealthy farmer and his two daughters. The farmer became involved with one of his serving maids, until one day she was found hanging by her neck from the clock tower on top of the stable. When the men who worked on the farm gently cut her down they found bruises on her neck that suggested strangulation. They were convinced she had been hung from the stable clock to hide a murder. Fingers pointed at the farmer, but nothing was ever proven. On his death, his daughters managed the farm until it was bought by the CEGB.

Some of the workforce at Wylfa had been employed at the farm when they were younger, and they remembered a portrait of the old farmer hanging in the hallway. They swore he was the restless spirit of the reception centre, forever tormented by thoughts of the murdered maid, cracking his riding whip in redemption and remorse.

Lady of Wylfa Nuclear Power Station

4

MERMAIDS, FISHERMEN AND SELKIES

Mermaids

In 1603, a chapbook was published that told of an encounter between Thomas Raynold, yeoman of Pendine, and 'a monsterous fish, who appeared in the forme of a woman, from her waste upwards'.

In 1782, Harry Reynolds, farmer of Castlemartin, spotted what appeared to be a merman with a tail like a conger eel, near Milford Haven.

In 1826, a mermaid with black hair, white skin and 'blameless breasts' was seen at Llanychaiarn, south of Aberystwyth, by another farmer who considered her modesty yet continued to watch for a further half hour.

And in 1858, Daniel Huws and a group of quarrymen from Porth y Rhaw, were at Trefin on their way from Fishguard to St David's when they saw a lady with long silver hair and the body of a fish. They asked what she was doing, and she replied, in Welsh, 'Reaping in Pembrokeshire and weeding in Carmarthenshire'. The west coast of Wales has spawned a shoal of fishy tails.

Pergrin, a fisherman from St Dogmael's, was pulling in his nets near Cemaes Head at the mouth of the Teifi, when he saw a mermaid combing her hair. He caught her and hauled her into his boat. She began to weep and wail and pleaded with him, in Welsh, to release her, and she promised to give him three shouts if he was ever in danger from the sea. So he threw her overboard and she disappeared into the depths. Time passed, until one cloudless day, Pergrin was out in his boat when the mermaid appeared and told him to haul in his nets. Three times she spoke, so he sailed for shore, and as he passed Pwll Cam, a great storm gathered. Pergrin reached safety, though twenty-seven fellow fishermen perished at sea that day, 1 October 1789.

A mermaid was caught in a fishing net at Conwy. She implored the fishermen to release her before she drowned in the air, but they refused. She dipped her tail in the tide to feel the water on her skin one last time, and cursed the people of Conwy to be forever poor. So poor, that if they were paid with a gold sovereign, they had to cross the estuary to Llansanffraid for change.

Early in the 1800s, a farmer from Treseissyllt found a mermaid stranded on the shingle beach at Aberbach. He picked her up, she wriggled and writhed, but he carried her back to the farmhouse, filled a bathtub with water, sprinkled it with a little sea salt, and dropped her in. She wept and pleaded to be released but he rubbed his hands and told her he had other ideas. So she cursed the men of the farmhouse to be forever infertile, so no child would ever be born there. When he grew old and alone, he rented the farm to a young farmer, told him about the curse, and said he was a lucky lad. The young farmer asked why, and the old man said, well, at least he'd never be able to get into trouble with his wife through flirting with mermaids.

The Llanina Mermaid

Mr Lewis Henbant, an old man from Llanarth, told the tale of a mermaid who lived on the rock at Carreg Ina. She became entangled in fishermen's nets at Llanina and implored them to release her. They cut her free, and in return for their kindness, she warned them of an approaching storm and saved their lives. There are many more stories about the Llanina mermaids.

In a rush-floored cottage at Traethgwyn lived a fisherman called

Gronw, and his daughter Madlen. On a warm heavy day in August, with a terrible storm brewing, Madlen was locking up the pigs and goats when she saw a ship flying a Saxon flag about half a mile offshore. She watched as it was struck by lightning and began to sink. Madlen ran and told her father, and while Gronw had no love for the Saxons, he would not see fellow fishermen drown. Madlen went with him and soon they were rowing towards the sinking ship. They pulled seven men from the sea, returned to save five more, while two swam ashore, although many more drowned.

Gronw took the twelve survivors to his cottage, gave them warm food and drink and dried their clothes by the fire. A tall, elegant man seemed to be their leader, but he spoke in a language Gronw could not understand, so Madlen fetched a monk from Henfynyw, who spoke Anglo-Saxon. The monk explained that the tall elegant man was Ina, King of the Saxons. In gratitude for saving his life, the King built a church on the spot where he was rescued, though he named it, not after Gronw or Madlen, but after himself, Llan Ina.

Time passed, the church flooded, a new one was built on the clifftop, and the story was forgotten. Now, when the tale is told, the King was rescued not by Madlen, but by a mermaid who lived on the rock at Carreg Ina.

Myra Evans, who told Madlen's story, was born in Ceinewydd at midnight between 1 and 2 November 1883, the night of All Souls, when the veil between this world and the Otherworld was at its thinnest. She collected fairy tales, gathered mostly from her father, Thomas Rees, a fisherman and sea captain who lost all his brothers at sea. Myra persuaded him to write down the stories and she kept them in a biscuit tin under her bed, so she could read them beneath her sheets when he was away.

Here is another of Myra's stories ...

Another Llanina Mermaid

In long ages past when the sea between the Rush Fields of Llanon and Ogof Deupen was land, on a poorholding named Tangeulan lived a widow woman, Nidan, and her son Rhysyn. They earned their living from the sea, he as a fisherman, while his mother salted and dried the herring and mended his nets after the seals bit holes in them to eat his catch.

Rhysyn had dark curly black hair and sloe-black eyes, he could sing and rhyme and tell a tale, and all the girls of Ceinewydd loved him. Quite a few of their mothers, too – and one lusty old grandmother. But Rhysyn had a taste for the exotic and he was engaged to Lowri, the new maid at the big house, Plas Llanina. She was from the south, hair of spun gold, buttressed of bosom, plump as a puffer fish, with a laugh like a fishwife, and he worshipped the very ground she walked upon. They were to be married on the next Gŵyl Mabsant, and the bidder had been sent from door to door to announce the wedding.

One evening, when the sky above Cardigan Bay was the colour of primrose, violet and campion, Rhysyn was pulling in his nets, singing a song about a girl with spun gold hair, when he saw, sitting on a rock in the mouth of Ogof Deupen, a mermaid. She was brushing long, tangled, red seaweedy hair with a mother-of-pearl comb, the evening sun cast shadows below her ribs, and her tail shone like quicksilver, though it was covered in limpets and goose barnacles.

Rhysyn was enchanted. He said, 'Beautiful lady, can I help you?'

The mermaid turned. 'Teach me the song that I hear you sing while I watch you fishing. Of the girl with spun gold hair. I love that song.'

Rhysyn rowed a little closer. 'Indeed I will teach you the song, but tell me your name?'

The mermaid said, 'Morwen, daughter of Nefus, King of the Deeps.'

Rhysyn sang his song, and such was the beauty of his voice, and the close-ness of this dark young man, that her skin flushed rose with embarrassment.

'No more. I will return every evening until I learn your song.' And she vanished beneath the water.

Rhysyn was not the kind of man to go falling deeply in love, the occasional flirtation had always been enough, and he was engaged to the buxom Lowri. But he returned the following moonrise, and many moonrises after that, until Morwen learned his song, and it soon became clear that she was entranced by him, and he loved that kind of power over a woman. One evening she declared herself. She invited him to swim with her, arm in arm in the Land of the Deeps.

He looked at her. A crab dangled from one ear, the shadows beneath her ribs looked as if they had been drawn with charcoal, barnacles and limpets on her tail were moving around unnervingly, so he told her all about Lowri, the maid of Plas Llanina.

Morwen began to weep and wail, she twisted her red, tangled hair between her fingers, tore it out at the roots, thrashed the water with her tail, causing waves to crash onto the beach at Cei Bach. Then the turbulence of rejection receded. 'You will regret your decision. My father will avenge this insult.' And she vanished.

Rhysyn went home, he became withdrawn and refused to go out fishing. He sat on the shore feeling his nets between his fingers and staring out to sea. Nidan noticed the change in her son. She called Lowri, but he was distant and silent with her, too.

On the morning of the wedding, the sky was full of primrose, violet and campion, and Rhysyn was sat on the shore, and there she was – Morwen, head and shoulders above the water. 'Rhysyn, son of Nidan, if you go to the church at Llanina, my father will take your land, from the Rush Fields of Llanon to Ogof Deupen, your mother's house at Tangeulan, and the lives of you and your bride.'

And she vanished beneath the waves.

Rhysyn had to be dragged to the church by his mother. As they walked through the door, the skies outside turned grey, but the moment he saw Lowri, looking so desirable in her white dress, he knew she was the only woman he would ever lose his heart to. A great storm gathered out at sea; it blew the waters of Cardigan Bay over the Rush Fields of Llanon, into the mouth of Ogof Deupen, over the house at Tangeulan, and through the doors of the church. Rhysyn was swept out to sea on a great wave, and as he was dragged down into the depths, a woman with tangled red hair held him in her arms, and as his lungs filled with water, his two legs became one and he swam like a fish.

All in the church were drowned that day, along with many of the coastal dwellers of Cardigan Bay, their horses and dogs, sheep and pigs. Dolphins swam where people once walked. If you listen, when the sky is full of primrose, violet and campion, just beyond Carreg Ina, you will hear the sound of church bells ringing from beneath the waves, announcing the marriage of Rhysyn and Morwen, as they swim forever, arm in arm, in the Land of the Deeps.

More Llanina Mermaids

The old man of Llanina told this tale by his fireside to T. Llew Jones.

In a mansion on the clifftop at Llanina lived a kindly old man with his three daughters, Branwen, Gwenllian and Nia. Men came in droves to woo them, but they loved each other more than they could ever love a man. One day the three sisters were on the beach when the King of the Deeps saw them and was mesmerised. All through the summer he watched them, until autumn turned to winter and the sisters stayed indoors, warm by their fireside.

One evening, a storm raged and the wind rattled the latch. Branwen put down her embroidery to see if anyone was there. After a while, she hadn't returned, yet the door still rattled. Gwenllian put down her spinning and went to look for her sister. After a while she hadn't returned, so Nia left her harp and went to look for her sisters.

In the morning the old man searched the beach for his daughters. A fisherman told him he had seen the golden hair of three girls swirling in the sea in the midst of the storm. The old man wept, for he knew his daughters had been taken by the King of the Deeps and they would be changed into mermaids.

Beneath the sea, the girls were filled with melancholy and wished only to return to their father. The King saw their sadness and knew he could not keep them. So he offered them their freedom, although they would no longer be of the land or the sea.

The following morning, the old man was on the beach when three white birds landed on his shoulders. He knew they were his girls, changed by the King of the Deeps into creatures of neither land nor sea, but of the air. And that is how the seagulls first came to New Quay, and the 'girls' became 'gulls'.

This story was written by T. Llew Jones of Pentre-cwrt, a descendant of the poets of Cilie. He wrote over a hundred books for children, many based on old folk tales, such as the legend of the smuggler Siôn Cwilt, the pirate Barti Ddu, and the trickster Twm Siôn Cati. Often there was more T. Llew than folk tale, yet the tradition has embraced him. Each year the master storyteller's birthday is celebrated on 11 October – T. Llew Jones Day.

The Fisherman and the Seal

There was a fisherman who didn't like fishing. The seals bit holes in his net to steal his herring, and it took forever to stitch it back together again. He preferred to throw his anchor overboard, lie back in his boat, dangle his feet over the side, and go to sleep.

One morning, some visitors offered to pay him to fetch them from Newport Sands and ferry them back to Goodwick in time for tea at two o'clock. The fisherman agreed. Taking tourists round the bay sounded far easier than fishing, and he would have time for a nap at lunchtime.

When he awoke, he could tell from the position of the sun that it was almost two o'clock. He would never be able to get to Newport in time, and the visitors wouldn't pay him, and he'd have to go fishing instead. He was wondering what to do when he heard a voice.

'What's the problem?' There was a seal staring at him.

'I didn't know seals could talk,' said the fisherman.

'You don't know much,' said the seal, 'Throw me a rope.'

The fisherman tied a knot in a rope, threw the knotted end into the sea, the seal picked it up between its teeth, and towed the boat all the way to Newport Sands in time to collect the visitors and take them to Goodwick in time for tea at two. They were delighted, for fishermen were usually late. They gave him a handsome tip and the fisherman gave the seal all the fish he could eat, and never once complained about his nets being bitten.

5

CONJURERS, CHARMERS AND CURSERS

The Dyn Hysbys

The dyn hysbys was a folk physician, a conjurer, soothsayer, astrologer, surgeon, vet, bonesetter, a specialist who could cure and curse. They used written charms, herbs and potions, incantations, lead bottles, snail water, bloodstones, snakestones, the laying on of hands, and the latest medical techniques. They were farmers, doctors, schoolteachers, tramps, preachers, showmen, shopkeepers and psychologists, and people travelled miles to visit the one they trusted.

Old Jenky

Dicky Davies

Abe Biddle

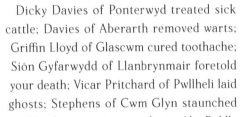

Dicky Davies of Ponterwyd treated sick cattle; Davies of Aberarth removed warts; Griffin Lloyd of Glascwm cured toothache; Siôn Gyfarwydd of Llanbrynmair foretold your death; Vicar Pritchard of Pwllheli laid ghosts; Stephens of Cwm Glyn staunched bleeding even in a stuck pig; Abe Biddle of Werndew found lost jewels and conjured hornets; Dick Spot from Llanrwst cast charms that left you dancing forever; Old Jenky of Trelleck had the Devil working for him; Dafydd Siôn Evan rode over Llanbadarn Fawr on an enchanted horse; Sir Dafydd Llwyd ordered a bull to gore to death a conjurer from Lampeter; Twm o'r Nant captured a spirit in a tobacco box in Llanfyllin after it had appeared as a boar, a wolf, a dog and a fly; and William Price of Llantrisant was a surgeon, bonesetter, physician, Chartist, nudist and vegetarian, who despised preachers, believed in free love, thought socks were unhygienic, cremated his son Iesu Grist (Jesus Christ) when cremation was illegal, and once cured a man of the drink by persuading him a family of frogs were living in his gut off the beer.

And then there was the infamous Dr Harries ...

The Conjurer of Cwrt-y-Cadno

John Harries was born in 1785, at Cwrt-y-Cadno in the Cothi Valley, Carmarthenshire. He was a cultivated man who dressed like a country squire, tall and well built, with blue wistful eyes. He trained as a physician in London, became a Fellow of the Royal College of Surgeons, and set up a practice in Harley Street with the astrologer 'Raphael'. When he returned to Cwrt-y-Cadno he opened a surgery specialising in skin diseases and mental illness, and a public house where he learned his customers' little secrets before they visited the surgery.

Dr Harries was a cunning man. He married the new-fangled medical techniques, learned in London, with the darker arts of the dyn hysbys. He developed three cures: the water treatment, the herbs treatment and the bleeding treatment (which did indeed employ leeches). The sick and sorrowful travelled from all over Wales to consult him, for he was said to have 'wonderful power over lunatics'. He could cast spells and lift curses, find lost cattle, tell fortunes, protect you from witchcraft, predict your death, and summon demons from a Book of Spells so powerful that it was padlocked and chained to his desk.

Dr. John Harries

Not everyone was impressed with the good doctor's abilities. The newspaper *Yr Haul* called him a charlatan and quack, and wrote, 'Because men insist on being foolish, they are left to consult Dr Harries, and go to expense on account of his lies and deceit ... he should be arrested and set on a treadmill for a few months, as happens to his fellow deceivers in England.'

Harries' reputation was sealed when he informed the police that a missing woman could be found beneath a poisoned tree. She was discovered in a shallow grave at the exact spot, and Harries was charged as an accomplice to murder. At the court in Llandovery he informed the judge, in Welsh, of his innocence, and added, 'You tell me which hour you came into the world and I will tell you the hour you will depart from it'. The case was dismissed.

Having predicted the date of his own death in 1839, Harries stayed in bed all day to see if he could avoid the inevitable, only for a fire to break out and in hurrying down a ladder to safety, a rung broke and he fell and broke his neck. As he was carried to the churchyard down a narrow roadway illuminated by flickering candles, the bearers found his coffin suddenly became weightless, as the Devil took his own. His son Henry continued the practice, and when the folklorist, vicar and writer, Jonathan Ceredig Davies, visited Harries's library in 1905, he found medical books, astrological almanacs, Latin and Greek tomes, but the padlocked Book of Spells had vanished.

In 2015, I was asked by the National Library of Wales to write a radio script about Dr Harries's Spell Book, which was in their archive. I was shown a small volume, the size of a school exercise book, bound in black with gold letters on the spine saying, 'A Book of Incantations', and a note, 'Donated by Mr Rhys Davys-Williams, Treforest, 26.8.1935'.

The first eleven pages contain spells, conjurations, exorcisms, astrological diagrams and incantations designed to summon spirits. There follows lists of patients and their treatments. On 29 June 1814, Griffith, Crygddy Mountain, was prescribed 'embrocation, cost 1s 6d'. There are also charms, including one for finding lost heifers and another written on the back of a bidding letter for a forthcoming wedding.

Bound into the volume is a four-page booklet advertising 'Gowland's Lotion, prepared by Robert Dickinson of Lincoln's Inn Fields, for Eruptions of the face and skin; pimples or blotches from surfeit or other cause, efflorescence or redness of the nose, chin, arms; Heats and that species of eruption and redness called Scorbutic Humours'. Also a copy of the 'Prophetic Almanack, published annually by William Charlton Wright, 65 Paternoster-row, London. 1825. Key signs used in astrological prediction, particulars of eclipses and other phenomena, a batch of celestial treats for every season, timely warnings, wholesome precepts, and poetical vagary.'

There is an invoice to Dr Harries threatening that 'adverse means will be resorted to' for the recovery of a debt. And another from Harries to Mr John Morgan:

> 1831. I hope you will not forget coming over to me to settel with me as soon as possible without further delayance. For I cannot wait your opportunity any longer for my Bill, your obedient servant, John Harries.

This is not the padlocked Spell Book, rather the random papers of an early nineteenth-century country doctor who used both conventional medicine and conjuring. However, the National Library is reputed to have the papers of the last dyn hysbys of Llangurig – unarchived, uncatalogued, scattered around the shelves like ashes at a funeral, ink still wet on the rustling pages, as if endlessly being written by an invisible hand.

Silver John the Bonesetter

John Lloyd was a farmer in the Harley Valley, who became a specialist in curing his sick animals. He used splints to set the broken legs of his sheep, he manipulated the knee joints of his cows, and applied herbal poultices to his poor pigs. When a miller's son broke his leg, John set the bone. The miller offered to pay, but John refused, so the miller gave him two silver buttons.

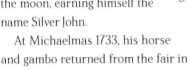

From that day, he began to treat people, yet he never took money for his services, only two silver buttons which he sewed onto his coat and waistcoat. On high days and holidays, he strode out dressed in his finest, with silver shoe buckles, a silver walking stick and a silver snuff box, until he shone more brightly than the moon, earning himself the name Silver John.

At Michaelmas 1733, his horse and gambo returned from the fair in Builth Wells without him. The following spring, Mary, daughter of the landlord from the Fforest Inn, was skating on Llyn Heilyn, when she slipped, fell face down and screamed. Staring up at her from below the ice were the frozen eyes of Silver John. When the ice melted, he was dragged from the water. All the silver buttons had been stripped from his coat.

His murderer was never found, but the children of Builth Wells sang this chilling song:

Silver John is dead and gone, so they came home a singin',
Radnor boys pulled out his eyes, and set the bells a-ringin'.

He is buried on the slopes of Great Greigiau, near Niblett's Quarry, in a grave where the grass grows bright green. His family, the Lloyds of Baynham continued to practise as bonesetters until the 1950s, when one of them held a surgery at the Horse and Jockey in Knighton, where he sold the family cure-all, Lloyd's Oil.

John 'Bonesetter' Reese, son of a Rhymney miner, had been taught the skills of manipulation by an ironworker called Tom Jones. When he emigrated to Ohio in 1887, he treated the mill workers and miners of Youngstown, who needed to be fit enough for work or they wouldn't be paid. He became chiropractor to the Pittsburgh Pirates where he was known as the 'Baseball Doctor', the ancestor of the most renowned bonesetter of all, Dr Leonard 'Bones' McCoy of the starship *Enterprise* ...

The Cancer Curers of Cardigan

In 1907, national newspapers carried reports of two elderly brothers in Cardigan who could cure cancer. The town was flooded with sick people looking for hope, causing consternation amongst those who were terrified of catching something contagious. Soon, they came from all over the world to the Welsh Lourdes to consult John and Daniel Evans of Pen-y-banc, Ferwig.

John was born in 1835 and Daniel three years later, the sons of a shipwright, who supplemented their small income as farmers, carpenters and shipbuilders by concocting herbal remedies. They collected plants from the hedgerows and woodlands, and invented an oil to treat skin blemishes, which they claimed could loosen the tentacle grip of cancer from healthy tissue. They kept the oil in small bottles, and applied it

John and Daniel Evans

with a brush, before squeezing the last drops back into the bottle. If anyone complained about hygiene, they were told to bring their own brush, which the brothers cleaned to avoid anyone stealing a sample of their secret recipe for scientific analysis. They treated everyone the same, rich or poor, and never charged, allowing people to pay only if they could afford to. Soon, they developed a reputation for successfully treating cases that defeated conventional doctors.

When some of their seriously ill patients died, the press and medical authorities turned on the Evans brothers, saying they were mixing arsenic and chloride of zinc with their herbs. However, John and Daniel continued to treat everyone who visited them, and turned down huge sums of money for their recipe, including £45,000 from a grateful American they had cured. John died in 1913 and Daniel in 1919, and the recipe was passed on to John's son, David Rees Evans, who continued the family tradition of medical herbalism.

Old Gruff

The author Marguerite Evans had developed writer's block, which she blamed on finding a pile of muddy potato peelings between her bedsheets after a disagreement with her cook. So her husband, the author Caradoc Evans, drove her to a whitewashed cottage at the end of a rutted track near Llangurig, to visit his friend Evan Griffiths. Old Gruff was a farmer, tall, burly, dignified, clean-shaven, white-haired, with twinkling blue eyes, a tweed coat and a Welsh flannel shirt open at the neck. When he wasn't riding up the mountain on his pony, he liked to sit in a high-backed

Evan Griffiths

stick chair with his fingers touching a mysterious blue stone that he used as a doorstop. For Old Gruff was a dyn hysbys.

Caradoc explained his wife's problem and the old man told them not to discuss it, she would be fine tomorrow, and he refused their offer of money. The following morning, the words flowed from Marguerite's pen and within three weeks her book was finished. They returned to Llangurig to thank Old Gruff, who explained that someone had wished her bad, so he had bent the wish by going to the mountain to draw strength, pray and think thoughts. Marguerite wanted to know how he knew this, but Caradoc told her it would not be wise to know too much. For Gruff lived by the Unseen.

An old farmer called Chickenheart moved to Llangurig from Hereford after his wife had died of overwork from looking after him. He lived in a red-brick farmhouse where flies poured out of the taps rather than water. Opposite was a white cottage where a bearded blacksmith lived with his widowed daughter. Chickenheart was mean-minded and the smith a gentle soul, if left undisturbed. Soon a feud grew between them.

After an argument, Chickenheart's cattle fell sick and dropped dead, his sheep were riddled with the fluke, injections didn't work, the vet's bill was running up, and his old dog Fly got run over and lost a leg. Chickenheart was convinced the smith had bewitched him, so he fetched Old Gruff, thinking he would be cheaper than a vet. Gruff walked round the house, paused in the bedroom, then gave Chickenheart a white envelope with some white powder in it, and told him to keep it by him and he would be bothered no longer by the blacksmith. Chickenheart offered a half crown, and Gruff refused it.

A woman from Aberystwyth was churning butter when a gypsy called and asked the pretty lady to buy a smidgen from her basket. The woman ignored her and carried on turning the handle. As the gypsy walked off cursing, the churning became heavier, the butter refused to set, and her arm nearly dropped off with effort. So she caught the bus over the mountains to Llangurig to see Old Gruff, having been careful not to tell her husband who would have said it was a waste of the bus fare.

Gruff asked if anyone had called asking a favour, so she told him about the gypsy. He explained that she should treat gypsies with respect, and never act rudely towards them. He gave her three small white stones to stand overnight in the dairy, and the following day her butter churned.

A young boy called Glyn from Llangurig bled freely if he cut himself. Once, he fell into a glass frame and gashed his arm. Tourniquets were applied but the cloths were soon soaked through, so he was carried to Old Gruff. The conjurer placed his hands on the blue stone and then on the boy's arm, went outside to the pump to wash the blood from his hands, and when he returned, the bleeding had stopped and there was colour in Glyn's cheeks.

One winter Old Gruff fell and broke his leg. The doctor told him he would never be able to ride his pony up the mountain again. Gruff said, 'Then it is time to die.' Marguerite and Caradoc visited him and she asked about the blue stone. 'Y Garreg Ddedwydd' ('The Blessing Stone'), he called it. It had been in his family for hundreds of years. It had come from Palestine and had been cut in two, but he didn't know where the other half was. As they were about to drive away, Old Gruff strode up his garden path, gave Marguerite the blue stone, stood by his white wooden gate, and waved them off. They never saw him again.

His funeral procession was a mile long. They came by trap, by car, on bikes, on foot, a farm wagon carried all the flowers, and he was buried in Llangurig churchyard in the grave of a giant.

Not long after, a young poet visited Caradoc and Marguerite in Aberystwyth. Marguerite told him the story of the stone and invited him to make a wish. Years later she asked him if his wish had come true. 'Not likely,' he said. 'I asked for fame, success, money.' His name was Dylan Thomas.

Margueritte Evans

HAGS, HARES AND DOLLS

Witchery

The last woman to be legally executed as a witch in Wales was Margaret ferch Richard in 1655. By 1736 the laws against witchcraft were repealed, cursing and charming were commonplace, and every town and village had a gwiddanes.

There was Dolly Llewellyn, the Queen of the Pembrokeshire witches; Old Moll from Gower, who left misfortune wherever she went; Ala, the Romani witch of Llanrug, left poisoned apples for unsuspecting children; the Old Hag of the Black Mountain chased little girls while croaking as a black crow; Beti Grwca from Ceinewydd was famed for love potions and mischief; Poor Hannah from Llandudno was burned alive in a cave on the Great Orme; Betty Foggy once stopped a ship being launched in Pembroke Dock;

Old Moll

Poor Hannah

Beti Grwca

Betty Foggy

Kate the Flanders witch lived in a Flemish farmhouse in Southerndown and turned herself into a hare to torment the local huntsmen who trampled the flowers in her garden; Mari Berllan Pitter from Pennant could stop horses with a whisper, made a waterwheel turn backwards, and could curse anyone except the local poet; Creaky Wheel of Llanbadarn Fawr stole potatoes in the middle of the night and if anyone complained, she threatened to break their heads with a sickle and have her daughter put the evil eye on them.

The Flanders Witch

Creaky Wheel

The Llanddona Witches

One stormy night an open boat came ashore in Red Wharf Bay, with a cargo of ragged men and women. The locals thought they were from Scandinavia, or Ireland, or had escaped from a sinking Spanish ship. They had no rudder or oars, which suggested they were criminals set adrift to drown as punishment. So the locals tried to push the boat back out to sea, but they were forced back by a spring of fresh drinking water that gushed like a fountain out of the sand. In the face of this, the strangers were allowed to make a home for themselves on the commons at the edge of the village.

The menfolk earned their living from smuggling. They had a trick of removing their red neckties and releasing black flies into the eyes of prying customs officers, so preventing them seeing the rum and brandy that passed by in front of their very noses.

The womenfolk were small with red hair. Siani Bwt was forty-four inches high and had two thumbs on her left hand. She rented a room in Caernarfon once a week, where she told fortunes. People flocked from all over to see her, so she draped old clothes across the room to keep her consultations private from the waiting crowds.

Big Bela, Lisi Blac and Elen Dal lived by begging, and if anyone refused to give them milk or potatoes, they cast spells, uttered curses, and helped themselves to whatever they wanted. Elen once asked a farmer's wife from Beaumaris for some butter and when the woman refused, her three cows sat on their haunches like begging dogs, gazing benignly and chewing slowly. Nothing would move them. Watching them was an old gnarled hare.

One of the Llanddona witches went to the market at Llangefni with her daughter. She placed a bid on a plump pig, and no one dared bid against her, save for one wealthy farmer. At the height of the bidding, he felt a hand in his back pocket and turned round to find the daughter. He knocked her to the ground and she lay there crying. He doubled his bid, bought the pig, and as the old woman helped her daughter to her feet, she cursed the hand that struck her helpless girl. Come winter, the pig died of a fever and the farmer's hand withered and hung lifeless by his side.

Here is one of the Tribe's spells, which was chanted at Y Ffynnon Oer for a man who had offended them. It cursed the man to break a bone when he crossed a stile, and not just any old bone, but his neck bone:

Crwydro y byddo am oesodd lawer,
Ac yn mhob cam, camfa,
Yn mhob camfa, codwm,
Yn mhob codwm, tori asgwrn
Nid yr asgwrm mwyaf na'r lleiaf,
Ond asgwrn chwil corn ei wddw bob tro.

Two of the Llanddona Tribe were known as Chwiorydd y Diafol, the Devil Sisters, who took their pleasure in cursing cattle, giving children nightmares, and casting spells on fishermen. They once went begging to a farm, but were turned away empty-handed and the sheepdog was set on them. As they walked away giggling, the barn burned to the ground and the dog dropped down dead.

At Pentraeth market they asked a flower-girl for a few coppers in exchange for telling her fortune. The girl refused, saying she had no money to spare. One of the sisters reached out a hand and touched the girl's flowers to make them wilt. But they didn't, for the girl was the youngest of seven sisters and the Chwiorydd had no power over her.

Goronwy Tudor had a birthmark above his breast which protected him from the Llanddona girls. Taking no chances, he nailed horseshoes above his door, placed rowan by the doorpost, grew Mary's Turnip in his garden, and sprinkled earth from the churchyard in every room. Nonetheless, his dairy became afflicted, the milk dried up, the cows gave blood, and he saw a hare suckling at their udders. Goronwy shot at the hare with a silver coin and it ran away screaming. He followed a trail of blood over the hill to a cottage, where he found Big Bela with a wound in her leg. She cursed him, so he collected some witch's butter from decayed trees, moulded it into Bela's shape, and stuck it with pins. Every pin caused her to scream with pain and blood to flow. So it was, until she released Goronwy from the curse.

Dark Anna's Doll

Old Liza lived in a ramshackle hut near Llanfairfechan, where she kept herself alive by begging for bread, milking the wild goats, and borrowing a turnip or a cabbage from a farmer's field. One morning she awoke to find a basket on her doorstep. She looked inside and found a baby girl, presumably left by the travellers. She carried the little orphan inside, named her Anna, and raised her as her own daughter. As Anna grew, she learned to love the kindness of her foster mother, though many saw old Liza as a fearsome old hag with a sharp tongue.

One day, Liza asked the farmer at Carreg Fawr for a little food in exchange for some lucky white pebbles she had collected from the stream. The ungrateful man set one of his hunting dogs on her. Anna screamed, Liza jammed her foot between the dog's bared teeth, wrapped her shawl around the girl to protect her, and kicked the dog off. They ran for their lives, with the dog gnawing at their ankles. When they reached home, Liza held her daughter, stroked her hair and dried her tears. She made a comforting bowl of soup with a couple of potatoes she had 'borrowed' from the farmer's vegetable patch, and sang lullabies until Anna drifted off to sleep.

That night, Liza found herself in a dark place. She scooped up some clay from the stagnant pool and mixed it with a little moss from the graveyard. By the light of a rush candle, she moulded it into the shape of the farmer, clothed it in bloodied fox fur and stuck two ivy berries on its face for eyes. With moonlight pouring through the window, she heated the figure on a griddle over the fire, muttered a spell, mixed in a little blood from the dog bites on her leg, took her hatpin and pierced the doll through the heart. At Carreg Fawr, the farmer stopped stroking his dog, wiped his forehead, scratched his chest, and carried on hunting. For Liza meant no harm to any living soul, so the spell could not work.

Come autumn, Liza passed over to the Otherworld, and young Anna was orphaned again. Neighbours brought her bread and milk and gave her paid work, sewing and darning, but at night she was alone with her thoughts. With each passing evening, her thoughts darkened, until they were black as peat. Anna remembered how cruelly the farmer at Carreg Fawr had treated them. By the light of the rush candle, she took hold of Liza's clay doll, pierced it with the hatpin, muttered a curse, and threw it into the fire. At Carreg Fawr, the farmer choked, clutched his chest, dropped his lantern and set fire to the hay in his barn. Next morning the neighbours found only a smouldering blackened skeleton.

No one suspected Anna. Why would they? She lived her life as a beggar girl, unseen and unloved, never betraying her emotions to anyone. She carved pegs from elder, carried them round in a wicker basket and sold them for a penny. In six months the elder softened and the pegs broke, so her customers bought more. She wrapped some of the pegs in scraps of cloth torn from her old frocks, cut a notch at the top which she filled with fox fur, drew eyes and a mouth with her sharpened fingernail dipped in blood, and sold them as peg dolls. It was never wise to refuse to pay her or send her away without food, for Dark Anna knew how to fashion a poppet.

'Voodoo dolls', or poppets, were quite common in Wales. In the Brecon Beacons, Farmer Trickitt turned an old woman and her son from his door. Back in her cave, she made a doll from the body of a burned rat, feet and limbs of a toad, white quartz from the cliff for bones, weeds for sinews, mountain herbs mixed with salt-water worms, pine gum, the heart of a black cockerel, clay from the river bed, water collected from a waterfall by moonlight and ivy berries for eyes. She breathed on it, passed it through the night air, heated it in the fire, doused it in the stream, and in his stone house across the valley, Old Trickitt dropped down dead as a doornail.

Hunting the Hare

Siaci lived with his old Nan at Ffrith Isaf, a lime-washed cottage on the hillside at Llanfrothen. He had three jobs: he ran errands for the vicar in Penrhyndeudraeth, caught crows for the landlord of the Oakeley Arms, and was employed as a beater by the squire of the local hunt.

He knew the land like the veins and blotches on the back of his Nan's hand, and never failed to raise a hare from a thicket. But there was one hare the huntsmen could never catch; one of those old gnarled hares that can outstare a greyhound, and weave through the old thorn hedges like dog rose and honeysuckle, unscratched by blackthorn and bramble.

The squire wanted this hare dead, but the vicar warned him it was enchanted and could only be caught by a jet-black hound without a single white hair on its body. The squire found such a dog in Powys, and after the owner haggled a high price, it was brought to Llanfrothen.

On the day of the hunt, Siaci was beating the bracken when the old hare broke cover, shrieked manically, and ran along the line of the old thorn hedge like dog rose and honeysuckle. The black dog was on its tail, red tongue lolling, unscratched by blackthorn and bramble, and it was gaining on the hare. Through woods, over hills, along streams, the men shouting, 'Hei, ci du!', 'Hey, black dog!'

Then the air was filled with a shriek as the dog's teeth sank into the back leg of the hare. Siaci shouted, 'Hei, Nan!' The dog's fur stood on end and it released its grip. The hare wrenched its leg free with a tearing of sinew and skin, and ran towards Ffrith Isaf with Siaci by its side. It leapt through the rhagddor and disappeared.

The men followed and the squire kicked open the door. The room was sepia and ochre, the air aromatic with spices, dried lavender hanging in bundles from the rafters, smoky bottles on sagging shelves around the walls, and a bubbling cast-iron cauldron hanging from a pot-hook over the open fire. An old woman, wrinkled as a raisin, sat in a stick chair while Siaci wrapped a bandage round her foot. Next to him was a bowl of red water. The hare was nowhere to be seen. Siaci's Nan blew the squire a kiss. 'My, what a moustache,' she said, 'Come on, cwtch up to old Nan,' and she patted the seat of her chair, puckered up her lips, and a thousand lines pointed towards the black hole of her mouth where a solitary yellow tooth wobbled in the breeze from her breath.

In the face of this wrinkled old woman, the fearless huntsmen of Llanfrothen ran for their lives, out the door, and over the hill. Before the squire could follow, the door slammed shut. 'I demand you open this door, madam, and let me out. Oh ...'

He emerged an hour later without his trousers, holding a primrose and smelling of lavender. His hair had turned snow white. He never, never went hunting again, and never spoke of what happened that day.

And Old Nan? Well, she taught Siaci how to write charms and invoke demons, and he became even more famous than the crafty conjurer of Criccieth. And who knows where she is now?

Hag

The Witch of Death

In 1574, ninety-two-year-old Siôn Gruffydd from Llandaff was lying in bed waiting for death. That night, a black shape appeared at the window, a figure with red eyes, a dark green face and black flapping wings. Siôn knew this was the gwrach-y-rhibyn – the death witch had come for him.

He closed his eyes and opened his arms to embrace her, when the room lightened. He peeped out of one eye to find she had vanished. He leapt out of bed, looked out of the window, and saw her land on the ground, fold her wings and enter the inn next door. The following morning Siôn felt better, so he rose from his deathbed and walked over to the inn for a beer, only to find that Tomos the innkeeper had died that night.

Stories of the gwrach-y-rhibyn are quite common in Wales. One lived in the Caerphilly swamp in the late 1700s. She had long black hair, talons for fingers and bat's wings. After the swamp flooded she moved into the town, wailing like a banshee and wringing her hands. The boys tried to catch her, but she flapped her wings, flew towards the castle and hid within its walls, where she still is, for all I know.

Another gwrach lived at St Donat's Castle in the early 1800s, where she flapped her leathern wings on the window and scratched her talons down the glass. She drifted through the village, roaring into the wind with arms outstretched, accompanied by black hounds with red eyes and fangs, bemoaning the death of the last of the Stradling family who had been killed in a duel in Montpelier. The castle is now the venue for Beyond the Border International Storytelling Festival.

A black lady lived in Tiger Bay where she beckoned to young sailors in the docks, back in the days when Cardiff was insignificant. She once asked a skipper for a ride in his boat, saying he would be handsomely rewarded. As he rowed out into the bay, the boat became heavier and heavier. She asked him to land, took him by the hand, and led him away from the Taff and through the woods. She brushed back her long black hair, smoothed out her dress, and he was eagerly anticipating his reward when she pointed at a stone, and vanished. He lifted it up to find gold. He used his money to become a dockside property developer, and never revealed his secret wealth until he was on his deathbed.

Gwrach y Rhibyn

64

DREAMS, MEMORIES AND THE OTHER WORLD

The Story of Guto Bach

'Don't talk to me, you silly young things – don't provoke an old man, now upwards of ninety years of age, by saying there were no fairies in Wales ... I tell you that fairies were to be seen in the days of my youth by the thousand, and I have seen them myself a hundred times.'

So said Cobbler Jig – real name, Siôn Tomos Siôn Rhydderch, shoemaker from Aberpergwm – who told this tale:

Guto Bach, son of Hywel Meredydd Siôn Morgan, looked after his father's sheep on the Rhos in Y Creunant. Guto was a daydreamer, always wandering off to play on the mountain. Once, he returned with pockets full of pieces of peculiarly white paper the size of crowns, with letters stamped on them. He said they were given to him by the little children on the mountain.

Guto Bach

One day Guto never came home. The whole neighbourhood was in a commotion, his father searched everywhere for him, but all he found were pieces of white paper with letters stamped on them. Time passed, and Guto never returned, until one morning his mother opened the door and there he was, sitting on the doorstep, looking not a day older than when he vanished, dressed in the same clothes, and holding a parcel. He told his mother he had been dancing with the fairies to the playing of a harp, and thought he had only been gone a few hours. His mother took the parcel from him. It contained white paper clothes without seams or stitching. Guto's mother burned them, and said no more.

After hearing this story, Cobbler Jig decided he would like to see the fairies for himself. He consulted a gypsy woman who told him to find a four-leaved clover and nine grains of wheat, and meet her at midnight on top of Craig-y-Ddinas. So he met the gypsy as arranged, and she placed the clover and wheat in her book, and washed his eyes with liquid from a phial. When his eyes cleared, he saw thousands of the little folk dressed in white paper clothes, all dancing round in a circle to a score of harps. All night they danced, until at sunrise they gathered in a line on top of the precipice, rolled themselves into balls and tumbled away down the hill and disappeared into the woods. After that Cobbler Jig saw them so often the people of Glynneath took no notice, either of him or the fairies.

Cobbler Jig was eccentric and jocular. 'One of the most entertaining persons I ever met with, and to those who understood Welsh, he was certainly a great treat,' explained Maria Jane Williams when she wrote down his story in 1827. Maria Jane was born in c.1795 at Aberpergwm House in Glynneath. She was known as Llinos (Linnet) for the beauty of her singing, and her playing of the harp and guitar.

When she was twenty, she began collecting fairy tales from the Vale of Neath, which she sent to an Irish antiquarian, Thomas Crofton Croker, who published them in the second volume of his *Fairy Legends and Traditions of Southern Ireland* in 1828, with an acknowledgement to 'the lady to whom the compiler is indebted'. Maria Jane became involved with another Irishman, John Randall, her father's gardener, with whom she had a child called Fanny – although some suspected Fanny's father was the rakish Earl of Dunraven, who kept a shooting box on his estate specifically for amorous adventures.

The Fairies of Pen Llŷn

Sir John Rhys

John Rhys was a farmer's son from Ponterwyd, Ceredigion, who became the first professor of Celtic Studies at Oxford University. He spent the summer of 1882 collecting fairy tales on Pen Llŷn, where he met Reverend Robert Hughes of Llanaelhaearn, who had seen the fairies riding 'wee' horses along the Pwllheli road one grey morning as he returned from his fiancée's house. Rhys explained, 'Story-telling was kept alive in the parish of Llanaelhaearn by the institution known as the pilnos, or peeling nights, when the neighbours met in one another's houses to spend the long winter evenings dressing hemp and carding wool ... When they left these merry meetings they were ready, as Mr Hughes says, to see anything.'

A Nefyn man was returning from Pwllheli Fair when he stopped at an inn at Efailnewydd. He didn't remember an inn being there before, but he stabled his horse, enjoyed a few beers, took a bed for the night and slept like a lord. In the morning he found himself lying on a pile of ashes with his horse tied to a fence post, nibbling his hair.

Griffith Griffith, a strong devout man from Perth y Celyn, Edern, set off at two in the morning to walk twenty miles to Caernarfon to pay his rent. He was passing through the heather between Llithfaen and Llanaelhaearn at the foot of Tre'r Ceiri when he saw a crowd of little men and women walking towards him, speaking a language neither English nor Welsh. He stood by the ditch to let them pass, and felt no fear. To Griffith, they were the tylwyth teg.

Alaw Lleyn of Edern, told the story of a woman who lived in a house on the beach at Nefyn, whose daughter disappeared for hours on end. The girl told her mother she had been playing at Pin y Wig, with some children who were much nicer than she was. The woman followed her daughter to the top of the headland where the girl pointed to her friends, and became excited when she saw their father was with them. The woman saw nothing, and forbade her daughter to visit the tylwyth teg again.

Lowri Hughes of Nefyn told a tale about her Nan, who was milking a cow at Garn Boduan when a dog came sniffing around. Nan kicked it away and it ran off, whining. It returned with a lame fiddler who asked for milk. She refused, so the fiddler began to play, and Nan found herself caught in an everlasting dance with the tylwyth teg, tormented forever by her own cruelty. Lowri's husband said the tylwyth teg lived beneath a sod on the old earthworks at Porthdinllaen, and were only seen when the weather was misty. The earthworks is now a golf course.

Elis Bach of Tŷ Canol, Nant Gwrtheyrn, was thought to be a changeling child. His father was a farmer, and all his brothers and sisters were the size of humans but Elis had legs so short his body almost touched the ground. He could run nimbly through the ruins of the Giant's Town on Tre'r Ceiri, and could easily round up the mountain goats for the Nant livestock markets.

At one market, Elis saw two men offering to pay over the odds for sheep. His mam invited them in for cawl, while Elis hid in a cupboard and overheard the strangers conspiring to steal all the sheep in the

Elis Bach

Nant. As the men were herding the stolen sheep up the corkscrew road, Elis followed on a separate path through the trees with his dog, Meg. He lay in wait at a bend in the road, leapt out in front of them, did a weird dance, frightened the lives out of them and chased them off towards Pistyll, while Meg escorted the sheep back down the track to the Nant.

The tylwyth teg still live under the old earthworks at Porthdinllaen, although you won't see them: too many golfers.

Gower Power

Willie John lived with his mam in a cottage at Llanmadoc on Gower, where he was famous for his home-brewed beer. The cottage was full of buckets and demijohns containing bubbling concoctions and intoxicating experiments with elderberries. One evening Willie's mam was feeding the hens when she heard a voice, 'Old lady, favour us with kindness'. It was the Verry Volk, standing next to a bed of primroses. They explained that they wished to reward the villagers for their kindnesses by giving them each a few grains of gold dust, but they needed to borrow a sieve to separate the grains from the nuggets. They pointed to the sieve that Willie used for straining his beer. Mam lent them the sieve and off they went down the path and over Llanmadoc Hill, without a thank you. 'You're very welcome,' she said. Later that night there was a tapping at the door, she opened it to find Willie's sieve leaning against the wall.

One Sunday after chapel, Willie strained some hops and brewed a cask of beer. By late summer it was ready, and he settled down in his chair by the fire and took a sup. Soon there was a sparkle in his eye and a twinkle in his toes, and he danced around the room to imaginary fiddles till his trousers fell round his ankles and his mother carried him up to bed. Every night this happened, and after only a very small tankard of beer. This was the strongest ale he had ever brewed, it was indeed. And what's more, the cask never seemed to empty. It was come-and-come-again beer.

Soon Willie John's beer was the talk of North Gower and the pubs of Cheriton and Llangennith emptied as the old farmers came down from the commons, the rowdy cockle girls walked from Penclawdd, and they danced all night to Phil Tanner's mouth-music. Willie and his mam

Willie John

soon had more money than they ever dreamed of. Then mam got to thinking. A dangerous occupation, thinking. She thought, 'the Verry Volk must have enchanted the old sieve before they returned it, bless them.'

Knowing the Verry Volk's business is to break the spell, and the cask slowly emptied, until the day came when Willie John drank the last drop of the finest beer that Gower had ever tasted. But when Willie's mam was cleaning the cobwebs from the cellar she found a little bag of gold dust, just enough to buy hops for Willie to brew another batch of beer next year.

The Curse of Pantanas

The farmer at Pantanas hated the fairies, what with all that singing and dancing amongst the wildflowers in his meadows. So he decided to be rid of them. He scythed down the flowers, ploughed up his fields, dug deep into the cold clay and sowed corn. When the fairies found their beautiful home destroyed, they vanished.

One summer evening when the corn was ripe for harvest, the farmer met a little man dressed in a red coat, who pointed a sword at his nose and said, 'Revenge!' That night his corn burned to the ground. The little red man appeared again, waved the sword around his head, and said, 'Revenge begins!'

The farmer told him not to be so dramatic, and to speak plainly. The little man explained that cutting down all the flowers and deep-digging the soil was no way to treat the land, and that there would be trouble, not for himself or his children, but for his children's children's children. Well, the farmer thought he'd be long beneath the cold clay by then, but he considered his great-grandchildren, and offered the fields back to the fairies. The little man accepted, but said the soil was already so deeply damaged, there would still be revenge. The fairies smoothed out the furrows and sowed seeds of cornflower and corn-cockle, and soon the meadows rang with singing and dancing, and the farmer went to bed with sheep's wool stuffed in his ears to shut out the racket.

Time passed, and memories of the curse dimmed. The farmer's great-grandson lived at Pantanas, a progressive lad called Rhydderch, who had turned the fields back to corn, always haggled a good price for his crop, and tolerated no red poppies or yellow rattle. He was engaged to Gwerfyl, the maid at Pen Craig Daf, and one winter evening, the two families were celebrating when they heard a voice from outside. It said, 'Revenge is here,' and a little old woman peered in through the window.

Rhydderch shouted, 'Go away, you old hag!' The little old woman said she had come to explain how to free him from his fate but for this insult he would be cursed forever, and she vanished. Rhydderch laughed and ordered the feasting to continue.

Later that night, Rhydderch escorted Gwerfyl home to Pen Craig Daf, they kissed, swore undying love, and he set off home into the cold frosty night. He never arrived. They searched the woods, the ditches, the caves and potholes at Raven's Rift, but Rhydderch had disappeared.

Time passed, generations were laid in the cold clay, and the curse, the lost boy and the fairies were all forgotten.

Rhydderch woke up with a headache, as if he'd slept too long. He was lying in a pothole at Raven's Rift. He remembered dancing with the fairies, and Gwerfyl would be worried about him, maybe angry. He walked to Pan Craig Daf to apologise, but couldn't find her. He ran across the valley to Pantanas, but no one recognised him. Everything seemed changed. The fields were neatly ploughed, hedges had been uprooted, woods felled, paths closed and ponds drained. There were fences everywhere. He was intrigued.

An old man asked who he was, and Rhydderch explained. The old man shook his head and said he had a dim memory of his grandfather telling him that a young man had vanished from Pantanas a century before, after dancing with the fairies. Rhydderch began to shake, the man held him by the shoulders, and in that moment he turned to dust and crumbled into the very same cold clay that his great-grandfather had first ploughed all those years ago.

Crossing the Boundary

Ifan Gruffydd of Rhos-y-ffordd near Llangefni, was a farmhand, writer, actor and teller of this tale:

My mother warned me never to go near Peter Green's cave in Henblas Woods, for it was well known that the fairies lived there, and they stole little children and kept them for a year and a day. I was told never to cross the boundary, and that boundary was the church. No doubt about it. I was scared of the fairies, though I loved to hear stories about them. And the cave was a lonely sort of place, silent and still, though everywhere was quiet in those days, you could hear footsteps half a mile away and know who it was.

We lived in a village of just a few houses, just Mam and me in this little old cottage. I liked being by myself. One Christmas, I was given a penny pistol, and I was thrilled to bits with it. Armed with my little pistol full of water, I went to the church and across the boundary into the

field where the reeds grew as tall as my armpits, and before I knew it, I was at Peter's cave. There was a little tent at the entrance, and a family of four eating their Christmas dinner. Two big greyhounds lay under a handcart, red tongues hanging like bloody blades over their chops, ears pricking up and flattening, as if they were ready to hunt at their master's command. I dropped my pistol. It was no use in the face of the fairies.

Well, before I could run for my life, the two children surrounded me. The boy counted the buttons of my coat, and chucked me under the chin. The girl drew her hand across my cheek, and kissed me, and oh, she was pretty. I was very young, but I'd fallen head over heels in love with her. I was terribly scared, but they gave me food, pheasants and hares, chicken and turkey, and I had a roasted Christmas dinner. I was sure Mam was worrying about me, so I stayed.

Soon enough I was happily playing with the children, and had given over the idea that they were the fairies. I played with them many times, and I loved it there. Dear me! I was fond of Juliana. Her father was a Scot, so people said, who had left home and married a dark girl from the Mediterranean. Juliana had inherited her mother's crow-black hair, and I had been told it was dangerous to mix with dark girls. Well, it made no difference to me, nobody could stop me going to Peter's cave.

One Saturday when I got there, they'd disappeared. Nothing left, only the dried rushes where they'd lain down to sleep, the ashes of the fire where they baked their potatoes, and the paths through the grass where we ran. Well, I was heartbroken. Juliana had gone, and I longed for her. I longed for her until she slipped from my mind completely.

When I grew up, I wandered the length and breadth of this old world, and found myself in France at the end of the First World War, in a camp in Dunkirk. It was my responsibility to look after the canteen staff who made meals for the soldiers who came on ships from the Middle East to be fed and rested. Then on they'd go to the next battle, and others took their places. It was a crazy place.

The French locals did a great trade selling things to the soldiers to take home as souvenirs. An old woman and her daughter came up to me and asked me whether they could set up a little shop near the entrance to the tents. Well, I did more than that for them. I lent the old woman a table to put her wares on, and I became very friendly with them. I'd call by for a chat early in the morning around ten, with a cup of tea each and one for myself. And the old woman told me stories, and the girl – oh dear me! – I'd completely fallen in love with her. Day after day we talked. The old lady told me she spoke fifteen languages, and could change from French to English to German, just like that.

I told her I could speak one language she couldn't – 'Welsh'. And she said, 'Rwy'n siarad Cymraeg.'

You see, she had lived in Wales with her late husband, so I asked whereabouts and she took out a postcard, it said, 'Llanfairpwllgwyngyllgogerychwyrndrobwllllantysiliogogogoch'.

Well, Christmas Day came and the old lady set up shop. I took them Christmas dinner from the cookhouse, and we chattered away, though the girl was quiet. Then she turned and looked at me and said, 'You lived with your mother in the cottage beyond the church.' I looked at her. Crow-black hair, dark eyes – it was Juliana. They had wandered the world, from one cave to another, one country to another, always being moved on, marginalised and dispossessed, until they found themselves here. At Christmas, just as it was when I last saw her at Peter's cave.

Well, when the war ended I came home. I don't know what happened to Juliana. I should have stayed with her, I know, but I couldn't decide, I was very young. Maybe I didn't think. This wasn't a movie. It was a true story, and a fairytale. There we are. That was my encounter with the fairies.

8

GOBLINS, BOGEYS AND PWCAS

The Ellyll

The American Consul to Wales, Wirt Sikes, was passing the Huntsman's Rest at Peterston-super-Ely, near Cardiff, when he encountered a group of men drinking from tankards, smoking clay pipes and discussing emigration to America.

Sikes, born in Jefferson County, New York, in 1836, was living a bohemian life as a writer, social reformer and independent newspaperman before he was sent to Cardiff by President Ulysses S. Grant. To occupy his time, he began collecting stories of encounters with pwcas and fairies, which he published in 1880 as *British Goblins*. The men from the Huntsman's Rest told him this tale:

Rowli Pugh and Catti Jones lived on a farm in Glamorganshire and they were known for their bad luck. Their crops withered, the roof leaked, the house was damp, their noses dripped, Catti had a weak chest, Rowli's back ached, they had no money and nothing to laugh at, at all. Their fortune was so bad they decided to sell the farm and go to America.

That evening, an ellyll appeared. It told them to light a candle before they went to bed and all would be well. Then it kicked

Wirt Sikes

up its heels and vanished, as they always do. That night Catti placed a candle by the bed and left it alight. In the morning, she woke up to the smell of fresh bread and a blazing fire, the tools were cleaned and sharpened, and the clothes and sheets were washed and starched. Catti left the candle alight every night and soon their crops were blooming, the cattle were content and the pigs fat. Even their noses stopped dripping.

This went on for three years until one night, while Rowli snored, Catti took it in her head to thank the ellyll. She stayed awake and, when he appeared, she watched him dancing around the candle. He looked funny, with his long pipe-cleaner arms and legs. Catti giggled, almost imperceptibly, just to herself, but he heard her and vanished. From that day, Rowli and Catti had to do their own baking and washing and cleaning, but they managed the farm well. They brewed their own beer and opened a fine alehouse at Peterston-super-Ely, so there was no need to discover America after all, and wouldn't that have saved a whole lot of trouble?

Ellyll

The Pwca of the Trwyn

One Christmas in the early 1700s, there was a knock on the door of the Trwyn Farm near Abercarn. The farmer, Job John Harry, opened the door and looked around but there was no one there. This went on each night for a month, until Job's frightened family became convinced it was a pwca. A neighbour offered to shoot it, and sat by the hearth with his gun in his lap and waited.

That evening, Job was walking home when the pwca jumped out in front of him, pointed its finger and said it knew about the man and he was a fool to think he could shoot something he couldn't see. It added that it had decided upon the one thing that pwcas do best, 'the tormenting'. When Job arrived home, he opened his door to find the neighbour being pelted by stones. The man dropped his gun and ran home to bathe his bruises. The pwca was nowhere to be seen.

The pwca moved in and lived in the oven, from where it could be heard scratching away on Job's fiddle in the middle of the night. If anyone complained it threw crockery around the kitchen, pelted them with stones and thumped them on their noses. One night it trod on Job's toes, ever so gently, and explained that while it was unsurpassed at 'the tormenting', it meant no harm. It said that Job was a good man, but he was surrounded by fools. So Job decided to learn to live with the pwca and all was well until an old man who lacked brains boasted that he could get rid of it, and threatened to stick it with a knife. The

Pwca

old man sat by the oven and waited, until he heard a voice calling him a fool for thinking he could stab a pwca, and he was pelted with stones until he dropped the knife and ran home.

The pwca grew quite fond of the girl who looked after the cattle, and resolved to help her out with the milking. She had never seen the pwca, until one evening it spoke to her from the oven. It asked why she never offered it food in return for its work. So each day, she left fresh milk and a slice of white bread by the oven as a thank you, until one day, feeling a little mischievous, she ate the bread and milk herself and left a stale crust and some water. The pwca was livid. It picked her up beneath the armpits with its fleshy hands, pinched her, bit her, tickled her and chased her all over the farm till she was blue bruised.

On Ash Wednesday, the pwca left as suddenly as it came. And we wouldn't have known it, but for Reverend Edmund Jones, who was born on the small farm of Penllwyn, Nantyglo, in 1702. He became fascinated with the Otherworld after discovering his teacher had taken part in a fairy funeral. So he sold his beloved books for £15 to raise money to build a chapel, gave his greatcoat and shirt to the poor, and set off with his beloved donkey, 'Shoned,' in search of tales of apparitions and devilry, preaching twice a day every day, well into his eighties. For his ability to see into the future, they called him 'Prophet Jones'.

Jones asked Job John Harry's son David why the pwca had come to the Trwyn. It was said to have arrived in a jug of barm carried by a servant, or it had rolled there in a ball of yarn, but David explained it was because his brother Harry, a scholar and clergyman, had been messing around with 'the conjuring'.

Red Cap Otter

Two daft lads were following otter tracks along the banks of the Dysynni near Llanfihangel y Pennant, when a small red creature dashed across the field in front of them and vanished down a hole beneath the riverbank. It wasn't a stoat or a weasel, so they reasoned it must be an otter, a small red otter. That would be worth a penny or two. So one lad held a sack over the hole while his mate poked a stick down another hole and wiggled it about. The creature ran into the sack, the lad tied a knot, threw it over his shoulder and off they went towards home, dreaming of fame and money. They heard a voice, 'Let me out, you dimwits!' They dropped the sack on the ground, and out jumped a little red man, who shook his fist at them, turned the air as red as his whiskers, cursed them to be dimwits for the rest of their lives, and ran away.

Sigl-di-gwt

Long ago in the Pant Teg farmhouse above New Quay, there lived a woman and her pretty babi. The woman worked till her fingers were red raw from washing, her back ached from lifting, and her breasts were sore from feeding. At the end of each day she walked the fields to collect the wool that the sheep had rubbed onto brambles and fences. She teased and carded and spun it into warm clothes for her pretty one.

One evening, the woman was spinning yarn by the light of a candle, singing a lullaby, 'Suo-Gan Gwraig Pant Teg', while her baby dozed in the cradle by the hearth. She was feeling drowsy when in walked a little old lady, dressed in a red and white-striped frock, a red cloak and black shoes with silver buckles. She peered through bottle-bottom glasses, squinted and spoke, without any how d'ye do, 'What would you give me if I were to spin all that wool for you, dearie? It'll take me but a few minutes, and you look so tired.'

The woman heard herself saying, 'Anything I possess would I give', thinking she had little of value.

'The deal is done,' said the little old lady, and she licked her thumb with a raspberry tongue and placed the top joint against the woman's thumb.

The little old lady set to spinning and within a beat of the babi's heart, all the wool was spun. The woman was delighted, for this would have taken her hours and her back would have ached. She thanked the little old lady and said, 'What can I offer you in return? Te? Bara caws?'

And in the blink of a crow's eye, the little old lady pointed her finger and snapped, 'Your babi'.

The woman was awake now. 'My babi? No, do not tease me, he is my life, my soul. I could never part with him. Undo your work, I would rather strain my sight.'

'A bargain is a bargain and is sealed by the tylwyth teg. It cannot be broken. For three days I will come, and on each day you will have three chances to guess my name. If you fail, as you will, your babi will be mine.'

The woman blurted out, 'Mari, Megan, Meinir?', but the little old lady danced away cackling, as little old ladies do in fairy tales. The woman thought it was all a dream, but next evening the little old lady returned and asked for her name. The woman said, 'Ceri, Caryl, Cerys?' and the little old lady danced away.

The woman tossed and turned in her sleep that night, and the following day she walked around clutching her babi to her breast and muttering names to herself, as if her senses were scrambled. She ran down the path from Pant Teg, wet ferns soaking her bare legs, took a drink from the well at Pistyll-y-Rhiw, and ran till she came to the bridge at Llanina. She sang her lullaby to the rattling stream and pleaded with the waters for help. In that moment, she heard singing coming from the other bank.

In a clearing in the trees she could see the little old lady, dancing around her spinning wheel, surrounded by wagtails, grey and pied, flicking their tails, chanting, 'Little she knows that Sigl-di-gwt is my name', over and over again. The woman could not believe her ears. She ran home and slammed the door just before the moon rose.

The little old lady came. 'Well, what's my name?' And she held out her arms.

'Siani?'

'No.' She began to claw at the babi.

'Siriol?'

'No.' She grabbed the babi.

'Perhaps it is Sigl-di-gwt?' said the woman firmly.

The little old fairy lady turned green, then red, and then steam poured from her ears, spittle from her mouth, green goo from her nose, and she leapt up and down in a towering rage, turned the air blue, stamped her foot three times, broke the floorboards and disappeared through the hole, never to be seen again.

9

BIRTHS, CHANGELINGS AND EGGSHELLS

Taliesin

There was a woman, an enchantress, a gwiddanes, a woman of the Otherworld. Her name was Ceridwen, and she lived by Llyn Tegid. She knew all the plants and roots and herbs in the forests; she brewed tinctures and potions and kept them in misty bottles on sagging shelves; she could set bones and draw out fevers. She gifted her giant husband Tegid Foel with enchanted armour so his flesh could never be cut in battle.

They had two children, Creirfyw, with her mother's ebony skin and father's strength, and Morfran, with his mother's dark soul and father's brains, and eyes so black the crows thought him their brother, though even the crows left him alone. He lived in the room at the top of the castle. They kept the door locked, just in case.

Ceridwen watched Morfran as he sat, breathing deeply, dark eyes staring, moving only to snatch a fly out of the air with those huge hands. How could a woman so otherworldly produce a grotesque like this? Yet, even a crow thinks its children are

Ceridwen

beautiful, so she decided to gift him with the powers of prophecy and inspiration. With that, he would be a dyn hysbys, a conjurer.

She gathered herbs, leaves, bark, fungi, slime moulds, breath and odours, using instruments carefully crafted by the light of the waning moon. She mixed powders and tinctures, built a great fire from peat and boiled the ingredients in a pitch-black iron cauldron, conjured from her own mind. The potion had to simmer for a year and a day, so she found an old blind beggar to sit and stir it, for he would never see what was in front of his eyes, and a guttersnipe named Gwion, a boy without a single thought in his head, who would not question why he pumped the bellows that kept the fire alight and the cauldron boiling.

A year passed and Ceridwen fetched Morfran from his loft and sat him by the cauldron. She told Gwion to pump the bellows one last time. There was a flame and a crack and the fire spat. Alarmed, Gwion stood up in front of Morfran, tried to protect his face, and three drops of the potion sizzled onto the back of his hand. It burned, he licked it, and swallowed the three drops.

Gwion had a thought. He had never had a thought before. It was inspiring. He knew what had been and what was to come. He knew Ceridwen was angry, and he was right. She roared with fury as the potion soured and turned to poison. Swirling with inspiration and prophecy, Gwion ran out of the door, as fast as a hare. Ceridwen screamed and gave chase as fast as a greyhound.

As her tongue touched the hare's back leg, Gwion dived into a river and swam as a salmon. Ceridwen shrieked and gave chase as an otter.

As her sharp teeth were about to bite into the salmon's flesh, Gwion leapt out of the river and flew as a bird. Ceridwen squawked and gave chase as a hawk.

As her claws tore into his back, he swooped into a barn, and hid as a grain of wheat. Ceridwen would never find him here.

Ceridwen clucked like a jet black hen with a red comb, spotted the grain that was Gwion, and swallowed him whole.

Ceridwen's belly grew, nine months passed, and she bore a baby boy. The child had a noble brow and bright eyes, and sang a song. She knew this was Gwion, and she resolved to be rid of him. She wrapped him in swaddling, dropped him in a leather bag, placed the bag inside a coracle, covered it with skins and set it free on the water. She watched it drift on the tide. Gulls pecked at it, gannets dived around it, fulmars spat at it, until it washed up on the shore south of the Dyfi estuary.

A young fisherman named Elffyn saw the bag, waded into the waters and pulled it ashore, hoping it might contain gold, for with gold he could be the poet he had always dreamed of. He found, not gold, but a baby. Elffyn sighed, but the baby sang a poem to him, prophesying that one day he would be worth more than gold. Elffyn showed it to his father. 'What have you caught, boy?'

Elffyn replied, 'A Bard.'

His father laughed, 'And what is the use of a Bard?'

The baby sang a poem so inspiring it charmed the birds from the trees and melted the old man's heart. 'Maybe there is a use for poets after all.'

They raised him and he became the finest poet in the Welsh language, and repaid their trust many times over. His name was Taliesin.

Bum das yg kawat.
Bum cledyf yn aghat.
Bum yscwyt yg kat.
Bum tant yn telyn,
Lletrithawdc naw blwydyn.
Yn dwfyr yn ewyn.

I have been a drop in a shower.
I have been a sword in the fist.
I have been a shield in battle.
I have been a string in a harp,
Disguised for nine years.
In water, in foam.

The Llanfabon Changeling

In a crumbling farmhouse called Berth Gron in Llanfabon lived a young mother and her baby boy and, oh, how she fussed over him. She drowned him in kisses, wrapped him in quilts by the fireside, and never opened the curtains for fear the sun would shine on him.

One day, she heard her cows bellowing and ran outside to investigate, only to find they were contentedly chewing the cud. She scurried back to the cradle, and found her baby looking plump and pink. Yet he stared through ancient eyes, grew wrinkled and wizened, grumbled and grizzled, and spat into the fire just to hear the sizzle.

The woman asked the advice of the old man from Caer Nos, a house built with stones stolen by night from Llanfabon Church. The old man rattled his teeth, sucked on his raven-head pipe, and told her, 'This may not be your babi. It may be an anwadalyn, a child left by the Otherworld.' The woman's heart missed a beat.

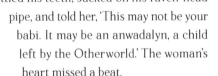

The old man took a hen's egg, blew out the contents, filled it with beer and gave it to the woman. He told her, 'Lay your kitchen table with seven glasses, break open the egg, pour out the beer, and say out loud so your babi hears, that you are brewing beer for the men who will bring in your harvest. Say nothing, do nothing, come and tell me what you hear.'

The woman could scarcely catch her breath, but did as she was told. As she stared at the flames of the fire, she heard a voice:

I was old before my time, I lived before my birth,
I remember the ancient oak, an acorn in the earth,
But I never saw egg of hen, brewing beer for harvestmen.

She went to the old man and told him what she had heard. He chewed his pipe, rattled his teeth and said, 'This is not your babi.' The woman was hag-ridden. He told her, 'On the next full moon, hide in the brambles at the crossroads by the Ford of the Bell, wait till midnight, say nothing, do nothing, come and tell me what you see.'

So on the full moon, she hid herself in the brambles at the cross-roads. As the clouds passed over, the moon turned red and she heard the sound of a solitary fiddle. Out of the night came a procession of strange people, dressed in pale crinolines and bonnets, waistcoats and bowler hats, and as they passed by there was her own baby, white as a wraith. She wished with all her heart to scoop him up, clutch him to her breast and run, but she didn't.

She went to the old man and told him what she had seen. He rattled his teeth, bit his pipe in two, and said, 'We must get your babi back.' He opened his battered old Bible box, took out a skin-bound book, blew away the dust, licked his fingers with a grey tongue, leafed through the pages and read out a charm. He told her, 'Take a black hen with no white feathers, build a fire of peat, not wood, close every door, window and mousehole, bake the hen on a spit, and watch the fire until every feather burns from the hen.'

The woman was near hysterical, but she took a black hen with no white feathers. She built a fire of peat, locked her doors and windows, stuffed rags in the mouseholes, wrung the hen's neck, skewered it and turned the handle of the spit. She waited and watched. She heard the fiddle tune from the crossroads, and in the flames of the fire she saw the procession of strange people. She held her breath. A child was crying, she could smell cooking meat, there was smoke, she was choking, suf-focating, when the last feather fell from the hen.

Silence. The fire dampened. The air cleared. A voice gurgled. She could hear her breath. She turned, and there was her beautiful baby, just as he had always been.

The Eggshell Dinner

David Tomos Bowen's mother told a story about the woman who lived next door to her in Glynneath, whose farmhouse was infested with fairies. It was one of those old longhouses where one half was the living room and the other half the cowshed, with a half-door connecting them. Whenever the woman was milking in the cowshed, she could see the little folk dancing in the kitchen, and whenever she was cooking, they were milking her cows.

One day, she was making supper for the reapers who brought in the harvest, when she heard singing and dancing upstairs, and a shower of dust fell from the ceiling into the pudding, spoiling it entirely. So she asked David Tomos Bowen's mother how to get rid of the troublesome fairies. 'Make only enough puddin' to fit in an eggshell, and boil it. Invite six reapers to dinner, and the fairies will see there won't be puddin' enough to fill six hungry bellies. They'll think there's no food in the house, turn up their noses and leave.'

So the woman filled an eggshell with puddin' and put it on to boil. She heard singing from the cowshed:

We have lived long in this world.
We were born at the beginning of time,
long before the acorn grew.
Yet we never saw a harvest supper fit inside an eggshell.
Something is wrong in this house,
we will not stay beneath this roof.

And the fairies vanished. Forever.

And that's how you get rid of the fairies, according to David Tomos Bowen's mother, and she should know.

The Hiring Fair

An old couple from Garth Dorwen, Penygroes, were weary with age. The old man's feet throbbed from standing on the hillside with his mangy sheep, and the old woman's back ached from milking her scrawny cows and scrubbing the dairy. They knew this could go on no longer.

So, on Calen Gaeaf, the first day of winter, dressed in their Sunday best, she in bonnet and shawl, he in bowler and waistcoat, they walked to the November Hiring Fair in Caernarfon. They strode up and down the line of young job seekers, all scrubbed faces and shining shoes, until they saw a small girl with thin red lips and raven black hair, who was twirling a penknife between her fingers. She told them her name was Elin and she was as strong as a carthorse and nimble as a mountain goat. A coin changed hands, and she was told to start work at first light the following morning. She followed them to the farm, walking three steps behind, clutching a sprig of rowan.

In the morning, Elin lit a roaring fire, milked the cattle, churned the butter, scrubbed the farmyard and placed a pot of salt-porridge to simmer on the hearth. In the evening she made cawl and fresh baked bread, sang songs and told tales. When the moon shone, she collected the coarse wool the sheep rubbed onto brambles, she carded it, dyed it, sat at her spinning wheel and wove bundles of warm blankets for bony old shoulders. By winter's end, the old couple had grown to love this dark girl who slept with a sprig of rowan on her pillow and an iron penknife by her side. She was the daughter they never had.

When the blackthorn bloomed and the days lengthened, Elin took her spinning wheel into the meadow and never returned. 'The tylwyth teg have taken her,' thought the old woman, 'they always do.' Soon, their backs ached and feet throbbed once more.

One evening a tall elegant man came to Garth Dorwen, saying he was from Rhos-y-Cwrt, and had heard the old woman knew the arts of the midwife, so she was to come with him, for his wife was in labour. His piercing eyes stared into the old woman's soul and she knew she could not refuse. He led her through fields and woods she had known since childhood, until they came to Rhos-y-Cwrt. He ushered her inside and showed her a scarlet bedchamber where a golden-haired lady was lying on a scarlet-draped four-poster bed, screaming.

She delivered the lady of a beautiful baby with golden curling locks. The man told her she was to stay for a month and care for his child, and she would want for nothing for the remainder of her mortal days. She could not refuse. He gave her an ointment to rub into the baby's skin, but warned her never to get it into her own eye.

A month almost passed, and she was rubbing the ointment into the baby's skin, when her left eye itched, she scratched it, and the ointment brushed her eye. In that moment, everything changed. Through her right eye she saw a scarlet-draped bedchamber, through her left it was a miserable dank cave, the four-poster bed was a mattress of rushes, and the golden-haired lady was raven-haired Elin.

Elin had run away from an arranged marriage to the tylwyth teg. She protected herself with a sprig of rowan and an iron penknife, until one night she was so tired after a hard day, she forgot the rowan and fell asleep. He had swept her away and laid her in his bed.

Elin told the old woman to say nothing, and her husband would be true to his word.

A month passed, the old woman returned home to find fresh milk, bread and cheese on her doorstep every day, the dairy scrubbed till it shone, and a fire blazing in the hearth. And so it was forever and a day.

Eleven months passed, and the November Fair rolled into Caernarfon. Prices were high, and word was that the tylwyth teg were there. They were, for the old woman saw Elin's husband spearing fruit from the stalls with a sword. Without a thought, she ran to him and asked after Elin and the baby. 'She is quite well,' replied the man. 'Through which

Elin

eye do you see me?' As the old woman raised her left hand, he took his sword, plucked out her eye, placed it in his sack, and vanished.

The old woman never saw the tylwyth teg again, but she still had her memory and she never forgot Elin, the raven-haired girl who slept with a sprig of rowan on her pillow and an iron pen-knife by her side.

The Baby Farmer

Cadi was a tall red-haired girl from Ynys Môn, who loved to dance with the fairies. They came through her keyhole at night, made a noise like the wind and danced a corelw around her room. They left her money, though she had never seen them, and felt she never should.

Cadi saved her money, and soon she had enough to get married. She chose a man as tall as herself, and they had a fine spindly child. One night at the fair, she told her husband how the fairies left her money. When they returned home, she tucked her baby snugly in his cradle, kissed him and went to bed. Next morning, she found a tiny wrinkled creature in the cradle, and she knew her own child had been taken. The fairies never came again, and she was left penniless to raise the wrinkled child. And she knew she should never have talked of fairy money.

Births, Changelings and Eggshells

Cadi became a baby farmer. She had so many babies, she couldn't count them all on her fingers. Yet poor as she was, she always dressed them well. All apart from her firstborn fairy child, who walked around in the filthiest of rags.

One day, Cadi went to the woods to gather sticks for the fire and she found a piece of gold. She knew it was fairy money and she mustn't speak of it. So she spent some of it on fine clothes for her children, hid the rest in the pot dog on the mantlepiece, and said not-a-word to her husband.

One day, a man knocked at her door, and told her she may be eligible for poor relief. She closed the door on him, rounded up her well-dressed children and hid them in the crog loft. She opened the door and showed the man her filthy firstborn and said she was oh-so-very-poor that she couldn't afford to dress her babies in anything better than rags. After the man left, Cadi went to the crog loft to fetch her precious ones, but they had vanished, gone to live with the fairies, never to be seen again.

DEATH, SIN-EATERS AND VAMPIRES

Poor Polly

David Siôn, a servant from Ystradfellte had heard more portents of death than most people; the groans of the cyhyraeth (banshee), the howling of the cŵn annwn (hellhounds), and the chirping of the aderyn gorff (corpse bird). One night he and a friend were crossing a bridge on their way home when they saw a light coming to meet them. It was a canwyll gorff (corpse candle). It hovered over the stream and they

saw a face reflected in the water. It was young Polly Siôn Rhys Siôn, a seamstress who worked with them at Ystradfellte. She was wearing the corpse candle on her ring finger, shielding it from the wind. 'Oh, not Polly,' they thought, 'she's far too young to have business in the grave-yard.' Yet a week later, poor Polly was carried over the same bridge towards her burying ground.

Welsh Wake Amusements

A wicked old farmer from Dolranog near Mynydd Carningli was lying in his coffin in the parlour usually reserved for visiting vicars. He had refused the minister's last request to repent, and died with a smile on his face. At his gwylnos, there was dancing to harp and fiddle, while his two nephews sang rowdy songs. In the past they would have raised the coffin on their shoulders and danced round with it, to let the dead join in the celebration, then tied a rope around the corpse's ankles and dragged him up the chimney feet first. But the old farmer wasn't one to dance. He didn't like flowers, either.

Before midnight, they heard the sound of galloping hooves, closer and closer, until the door burst open and a blast of icy wind blew out all the candles. You could have heard a needle drop on a sheep's fleece. Then the door slammed shut and the hooves were heard again, fainter and fainter. They lit the candles and continued singing and dancing till the early hours.

Before they left, the old man's two nephews went into the parlour to pay their last respects. The coffin was empty. They looked round the room but there was no sign of the corpse. So they filled the coffin with stones and nailed on the lid, and made a pact never to tell a soul that the Devil had taken their uncle, and no one would have ever known, if I had not told you.

The Fasting Girls

In 1770, Thomas Pennant, the curious traveller, visited forty-seven-year-old Mary Thomas of Tyddyn Bach, Llangelynin, near Tywyn.

Mary was seven when she contracted scarlet fever. She was seized with inflammations and swellings every spring and autumn. She could not bear to be touched on the left side, and her pain was relieved only by the application of a sheep's skin freshly taken from the animal. Her parents took her to Holywell for a cure, but when she was twenty-seven, the fever struck again, more violently this time, and for over two years she ate nothing.

When she recovered, she thought she had been asleep for only a day. She asked for food but couldn't keep anything down, other than water smeared on her lips. She took the sacrament, after which she managed a few drops of wine and a little bread and a nut-kernel of egg. Pennant described:

Her eyes weak, her voice low, deprived of the use of her lower extremities, and quite bedridden; her pulse rather strong, her intellects clear and sensible ... she takes for her daily subsistence a bit of bread, weighing about two penny-weights seven grains, and drinks a wine glass of water: sometimes a spoonful of wine, but frequently abstains whole days from food and liquids. She sleeps very indifferently: the ordinary functions of nature are very small, and very seldom performed.

Following Pennant's visit, news spread of the miracle girl. She was visited by George III's brother, Prince William Henry of Gloucester, and a nobleman who donated goods worth £50. Some locals suspected she was performing for the tourists, and filling her belly after dark. Others said it was gweledigaeth, 'trance'. When she was in her mid-eighties, visitors described her as a mere skeleton, with a brown complexion and jet-black eyes, an unusually large head, leathery skin and sucking soup through a hollow goose

Thomas Pennant

quill, arms nothing more than skin and bone; the muscles of her legs wasted away, though her memory was sharp, and she could hear conversations a considerable distance away.

By 1812 she had moved to a cottage at Friog near Dolgellau, cared for by her neighbours and surviving on bread dipped in beer. She baked her own bread in a pot on a tripod, kneading it while she lay in bed. She died in 1813, aged around ninety.

By the 1860s, fasting girls like Mollie Fancher, the Brooklyn Enigma, had become newspaper celebrities. Sarah Jacob was born in May 1857 near Llanfihangel-ar-Arth, Carmarthenshire, the daughter of a church deacon. When she was nine, Sarah fell ill with scarlet fever, and as she recovered she lay in bed, wrote poetry, read her Bible and refused food. She became a local curiosity; folk came to visit her. She seemed healthy enough – big wide eyes, plump rosy cheeks, red lips, flowers and ribbons in her hair, 'like a lily amongst thorns,' said one perceptive visitor.

Yet she never ate or drank. They said her sister passed her food when they kissed, like a mother bird would feed her fledgling. Her friends said she never ate much anyway. The vicar wrote to the newspapers about the miracle girl who was living on air. Visitors caught the train on the newly opened railway line, bringing gifts of money and flowers, hoping to find cures for their ailments or to witness the freak show. By 1869 she had lived for two years without food or drink.

Guy's Hospital in London organised an experiment. Nurses watched Sarah round the clock, with instructions not to give her food unless she asked. She didn't, and just over a week later she died. Her parents were convicted of manslaughter; her father Evan served a year's hard labour in Swansea Gaol, her mother Hannah six months, and soon the story of the Welsh Fasting Girl was forgotten.

Evan Bach Meets Death

When Evan was sixty, Death came to visit. Evan told Death it was foolishly soon, that he had plenty to occupy him, his garden needed digging, there was the dog to feed, and Mrs Morgan would be inconsolable, but Death said he had set his mind on a man of sixty.

Evan's eyes lit up. He suggested Billy James in Newton, 'He's weary of life, he'd be glad to go.'

Death said he wanted a healthy man.

Evan coughed, thumped his chest, spat into the fire, and said, 'Well there's Dewi Mawr of Pyle, he can walk forty miles a day and not be breathless.'

Death smiled, but Evan was getting into his stride.

'There's Ned of Merthyr Mawr, Jack o' Cornelly, old Uncle Dick o' Newton, all over eighty, miserable as sin, and no one to mourn over them.'

'Too old', said Death.

Evan suggested, 'A game o' cards?'

Death said that, contrary to popular belief, he wasn't a gambler.

'I could give you my savings,' said Evan. 'It's a tidy sum.'

Death said he had little use for money where he came from, but maybe they could do a deal.

Evan agreed.

Death told him he must be more generous, and give money to the poor.

'Indeed,' said Evan.

He must visit his poor old Aunt Molly.

'Yes, indeed,' said Evan.

He must help his nephew repair his old fishing boat.

'Yes, agreed.'

And support fundraising events, even if they involved fancy-dress.

'Agreed, yes indeed.'

If you fail, I will come for you.

Evan asked, 'Then will I live forever?'

No, said Death, only till a hundred.

Evan said he would be quite satisfied with ninety-nine. So he took his Aunt Molly to live with him, bought his nephew a new fishing boat, and gave a few extra coins to the orphanage. But as he approached ninety, he slipped back into his old miserly ways, and Death came for him. Evan pleaded for the other six years, for he still hadn't dug his garden.

Too late.

Death took him.

Modryb Nan

Jack's Nan often disappeared from her home in Neath for months, even years, but she always returned. She had a man in Bridgend, they said, for he had twice been seen visiting her, dressed in a long grey cloak and a slouching grey hat. Jack had never seen his face, but had heard the rattling of keys as he walked.

One night Jack heard three knocks on the door. Nan shouted, 'Who's there?'

The answer came, 'You know me.'

Jack peered over the banisters and watched Nan open the door. A stranger in a grey cloak entered. 'I am come for you,' he said.

Nan shivered and said she wasn't ready, it was a cold night and she was warm by the fire.

The stranger threw off his cloak to reveal a bag-o'-bones, and said, 'This is the third time of asking, tonight I claim my bride', and he took Nan by the hand and held her round the waist and they began to dance, whirring wildly round and round the flagstone floor, until Nan fell to the floor. Death put on his cloak, threw open the door, and as the icy wind blew in, he grabbed Nan by the arm and was gone. The last Jack saw as he wiped the frost from the window, was a grey skeletal horse flying away like lightning with Nan in front and Death behind.

And this time Modryb Nan never returned from her Dance with Death.

Sin-Eaters

A long, lean and lamentable old man lived in a cottage at Llangorse in the late 1600s. He was paid sixpence to eat a loaf of bread and drink a maple wood bowl full of beer from the chest of a corpse, so consuming the sins of the dead. In the 1850s another sin-eater lived in Llandybie, remembered as a pariah in the community, paid 2s 6d to eat a plate of salt and bread from the corpse's chest, while muttering an incantation. In Llanllyfni, a family placed a potato or freshly baked cake on the corpse, and then left the coffin under the Coeden Bechod, the Tree of Sins, where the sin-eater ate it after dark.

A highwayman frequented the road through the Usk Valley from Brecon to Abergavenny. No one knew his identity, but suspicion fell upon a gentleman who lived in a fine house in Crickhowel, whose piebald mare was seen by night carrying a masked rider. On his death around 1850, the funeral procession stopped outside the sin-eater's house.

Sin-Eater

He was a gaunt old man with a sallow complexion, sunken eyes and long grey hair. He ate bread and drank beer over the corpse in exchange for a silver coin, and the gentleman was laid to rest in Crickhowel cemetery. Strange tales were told of the ghost of a masked man on a piebald horse who held up carriages on the road from Brecon to Abergavenny. When he removed his mask, he revealed a gaunt old man with a sallow complexion, sunken eyes and long grey hair.

Vampires

In *La Dame de Pique, or The Vampire, a Phantasm Related in Three Dramas* of 1852, Dion Boucicault wrote:

> The Peaks of Snowdon – The moonlight is seen to tip the highest peaks and creeps down the mountain side; it arrives at the ledge, and bathes the body of Alan Raby in a bright white light – After a moment his chest begins to heave and his limbs to quiver, he raises his arms to his heart, and then, revived completely, rises to his full height. Alan (addressing the moon); 'Fountain of my life! Once more thy rays restore me. Death! – I defy thee!'

Boucicault himself played the part of the vampire who climbed Snowdon on the stage of the Princess's Theatre in London in 1852, forty-five years before Bram Stoker's Dracula washed up in Whitby. However, Alan Raby was not a normal Welsh vampire.

A man bought an old four-poster bed at a bankruptcy sale in Cardiff for his wife and four-month-old baby to sleep in while he was away. On the first night, the baby griped and grumbled. On the second night, it wept and wailed till the woman called the doctor, who prescribed a powder to help it sleep. On the third night, it shrieked and howled, and she clutched it to her breast until it died in her arms. On its throat was a red mark with a spot in the middle that was oozing blood.

When the man returned, he vowed revenge on the creature who had killed his child. He slept in the bed and waited. On the first night he woke thinking there were hands clawing at his neck, the second he swore he was being strangled, and by the third he found blood oozing from his throat. For, you see, this was a Vampire Bed.

One Friday evening in the early 1700s, a pious Dissenting minister was riding his grey mare towards an old farmhouse in Glamorgan, where he was to stay before delivering a sermon the following evening. He was greeted warmly by the landlady, ate a hearty meal, was accommodated in the guestroom, slept splendidly and was up with the lark.

In the morning light, he noticed the room contained some fine old Tudor furniture. He sat by the mullioned window in a worn leather armchair and read his Bible. He felt himself dozing, and when his eyes opened he saw blood flowing heavily from the back of his left hand. He rinsed it in the washbasin, and when the bleeding finally staunched he looked at the wound and found it had the appearance of a bite. Maybe he had scratched himself on a nail, though surely the mark would have been on his palm. No, it was a bite. He wrapped his hand in a kerchief, and that evening delivered his sermon with its accompanying magic lantern show, which he considered was favourably received.

That night he couldn't sleep, and not from the lingering excitement of his performance. It was as if a dog was gnawing his flesh. He lit a candle and pulled up his shirt to find his ribs covered in bites that were pouring blood.

In the morning, he went to the stable to saddle his grey mare, and was alarmed to find it had exactly the same bite-marks on its neck. He complained to the landlady. 'Madam, I believe a vampire walks your house.' The landlady looked sheepish, and explained that two other ministers had suffered the same treatment. The house used to be a Dower House, and when it was converted into a farmhouse, several rooms were blocked off, along with the previous tenant's library and his dusty old books and belongings, though a few of the less woodwormy pieces of furniture were scattered around the farmhouse, including the armchair and bed.

The previous tenant was an old antiquarian who was not pleasantly disposed towards ministers, and he had indeed returned as a vampire. Several ministers had tried to exorcise the creature, but it refused to leave the library. A dignitary of the Church of England tried to lay the spirit but it bit him on the left hand and leg and he walked away, perspiring greatly.

The vampire only left when its furniture was sold at auction. There is no record of the unsuspecting soul who bought the lot, though in 1840 a handsome Elizabethan chair was advertised by an auction house as a 'Vampire Chair', after it was discovered that anyone who sat in it found their hands scratched till they bled. You see, Wales is not a land renowned for its darkly tormented souls who drink blood in the fevered imaginations of gothic writers, but it does have vampire furniture.

An old Carmarthenshire miser was said to be able to suck blood from a stone. He had accumulated so much wealth but always haggled with the shopkeepers, beat them down in price and never paid his workers a living wage. When he died, he was laid out in the parlour, and in the morning the undertaker found strange scratches on the body. Everyone agreed they had been caused by a vampire who had been unsuccessfully trying to get some blood out of the old misery.

Vampire

The Zombie Welshman

An English knight, William Laudin, told the Bishop of Hereford that an evil Welshman had died 'unchristianly' and was returning each night to summon his fellow villagers to the grave. People fell sick and died, and only few were left alive. The bishop explained that an evil angel was living inside the body of a lost soul, and he advised William to exhume the Welshman, cut off his head with a spade and sprinkle him with holy water. William followed the bishop's instructions, but the zombie Welshman

continued to walk. One night it came for William, who drew his sword, chased it back to the grave and cut off its head, again. This time, it stayed dead, and the ravage of the pestilence ceased, according to Walter Map in the late twelfth century.

11

CHAPEL, CHURCH
AND DEVIL

The Devil's Bridge

Megan Llandunach was standing on top of the gorge above Pontarfynach, gazing at the waterfalls far below, clutching a piece of string attached to a shabby mongrel and weeping into the wind, when she became aware of a man behind her. She turned and there stood a monk, dressed in grey robes with a hood pulled over his face so his eyes shone from the shadows. She looked down at his feet. They were cloven. He spoke, 'Why do you cry so, my dear?'

She dried her tears and wiped her nose, 'Because my wayward cow has wandered to the other side of the gorge, and I am too weak and feeble to climb down and up the other side to fetch her.'

Diafol

The Devil, for it was he, offered to build her a bridge, providing she gave him the soul of the first living creature that crossed over. She dried her tears and wiped a dewdrop from her nose, while the Devil dreamed of beef soup. He gathered stones from all parts of Wales and Ireland, pausing only once to avoid being preached at by the

Chapel, Church and Devil

Vicar of Llanarth, and soon a fine bridge spanned the gorge. He proudly showed it to Megan, expecting praise. Instead, she whistled her cow to stay, pulled a stale loaf from her pocket, threw it across the bridge, and her shabby mongrel gave chase. The Devil threw his head back, exposed his red skull and deep eye sockets, and let out a howl that made the river freeze over. Then he shuffled off, with the soul of a shabby mongrel on a piece of string trailing behind him.

This folk tale has long been entwined with tourism. In the late 1700s the name of the village was changed from Pontarfynach, the Monk's Bridge, to the Devil's Bridge, to attract visitors to the newly built Hafod Hotel and estate. In the 1920s the Great Western Railway published the story in *Legend Land*, a book of Welsh and Cornish fairy tales designed to encourage people to visit the west by train. Now the story is told on a notice board in the village for those disembarking from the Vale of Rheidol Railway, so avoiding the unnecessary employment of storytellers.

Devil's Bridge

Huw Llwyd's Pulpit

Huw Llwyd of Cynfal Fawr was a bard, military man and conjurer, renowned for delivering weird and wonderful midnight sermons from a rock amongst the cascades by the River Cynfal. He frequently commanded his congregation to go on a mission for God, engaged in a lengthy feud with his neighbour, the poet and archdeacon Edmund Prys who had accused Huw of plagiarism, and once persuaded the Devil to shoot himself in the mouth, so inventing the taste of tobacco.

Huw Llwyd

Huw was invited to investigate a series of robberies at an inn near Betws-y-Coed which was run by two fair-haired sisters. Visitors invariably enjoyed an enchanting evening in the company of the ladies, though in the morning they would find their pockets empty. So Huw arrived and asked for a night's lodging, saying he was a weary traveller on his way to Ireland. The sisters made him a fine meal, he amused them with tall tales of his adventures in countries he had never been to, and they purred with pleasure.

At the end of the evening, Huw went upstairs, locked the door, lay on the bed, placed his clothes and sword by his side, closed his eyes and pretended to sleep. Before long, two black cats came down the chimney, chased each other around the bed, and played with his clothes, turning them over and over in complete silence. One cat licked Huw's face while the other put its paw into his pocket and pulled out his purse. Without opening his eyes, Huw lifted his sword and cut off the cat's paw. There was a howl of pain and both cats disappeared up the chimney as if their tails were on fire. Huw felt in his pocket and took out a human hand.

Next morning at breakfast, only one of the sisters appeared. Huw insisted on offering his thanks to the other sister and burst into her bed-chamber, where she lay on the bolster looking pale. She held out her left hand, but Huw refused it, saying he only kissed a lady's right hand. He pulled the severed hand from his pocket, touched it to his lips, threw it onto the bed and told her that he would be watching her. And he walked out of the room backwards, to keep both sisters in his sight.

When Huw was preparing for death, he instructed his daughter to throw his books into Llyn Pont at Rhyddu. The books contained all his notes on astronomical lore, the medicinal value of herbs, the white art of astrology and the black art of magic. His daughter was a learned girl and she could not bear to part with her father's books. Huw asked her again to throw his books into the lake, so she hid them. He told her a third time, explaining he would not rest in peace knowing his wisdom may fall into untrustworthy minds. She knew she must carry out her father's last wishes. As she threw the books into the water, a dripping hand emerged, caught each one and carried them down into the depths.

At that moment, Huw Llwyd died – without knowing that his clever daughter had lovingly copied out all his spells.

The Church that was a Mosque

St Patrick was on a mission from Pope Celestine to introduce Catholicism to the unruly Irish when he was shipwrecked off the north coast of Ynys Môn. He swam ashore at Middle Mouse, a small island off Cemaes, which he named after himself – Ynys Badrig, Patrick's Island. He reached the shore at Patrick's Cove, drank from Patrick's Well, lived in Patrick's Cave, and he built Llanbadrig, Patrick's Church, one of the most unique buildings in Wales, all thanks to another explorer and traveller.

Henry, third Lord Stanley of Alderley in Cheshire, was born in 1827. He was the author of many travel books, a vocal critic of British colonialism, a linguist who spoke Persian, Turkish and Arabic, and a man who swore he would never marry an English woman. While in Istanbul, he fell in love with a lady called Fabia and converted to Islam. They married in Algeria in 1862 under Islamic law, then renewed their vows in Istanbul in the presence of the British Consul. While living in Geneva, he discovered Fabia was actually Serafina Fernandez Funes of Alcandete and was a bigamist, so on the death of her first husband, Henry married her a third time.

In 1869 Henry inherited the title Lord Stanley, along with much of Ynys Môn, including Llanbadrig Church. He returned to Britain, married once more in the eyes of his friends in London, and finally for his family in a Catholic church in Macclesfield. Then he took his seat as the first Muslim in the House of Lords, adopting the name Abdul Rahman. His beliefs were both humble and deeply rooted in Muslim theology. In 1884 he transformed St Patrick's little church at Cemaes into a mosque, with deep-blue tiling, Arabic iconography and geometric patterns in the stained-glass windows rather than the virgin birth.

He died on 21 Ramadan 1903, and was buried in unconsecrated ground at Alderley. At his funeral, the new Lord Stanley removed his hat, only to be nudged by Nancy Mitford, who told him, 'Not your hat, you fool, your boots.'

St Patrick could never have guessed that his attempts to introduce Catholicism to the Irish would have led to the introduction of Islam to Wales, and Lord Stanley could never have known that his beautiful mosque would one day stand in the shadow of Wylfa Nuclear Power Station.

The Chapel

A shipwrecked Welshman found himself washed up on a desert island. He built a house, then another and another, until he had a whole village. One day a tramp steamer was passing, the captain went ashore and was surprised to find the man had built two chapels, so he asked why the need for both. The man explained, 'Well, this is the one I go to. And this is the one I don't!'

12

SHEEPDOGS, GREYHOUNDS AND A GIANT CAT

As Sorry as the Man Who Killed his Greyhound

Around 1200, Llewelyn the Great and his wife Joanna, the illegitimate daughter of King John, were living at Aber in Gwynedd with their baby boy. They loved nothing more than chasing wolves through the forests with their pack of hunting hounds, and Llewelyn loved one of these dogs as much as his own child. Gelert was gentle as a lamb, whiter than a swan, stronger than a lion, faster than a tiger, and was always at the head of the pack when the horn sounded. No wolf had escaped Gelert's jaws for six years.

Llewelyn and Joanna were staying at one of their hunting lodges in the forest. They tucked their child safely in his wooden cradle by the hearth and set off with their hounds. They killed three wolves, and blew their horns to call the dogs to return, but Gelert did not appear. Llewelyn feared his favourite hound had been slain by a wolf.

They returned to the hunting lodge to find Gelert lying by the over-turned cradle, blood caked to his fur and dripping from his chops. Thinking Gelert had slaughtered and eaten his child, Llewellyn ran his sword through the dog's heart. Then he went to the cradle and saw, lying on the flagstones, the body of a huge wolf. He lifted up the cradle and there was his child, safe and sound. The gruesome truth dawned. Gelert had followed the wolf to the house, knocked over the cradle to hide the baby, and fought off the wolf. Llewelyn stroked the dying hound, and Gelert licked his hand. He buried the dog near the river, placed a slate slab over the grave, and the village was named Beddgelert (Gelert's Grave).

This story was thought to have been brought to Beddgelert from South Wales in the late 1700s by David Prichard, landlord of the Goat Hotel, to encourage tourists to visit the village and part with their money. By 1800, the story had gone viral, popularised by the poem, 'The Grave of the Greyhound', written by William Spenser when he stayed at the Goat that same year.

However, a version of the story was known long before David Prichard moved to the village. The 'Fabula de Beth Kilhart' was written around 1592 and tells of how Llewelyn and Johanna Notha brought a dog from England that 'excelled the Swan, or the snow in whiteness, the lamb in gentleness, the tiger in swiftness, and the Lion in strength of jaw and courage, whose name was Kill-hart'. They chased a hart (a stag) across Gwynedd, and in the resulting fight, the hart and dog killed each other. The dog was buried at 'Bethkilhart'. This story was said to been taken from an early thirteenth-century manuscript, raising the intriguing thought that Llewelyn told his legend in his own lifetime.

A Fairy Dog

A farmer found a bedraggled black dog by the roadside between Pentrefoelas and Hafod y Gareg. As the little dog stared up at her with watery eyes, she remembered a story about her cousin from Bryn Heilyn, who once found a black dog, took it home and treated it cruelly. The fairies came and asked the woman if she would prefer to travel above the wind, below the wind or in the wind. She said, 'Below the wind', so they carried her through the air, just far enough above the ground so her legs were scratched by brambles and her body was dragged through hedges, until she was torn to shreds.

Now the farmer had no wish for this to happen to her, so she took the dog home, made it a soft bed by the fire, fed it chicken bones and ham shanks, and told it fairy tales. The fairies came and thanked her for looking after their dog, and asked if she would like a clean cowshed, or a dirty cowshed. Now, the farmer knew you couldn't have a clean cowshed unless you had no cows, so she said, 'A dirty cowshed, os gwelwch yn dda', and they gave her two cows for every one she owned and she lived on the finest milk, butter and cheese for the rest of her days.

A Gruesome Tail

Old Shemi Wâd had a shotgun with a barrel that was bent at right angles so he could shoot round corners. He was out hunting one day on Parrog Marshes when he tried to shoot a hare, but there were no corners on the marsh so he missed. He told his retriever to fetch a hare and the dog was off, lolloping through the long grass. Well, the poor dog didn't see a scythe blade that some daft lad had left lying there pointing upwards, and he ran right through it, slicing himself in two.

But Shemi's dog was indestructible. He called his two half-dogs, and went through his pockets. He found a bit of old cheese, some maggots, matches, baccy and a tin of ointment. He opened the tin, took the left half of his dog, tucked it between his knees, and spread the ointment all over the cut. Then he did the same with the right half. He fumbled in his pockets again, found a needle and cotton and sewed his dog back together. It wasn't till he finished that he realised he'd sewn the two halves the wrong way round, so that one head faced forwards and the other backwards. Well, now the dog could run both ways and catch two hares at the same time. Best dog old Shemi ever had.

Cath Palug

Coll ap Collfrewy, a swineherd from Cornwall, owned a huge white sow called Henwen. She was so enormous the people feared she was about to give birth to something evil, so they chased her into the sea. Coll grabbed hold of her bristles and held on while she swam to Wales.

Henwen walked ashore and passed through Maes Gwenith in Gwent, where she gave birth to a grain of wheat and a bee. The seed germinated and the bee pollinated it, and there grew the finest wheat fields in Wales. As she passed Llonion in Pembroke, she gave birth to a barley grain and a bee, and there grew the finest barley fields in Wales. At Llŷn in Arfon she gave birth to a grain of rye and a third bee, and that made the finest rye bread in Wales.

At the Hill of Cyferthwch in Eryri, she gave birth to an eagle and a wolf cub, and by the time she reached Llanfair in Arfon, she was pregnant again. This time, she gave birth to the most monstrous creature that Coll had ever seen. A little black kitten. It looked so evil, he decided to drown it. He picked it up by the tail and threw it from the Black Rock into the Menai Straits, though the kitten refused to drown. It swam to Ynys Môn, where the sons of Palug pulled it from the water, but they must have wished they hadn't. It grew and grew, until it rampaged through the island, tearing hundreds of warriors to shreds with its sharp claws. Little wonder it became one of the three plagues of Ynys Môn.

The French romances tell how Cath Palug was known as Capalu, and had the body of a horse and the head of a cat with red eyes. In a twelfth-century satirical story, it kills King Arthur and takes the throne of Britain for itself. In the Welsh story, it is finally slain by Cei, one of Arthur's knights.

The Sheepdog

A Welsh MP went to the Royal Welsh Agricultural Show, just to be seen. Trying to cosy up to a grizzly local farmer, the MP admitted, 'I can't speak Welsh but I understand every word you say'. The farmer replied, 'Just like my old dog Meg, here.'

HORSES, FAIRY CATTLE AND AN ENCHANTED PIG

The Ychen Bannog

Huw Gadarn, known as Huw the Mighty, was the first farmer in Wales. He had returned from the Summer Islands of the Mediterranean, where he had learned how to use a plough and how to domesticate wild and hairy creatures.

One day, he was called upon by the poor people of Dyffryn Conwy, who were being terrorised by an afanc, a wild, hairy creature with a scaly tail and huge yellow teeth, which had emerged from a pool to terrorise the land by causing floods and eating people. So it was, Huw the Mighty arrived in Conwy with his plough and two long-horned oxen, the Ychen Bannog, the children of the Spotted Cow.

Huw explained that the afanc was attracted to maidens, so he chose a reluctant local girl as bait, dressed her in a pretty frock and persuaded her to sit beneath a tree by the pool with a wreath of flowers in her hair. He told her to keep still and look alluring, while he hid and waited. Late in the day, the afanc crawled out of the pool, dripping

Ychen Bannog

with pondweed and gnashing its yellow teeth. It stared into the girl's eyes, laid its head on her lap, placed its claw on her breast and fell asleep. The brave girl held her breath as Huw quietly wrapped the hairy creature in chains and tied it to the Ychen Bannog, but as they dragged it away, it awoke and in its rage tore the girl's breast.

The Ychen Bannog dragged the afanc to Llyn-y-Foel, but the strain caused one of the oxen's eyes to pop out of its head, and where it dropped to the ground it formed Pwll Llygad yr Ych, the Pool of the Ox's Eye. They hauled the afanc through Bwlch Rhiw'r Ychen, the Pass of the Oxen, through Nant Gwynant and dropped it in remote Llyn Glaslyn, where there was no one to terrorise.

It was last seen in the eighteenth century, flying over the lake like a toad with wings and a tail, shrieking terribly. And Huw the Hero was last seen on a Mediterranean island, hiding from an angry Conwy girl with a scarred breast.

In Welsh, 'afanc' means 'beaver'. According to Gerald, the last beavers in Wales lived on the banks of the Teifi at Cilgerran in the late twelfth century, where they built intricate dams and homes in the shape of willow bowers. If a male beaver was cornered by hunting hounds he gnawed off his own genitals and offered them in exchange for his life. And if the beaver had already been pursued, he would turn around, lift up his tail and show the dogs they already had his prized possessions.

Afanc

The Ox of Eynonsford Farm

At Eynonsford Farm near Reynoldston on Gower stood an old thatched longhouse with a kitchen at one end and a cowshed at the other, where the farmer kept his prize ox. One summer night, he heard music coming from the cowshed. He shone his lantern inside and there were the Verry Volk, scurrying around the pebbled floor and dancing on the back of his prize ox. When the music stopped they fed the ox some herbs, and it dropped down dead. They swarmed over the body, skilletted it into a thousand steaks and laid the bones on the floor. They lit a fire outside, roasted the ox and feasted through the night. Then they went back into the cowshed, reassembled the bones into the shape of an ox, stretched the hide over them, and there was the farmer's ox, alive as ever and good as new. Except, one of the bones from its foreleg was missing. They searched everywhere, until the sun rose over Cefn Bryn, and then they vanished. The farmer went into the cowshed and there was his lopsided ox, with one foreleg longer than the other, walking with a limp.

Ceffyl Dŵr

A fisherman and his grandson landed their boat in Oxwich Bay, and walked by lantern-light up the track to the church, where they saw a white horse. It made no sound, pranced on its hind legs, poured breath from its nostrils, passed through the closed gate into the churchyard and vanished. The fisherman put his arm round the boy and told him it was past his bedtime. It was a ceffyl dŵr, a water horse.

Ceffyl Dŵr

A weary traveller was walking across the Vale of Glamorgan when he came to the ford over the River Ogmore. He saw a white horse, nibbling the fresh grass by the water's edge. The horse offered to carry him over the shallow river to save his poor feet from getting wet, so he climbed on its back and held on to its white mane. The horse galloped away until they were travelling as fast as lightning, when the man noticed the horse's hooves weren't touching the ground. The horse vanished and the man fell to earth, where the horse ate up his remains.

A man was resting by the cascades near Glynneath, when a water horse appeared from the river and shook itself dry. The man climbed onto its back, the horse flew through the air and, as the moon rose, he found himself falling onto the hillside. Dazed and shocked, he climbed down the hill and found himself in Llanddewi Brefi in Ceredigion, over fifty miles from Glynneath.

A man caught a white horse in Carmarthen Bay, took it home and used it as a carthorse. One day, he noticed its hooves were pointing the wrong way and realised it was a ceffyl dŵr – too late, for it escaped from its bridle, dragged the man into the sea and he was never seen again.

A ceffyl dŵr was seen around Flemingston in the Vale of Glamorgan in the early 1800s. One December evening on the full moon, with snow in the air and visibility poor, a traveller was walking to the Old Mill near Aberthaw when he realised he was lost. He saw a small horse ridden by a long-legg'd man. The horse's shape was outlined in light so the man followed, hoping it would lead him to a village. He found himself at the Old Mill when the horse vanished. That night the valley flooded, and the man believed to his dying day that he had been guided to safety by the ceffyl dŵr.

The Horse that Dropped Gold

There was an old man who had very little money and nowhere to keep the little he had. He didn't like banks, so he fed his few coins to his horse. Every time the horse dropped dung he took a coin, then fed the rest back to the horse.

One day a fair came to town and the old man wanted to go. He knew he had two sovereigns in the horse, so he waited till the horse dropped dung and cleaned his sovereigns. He knew if he spent them, there would be no more money in the horse.

A rich man was passing by and saw a horse that dropped gold, so he asked the old man if he would sell it. The old man said he could never part with his dearest friend, for they had travelled together for years and shared many adventures. But the rich man offered more and more money and eventually the deal was done. The rich man placed the horse in his stable and waited for it to drop dung. Then he put on a little pair of white gloves and searched through the steaming mound. He found no gold, and realised he had been taken for a fool.

He complained to the old man that the horse did not drop gold. The old man asked him what he fed to the horse, and the rich man told him only the finest oats, straw and hay. 'Well, there you are then,' said the old man. 'If you don't feed your horse gold, how do you expect him to give you gold?' The rich man demanded his money back, and the old man said he'd see him on the back of the Devil first.

So the old man is a little richer, and the rich man is a little poorer. And isn't that how it should be?

The King's Secret

Pen Llŷn was once ruled by March ab Meirchion of Castellmarch near Abersoch, a pompous old soul who had a secret. March had the ears of a horse. To hide his ears, he grew his hair long and high like a beehive, and wore a tall stovepipe hat. Every barber he employed had discovered his secret, so he cut off their heads. One young barber found the ears but, valuing his head, said nothing.

'Have you anything to tell me, barber?'

'Nay, Your Majesty.'

'Did you say "Neigh"?'

But the secret was too big. It burned a hole in the young man's heart till he was fit to burst, so he whispered his secret to the earth. 'March has horse's ears.'

The earth giggled.

In time, reeds grew on the earth, and an itinerant piper cut them to make a new set of pipes. That evening, he played at a feast organised by March to celebrate himself when the pipes began to sing, 'March has horse's ears!', louder and louder, until March was about to order the decapitation of everyone in Pen Llŷn. Then he realised, 'March, you are a fool. You cannot even see your own ears. Why be embarrassed about something you can only see with a looking glass?' And March laughed, a great belly-laugh, and everyone on Pen Llŷn has been laughing ever since.

On the travellers' camp and caravan site between Abersoch and Castellmarch was a cafe. It was little more than a pre-fab, though the walls were decorated with painted murals depicting scenes from the March's story. One was of the pompous old king with his horse's ears, an image that sparked a lifetime's interest in book illustration, folk art and visual storytelling. The cafe was demolished quite recently. The paintings hadn't been thought worth saving. They were hardly Lascaux or Bayeux, just a childhood memory – my own guilty secret.

The Undertaker's Horse

Back in the days before tractors, the horse was King of Gower. There was one old Clydesdale called Blossom who lived near Rhossili, and her job was to pull the lifeboat down to the sea whenever she heard the boom or saw the flares. She always reached the quay before the lifeboatmen, and had helped save the lives of many a lost soul.

Blossom had reached the end of her working life and was ready for the Knacker's Yard, but the lifeboatmen could not bear to think of her ending her days as glue. So they gave her to the local undertaker, for she walked slowly enough to pull coffins to the church at an appropriate pace.

One day, she was pulling a coffin to the door of Port Eynon Church. Not even the horse brasses round her neck rattled to disturb the sombre thoughts of the mourners. The undertaker climbed down from his seat and the bearers in their black top hats were about to lift the coffin when the boom went off. Old Blossom's ears pricked up. She saw the flares. Someone needed help.

Off she galloped as fast as her old legs could carry her, down to the quay to launch the lifeboat, the coffin bouncing up and down on the

Undertaker's Horse

cart behind her. The mourners watched their dear departed depart, and the funeral continued without the corpse, as if nothing unusual had happened, though the relatives complained that they had paid for a cremation, not a burial at sea.

The Boar Hunt

Ysbaddaden Bencawr, Old Hawthornbush, the King of the Giants, had given Culwch a series of impossible tasks in his quest to win the hand of the giant's daughter, Olwen. One of these tasks was to cut the comb from between the ears of the enchanted Irish wild boar, Twrch Trwyth. Now, read on ...

King Arthur resolved to help Culwch in his impossible quest. He summoned the finest warriors from Britain, and the finest dogs and horses from Brittany and Normandy, and this mighty army sailed to Ireland where the Irish greeted him with gifts and offers of help. They went to Esgair Oerfel where the dogs were let loose on Twrch Twyth and his seven boars. They fought from dawn to dusk, until one fifth of the men of Ireland were slaughtered.

Twrch Trwyth

On the third day, Arthur fought Twrch Trwyth, and the battle lasted nine days and nine nights, and in all that time Arthur slew only one insignificant piglet. Culwch asked why the boar was so difficult to defeat, and Arthur explained, 'Twrch Trwyth was once a King who indulged in every sin known to man, so God punished him by changing him and his courtiers into wild boars'.

Arthur sent one of his men in the form of
a bird to invite the boars to talk. Grigun, a
boar with silver bristles, told the bird that
it was bad enough being turned
into boars without having to
fight the mighty Arthur as
well. But if Arthur wanted
the comb from between Twrch
Trwyth's ears, the only way was to kill
him, and that would never happen.

Twrch Trwyth and his army
of boars swam to Wales, pursued by
Arthur and his warriors in their ship
Prydwen. Arthur landed at Porthclais in Dyfed and tracked down
Twrch Trwyth, but not before the boar had slaughtered every man
and beast in Daugleddyf. At Preseli, Arthur arranged his warriors on
the two banks of the Nyfer, while Twrch Trwyth stood his ground at
Cwmcerwyn. There was a terrible slaughter, and every warrior who
fought the boar was torn apart. Arthur chased him all over Dyfed until,
one by one, all his boars were slain and Twrch Trwyth stood alone, and
made for Cornwall.

Arthur summoned all the warriors of Devon and Cornwall to meet
him at the mouth of the River Severn, on the banks of the Hafren.
He told them, 'Twrch Trwyth has slaughtered too many of my men.
He will not leave Cornwall alive. I will fight until one of us stands.'

Culwch spoke for all the warriors and they stood by Arthur. They
caught up with Twrch Trwyth and drove him into the Hafren. They held
him firmly by the feet, while Mabon ap Modrun grabbed the razor and
Cyledyr Wyllt took the shears, but before they could remove the comb,
the boar dragged them onto the land. He dragged them, grunting and
squealing, into Cornwall where the boar savaged them with his terrible
tusks, then retreated, his white tusks dripping with blood. Arthur and
his knights drove Twrch Trwyth into the sea, where Culwch managed

to cut the comb from between his ears. No one knows where Twrch Trwyth went, but as he swam out to sea, he dragged two of Arthur's finest warriors with him.

Arthur returned to Celliwig in Cornwall to wash his wounds, while Culwch embarked on the next of the impossible tasks to help him gain the hand of Olwen.

EAGLES, OWLS AND SEAGULLS

The King of the Birds

Back in the old Welsh Dreamtime, the birds decided to elect a King. They called a parliament, they came from North and South, big birds and little, colourful and drab, cooing and squawking, and they agreed their King would be the bird who could fly the highest. They all knew the eagle would win, for he could soar high over the mountains of Eryri.

As Eagle prepared to fly, a little wren jumped onto his back and hid amongst his feathers. Eagle flew higher than any other bird till he could fly no higher when Wren jumped from his back, flew just that little bit higher, sang as loudly as he could and landed back on the eagle.

The King

So, Wren had won, and the birds were furious. How could such a tiny, cheeky loudmouth be their King? They decided to drown him in their own tears. They took it in turns to weep into a pan until it was full, but clumsy old Owl knocked it over and spilt the tears, so she was chased away and cursed to fly by night to escape their wrath.

Watching this, Wren understood that he would not be a popular monarch, so he abdicated in favour of the eagle, happy that a little bird with a loud voice could be heard above all the twittering.

Are you listening, Your Highnesses?

The Ancient Animals

In the Woods of Gwernabwy in Scotland lived a wise old Eagle and, oh, he was a gloomy old soul. His wife had died, his children and grandchildren had inherited the woods and mountains around, and he was all alone in his melancholy. So he decided to cheer himself up by getting married again, wise old bird that he was. Not to a young fledgling, oh no, for he would never be able to satisfy her needs. No, his wife must be older than himself. But who?

Then he remembered. Owl of Cwmcawlwyd. She was reputed to be older than the rocks, but he wanted to know exactly how old she was. Eagle needed wisdom, so he flew to Wales to see his friend, the Stag of Rhedynfre. He asked Stag if he knew how old Owl was. Stag said, 'See this withered old stump of an oak tree? An oak is three hundred years in growing, three hundred years in its prime, three hundred years decaying, and three hundred years rotting into earth. When I was a fawn, I remember this tree as an acorn and even then, Owl was a wrinkled old bird. But if you don't believe me, there is one much older than I. Ask the Salmon of Llyn Llaw.'

Eagle went to see Salmon and asked if he knew how old Owl was. Salmon said, 'See the number of scales and spots on my back and belly, multiply those to the number of grains of spawn in my body, that's how old I am, yet when I was a fry, Owl was a wrinkled old bird. But if you don't believe me, there is one much older than I. Ask the Ousel of Cilgwri.'

Eagle found Ousel sitting on a pebble, and asked how old Owl was. Ousel said, 'See this little pebble, a child of seven years could take it in his hand, but there was a time when three hundred of the strongest oxen could not pull it. I have cleaned my beak upon it once every night before going to sleep. I have no idea how old I am, but I have only ever known Owl as a wrinkled old bird. But if you don't believe me, there is one much older and wiser than I. Go to Ceredigion, ask the old Toad of Cors Fochno. He gibbers incomprehensibly, but he is older and wiser than the very earth itself. If he does not know the age of the Owl, no one does.'

Eagle flew to Cors Fochno and found Toad sitting in the middle of the swamp, wrinkled as a walnut, breathing and blinking. He told Toad that he was marrying Owl, but hadn't actually asked her yet, though she was certain to agree, but he only wanted to marry her if she was unimaginably ancient. So how old is Owl? Toad blinked, and breathed, and said, 'I only eat dust. And I never eat half enough dust to fill my belly. See those hills? I have eaten all the dust in the valleys of Wales, though I have only eaten one grain a day, for fear I eat all the earth before my death. That would not be sensible or sustainable, now would it? You see, I am as old as the rocks, yet when I was a tadpole, Owl was a wrinkled old harridan, forever chattering, "ty-hwt-ty-hwt", all through the long winter nights, frightening the children, boring the ancestors, disturbing my sleep. Marry her, and take her away with you. Dimwit.'

So Eagle married Owl, and all the animals in Wales came to the wedding, all except for Toad. Maybe he forgot, or he fell asleep, or he was busy breathing and blinking. Maybe you should ask him? He's still there, in the middle of the quivering bog, the wisest creature in Wales, wiser even than the Bards. But if you try to walk out across the peat to seek his wisdom, you'd be sucked down into the deep, dark bog long before you reached him. That's why he says, 'Dimwit, dimwit, dimwit'.

The Old Toad of Cors Fochno

Shemi Wâd and the Seagulls

Shemi was born in Fishguard in 1815, where he lived in a whitewashed cottage in Broom Street. He earned his pennies by gardening, growing fruit and veg, pig sticking for the local farms and telling tall tales to anyone inclined to listen. He smoked, drank, scratched himself in public and didn't believe in washing. That's why he got fleas. One of them was a singing flea who lived beneath his bed in a saucepan he used as a chamber pot. The flea sang rude sea shanties from the tops of old matchsticks, and no one sang better than Shemi's singing flea.

One sunny day Shemi took his fishing rod and tramped down the hill to Parrog to catch mackerel. He sat down on his favourite rock and emptied his pocket looking for maggots for bait. He pulled out string (long), string (short), a tin of baccy, a box of matches, a spare box of matches (just in case), a piece of cheese, an unwashed hanky, two coins, a sweet covered in fluff and a stale currant bun. But no maggots. So he broke off a piece of the currant bun and threaded it on the hook.

It had been a long hard day doing nothing-much-at-all and he fancied a nap, so he tied the rod to his tummy with the string, and dreamed of nice fat mackerel for tea. As the tide went out, the sharp-eyed seagulls spotted the crumbs on the end of his line and swallowed them down, hooks and all. At that moment Shemi snored loudly, startling the seagulls who took off, pulling the fishing line and fisherman behind them. Shemi found himself flying through the air and over the sea towards a green land and a grey city.

Then the fishing line broke, down Shemi fell and landed with a thump in a flower bed. He checked that his sou'wester was still on his head and asked a couple of passing ladies where he was, but they couldn't understand a word he said. This was clearly Central Park in New York, where they don't speak Pembrokeshire. He was feeling tired after his long flight, so he climbed inside an old cannon that reminded him of the one in Fishguard, and went to sleep.

At nine o'clock the next morning there was a loud bang and Shemi woke up to find himself flying over the sea once again, but this time without being attached to seagulls. He landed with a thump outside the Rose and Crown in Goodwick, picked himself up, checked his sou'wester was still on his head, looked around to make sure no one was looking, went inside, ordered a pint of cwrw and told the landlord all about his walk to the pub that day. The landlord he didn't believe a word. A flock of seagulls couldn't have pulled old Shemi over the sea to New York. It must have been Dublin. That's much more believable, now, isn't it?

Iolo's Fables

Iolo Morganwg described himself as a rattleskull genius, loud but with little substance. He was an eighteenth-century stonemason, writer, antiquarian, lyrical poet, myth-maker, folk song collector, pacifist, political radical, argumentative dreamer, failed farmer, laudanum addict, fierce opponent of slavery, owner of a fair trade shop in Cowbridge, creator of the Gorsedd, writer and collector of manuscripts in the tradition of William Blake and supporter of the French Revolution who met Tom Paine and Benjamin Franklin. He walked everywhere with a staff and a backpack containing his precious flute, and a nosegay of stories and songs. In his desire to create a Welsh identity and mythology, he wrote several Welsh animal stories in the manner of Aesop, which he called *The Fables of Cattwg the Wise:*

The Mole and the Lark

A mole emerged from his dark dank tunnel, attracted by the bright sunlight and the song of a skylark. 'Oh, how I wish I could fly as free as the lark and sing as sweetly,' thought the mole. Just then, a sparrowhawk flew over a hedge, snatched the lark in its talons and flew off. The mole retreated down his hole, thinking it was far better to be a mole, safe in the dark dank tunnels with only earthworms for company.

The Hog and the Cuckoo

A hog was tied to an apple tree in the orchard, when he heard a cuckoo singing from the topmost branch of the tree. He pointed his snout upwards, and said, 'Why on earth do you climb up so high to sing coo-coo, for no pig cares a straw for your song?'

The cuckoo replied, 'I sing because the sun shines and people listen all spring for my song, and because I am not tied to a tree by a rope attached to a ring through my nose.'

The Woodpigeon and the Magpie

Magpie was watching a woodpigeon making a mess of building her nest. He explained that she was doing it all wrong.

'I know!' said Woodpigeon. But she ignored Magpie's sage advice and carried on in her messy way.

Magpie told her, 'You need to weave the sprigs in with the twigs, neatly this way and that way, and then you will build your nest correctly.'

Woodpigeon said, 'I know! I know!', but she kept on making a mess, saying, 'I know! I know! I know!'

Magpie was exasperated, 'If you know all this, why don't you do it?'

But Woodpigeon went on in her own scatty way, for it is not easy to make a nightingale out of a crow, or to put brains in a gate post.

The Nightingale and the Hawk
Nightingale was proud of her melodious voice. Thrush called her an angel and Blackbird declared his love for her in poetry. But Nightingale declaimed that she would only listen to birds more heroic than thrushes and blackbirds. What pomposity, they thought, and so did Lark, Linnet and Cuckoo, so they all left her. Nightingale sat all alone, until Hawk spotted her and declared his love for her. She fluttered with flattery at this handsome Hawk and invited him a little closer. So Hawk snuggled up, plucked out all her feathers and ate her up.

Why the Robin's Breast is Red

A boy was throwing stones at a robin when his grandmother grabbed him by the ear. She told him that the bird's red breast was burned there by the fires of Hell, where he goes to deliver drops of water to cool the souls of those in torment. So never hurt a robin, for one day you may need those cooling waters.

Toad

DRAGONS, HAIRY THINGS AND AN ELEPHANT

The Red and White Dragons

Lludd, King of the Brythons, was a wise ruler who built houses for his people, protected them with walls and and provided them with enough food to fill their bellies.

Lludd loved his brother Llefelys well, and arranged a marriage between him and the King of France's daughter, and so the Brythons and French became brothers, too.

As time passed, three plagues fell upon Brython. The first was that every word was carried on the wind, every conversation overheard, until there were no secrets left. The second was a pitiful shriek that was heard on Mayday eve, which drained men of their strength, women miscarried, young people lost their senses, nothing grew on the earth and no fish swam in the seas. The third was that food was disappearing from the nation's food stores and the people's bellies rumbled with hunger.

Lludd asked for help from his brother Llefelys. They met on a boat in the middle of the sea between Brython and France and spoke through a copper tube so their words could

Dragons

not be stolen. Llefelys explained that the first plague was caused by an invading people called the Coranians, who had spies everywhere and were stealing secrets. The second plague was caused by an invading white dragon, and the shriek was the pain of a native red dragon. The third plague was caused by an invading giant who had enchanted the country in order to steal its food supplies.

So Llefelys conjured a potion extracted from the crushed bodies of insects soaked in water, which he threw over the Coranians, poisoning them but leaving the Brythons unharmed. So ended the first plague.

Llefelys then told Lludd to go to the centre of his Kingdom in Oxford, dig a pit, place a cauldron in it, fill it with mead and cover it in silk. This he did, and the white dragon appeared and was attacked by the red dragon until, exhausted as pigs, they dropped into the cauldron, swallowed the mead and fell asleep. Lludd dragged the two drunken dragons to Dinas Emrys in Snowdonia, imprisoned them in an underground stone cell, and so ended the second plague.

Llefelys now told Lludd to wash himself in the bath by his bed until his eyes were clean. He saw the giant carrying a hamper of food from the stores, drew his sword and they fought until the man pleaded for mercy. From that day the giant served only Lludd, the people's bellies rumbled no more, and so ended the third plague.

When Lludd and Llefelys passed over to the Otherworld, Vortigern became King of the Brythons. Vortigern had betrayed his people to another invader, the Saxons, and had fled to Snowdonia where he began to build a castle, but every night the walls fell down. His advisers told him it was a sign that the Gods were displeased with him, so he must appease them by sacrificing a boy born of a virgin and smear his blood on the foundations.

They found a lad called Emrys Wledig, but Emrys was a cunning child who told Vortigern that his advisers had it all wrong, that it was nothing to do with the Gods. Oh, no. The problem was caused by trying to build the castle on top of an underground cell where two dragons were sleeping, and if these dragons awoke, they would fight, and if the white dragon won, the Saxons would invade Vortigern's land, but if the red dragon won, the Brythons would repel the invaders.

The boy was clearly speaking nonsense, so Vortigern continued to build his walls. The dragons awoke and fought with tooth and claw until the red dragon defeated the white and the Saxons were repelled. The treacherous King was chased by his own people to Nant Gwrtheyrn where he leapt to his death from the cliffs at Carreg y Llam. The land became known as Cymru, and the people of Wales chose as their emblem the red dragon.

And young Emrys Wledig? Well, he grew to be a great conjurer named Myrddin, or Merlin.

Serpents, Carrogs, Vipers and Gwibers

Dragons, serpents, gwibers, wyverns, carrogs and vipers were once as common as pheasants in Wales. Wherever they appeared, heroes were called upon.

A dragon was eating people in Denbigh, when Siôn y Bodiau, who had two thumbs on each hand, cut off its head and carried it through the town shouting, 'Dinbych!'

Gwiber

A flying stony-skinned serpent was lured into the river at Newcastle Emlyn by a soldier waving his red flannel uniform, who shot it in the fleshy underbelly, filling the river with blood.

A carrog was killed in a meadow near Conwy, where young Nico Ifan kicked its body, caught his leg on a fang, and poisoned himself to death.

A wyvern terrorised Moel Cynach where it hypnotised and ate people, until a passing shepherd found it asleep, drove a stake through its eye and buried it at Bedd y Wibr, the Viper's Grave.

A gwiber near Llanidloes drank cattle's blood, set fire to the forests and filled the River Severn with green slime, before a fisherman slew it and turned the meadow red with its blood.

Another gwiber was terrorising the folk of Llanrhaeadr-ym-Mochnant, so they built a pillar out of boulders, wedged iron spikes into it, draped it in scarlet cloth and set fire to it. The gwiber thought it was another fire-breathing creature, attacked it and tore itself to shreds on the spikes.

A man from Penmachno was told he would die of a viper's bite, a broken neck and drowning, which he thought couldn't possibly happen, until he met a viper that bit him on the hand. He tried to run, tripped over a rock, broke his neck, fell into the river and drowned.

A serpent was so repulsed by the smell of St Samson that rather than fight him it ate its own tail, then its body and finally its head before it vanished.

The woods around Penllyn in Glamorgan were inhabited by terrible and beautiful serpents covered in scales that shone like jewels, with crests the colours of the rainbow. When disturbed they glided on sparkling wings, and when they were angry they flew over people's heads with outspread tails covered in feathers like a peacock's. An old man said he had killed many of them, for they were worse than foxes for taking his poultry. An old woman said they had a king and queen, and they lived in the woods around Penmark and Beaupre. Her grandfather was attacked by one, so he shot it and kept the skin and feathers.

In 1812 a fearsome gwiber with a long body, short wings and glaring eyes, appeared in a grove near Plas y Faerdref in the Vale of Edeirnion. A hunt was arranged and when it was cornered, the mighty huntsmen found they had been chasing a cock pheasant who had strayed from a neighbouring estate.

The Marvellous Lizard of Cefn lived in a cave near St Asaph which was renowned for archaeological discoveries, including bones of elephants, rhinos and hippos, and for being visited by Charles Darwin in 1831. In October 1870, reports appeared that a monstrous scaly creature had been slain by a heroic Welshman. People queued to see the remains of the creature in return for an admission fee. It turned out to be a crocodile from a travelling menagerie that had died and been brought to the cave by Mr Thomas Hughes, chimney sweep from Rhyl, who was earning himself a pretty penny from the tourists.

The Welsh Yeti

Not far from Llyn Gwynain near Dinas Emrys, was a cave called Ogo'r Gŵr Blew, where lived a gŵr blewog, a hairy thing. It was partly human, with a body covered in thick black hair and the talons and teeth of a beast. It prowled round the farms, slaughtered cattle and carried them away to its lair in the mountains. When it had eaten all the cattle, it developed a taste for people, particularly children. Parents bolted their doors and windows.

One young widow was so terrified by the thought of her babies being eaten by the gŵr blewog, she lay awake every night to protect

Gŵr Blewog

them with a lamp in one hand and an axe in the other. One night she heard footsteps outside the cottage, the door latch rattled and there was a howl. She held her breath. A hairy face appeared at the window, a claw smashed the glass and reached in. The woman dropped her lamp and hacked at the arm with the axe. There was a shriek of pain and footsteps faded into the darkness.

In the morning the villagers found the woman cowering in a corner, clutching her babies to her, shaking with fright and staring at a severed claw lying on the floor in front of her. They followed a trail of blood to a cave strewn with bones, but there was no sign of the gŵr blewog. They burned the claw on a fire of rowan wood, buried the ashes outside the church wall and covered it with soil from the churchyard. The village was troubled no more, but a ghostly hairy shape was often seen prowling round the gravestones searching for its severed claw.

The Wiston Basilisk

On Wiston Bank lived a basilisk. It had yellow and black skin, poisonous breath and eyes in the back of its head that could turn you to dust with one glance. It was said that anyone who looked at the basilisk without being seen would inherit the estate of Castell Cas-wis, near Haverfordwest. Several tried, and all were turned to dust, until a young man called Jac had an idea. He climbed inside a barrel, the lid was fitted firmly and he rolled past the basilisk, peering through the bunghole, singing, 'Basilisk, Basilisk, I can see you but you can't see me'. Jac inherited the castle, though he had to live in a barrel for the rest of his life.

Shaggy Elephant Tales

Ask anyone in Tregaron about the elephant that died there, and they will all tell you a tale, though not necessarily the same one. Here is the true story. Honest, it is.

In 1841, William Batty was manager of an amphitheatre on the south bank of the Thames in London, where he presented exotic circus phantasmagoria. There was a whole family of Battys, Lena the equestrienne, Thomas the lion tamer who had been scarred by a tiger, Madame Frederica and her amazing performing dogs. And then there was brother George, a man of entrepreneurial abilities, who reasoned there was a whole country out there who wanted to see wild animals.

So it was, one evening in May 1848, Batty's Travelling Menagerie pulled into the village square in Tregaron on its way to the fair in Cardigan, with wagons containing exotic creatures, Indian and African leopards, crested porcupines, a magnificent specimen of the drill baboon, a young Russian bear, a pair of Irish badgers, a handsome blue macaw (very rare), and 'Rajah,' a seven-year-old Indian elephant, very docile, trained to carry children. After a night's lodgings at the Talbot Hotel, they moved on, leaving behind a thin drizzle, an irate preacher who took offence at them for travelling on the Sabbath, and a sick Indian elephant.

The townsfolk were bemused by the poor creature, but did their best to care for it. They kept it warm and brought it water, and one small boy whispered into its ear and stroked its wrinkled skin. Some said it had swallowed contaminated water from the mines in the hills and was dying of lead poisoning. They wrote to the local newspaper declaring their concern for the suffering of this strange animal. The preacher wrote, too, condemning the blasphemous Batty to everlasting Hell.

A week later, the elephant had vanished, and this is when the stories began. Some say it was buried at the back of the Talbot Hotel, although a recent archaeological dig organised by University of Wales, Lampeter, failed to find it – much to the amusement of those who believe it's under the car park or on the other side of the hill. Another theory says that hunger drove the locals to make a jumbo cauldron of cawl. Yet the suspicion remains that it lived a contented life on a farm in the hills, fed on bara brith and unseen by prying eyes, like all the other elephants who have lived peacefully and undisturbed in the wild west. Apart from the one that fell through a bridge onto a train on the Cliff Railway in Aberystwyth. But that's a very tall tale indeed.

SAINTS, WISHES AND CURSING WELLS

The Shee Well that Ran Away

A water ogre lived on the Ewenny River, where three springs met at a spot known as the Shee Well. It stole the heart of any girl who washed her clothes in the river, and imprisoned them in the well. Only one girl escaped, and she never spoke of what had happened to her. In time, the Shee Well grew tired of the ogre's unpleasant behaviour. It wept and wailed, and ran away to live in a cave in the hills, taking the river and all the fish with it.

The ogre had no water to drink, no fish to eat and the dry riverbed became infested with toads and snakes. It pleaded with the Shee Well to return. The well agreed, on condition that the ogre set the girls free and then looked after the meadows and the forest. The ogre agreed, the well returned, the forest flourished and fresh, sweet water flowed through the valley once again, which is now a place of peace and tranquility.

It is said that if a girl washes her underwear in the river, carries it home between her teeth and places it by the fire to dry, then she will see her future husband in the flames. And if she doesn't like him, she can turn her underwear round and he will disappear.

St Dwynwen

Dwynwen grew up on Ynys Môn some thousand and a half years ago, one of twenty-four daughters of King Brychan. History does not record whether they all had the same mother. He was an early Christian, who filled his daughter with compassion and piety. She was a little cold, but she was changing. She was bleeding.

She visited the wishing well at the top of the hill, no more than a hole in the ground filled with muddy water and three brown fish. She wished for a man – just to see him naked, you understand. Then she flushed, embarrassed at her boldness. She ran down to the river, threw off her clothes and was about to dive in the cooling waters when she sensed someone behind her. She turned, and there was a man with shaggy black hair and a thin red mouth full of shark's teeth, staring through dark furrowed eyebrows.

'I know you, Dwynwen.'

'And I know you, Maelon.'

Then her wish came true. Maelon removed his clothes. She didn't know where to look, she closed her eyes, touched her fingertips together to pray for guidance from the angels, but her eyes kept opening. The heat inside Maelon passed into Dwynwen. She was on fire, about to combust, yet her eyes stared coldly at him and she wept frozen tears. Her stare penetrated the back of Maelon's neck and travelled down his spine. His heart slowed, the blood in his veins froze and he was turned into a block of ice.

She walked for three days, then returned to the well at the top of the hill. She asked the three brown fish for three wishes.

Dwynwen

142

Wish one, compassion. Defrost Maelon. She watched from the hill-side, as life returned to his body. Would he run to her, scoop her up in his arms and kiss her gently? No. He ran.

Wish two, redemption. No man would come closer than an arm's length and a palm's width of her for the rest of her life.

Wish three, consideration. Let others find true love. They may not recognise it when it bites them, but they must have the chance.

She left home and lived her life on Ynys Llanddwyn, in celibacy and solitude. Women were inspired by her, visited her, a commune grew and then a convent. The Church recognised her piety and proclaimed her a saint of true, albeit doomed, love. A shrine was built to her on the island, pilgrims left offerings and money and a Dean of Bangor Cathedral built a fine house for himself on the gratuity of visitors. Dafydd ap Gwilym wrote odes to her, and asked her help to win a lady's heart.

Then she was forgotten until the 1960s, when young lovers in Wales began to celebrate 25 January, St Dwynwen's Day, with cards and flowers. She is not forgotten, just strangely remembered.

Dwynwen's Well

Gwen, a fisherman's daughter from Ynys Llanddwyn, was being courted by Gwilym, a woodcutter from Cerrig Mawr. He was a good-looking lad, and he knew it. Stories of his philandering preceded him.

One evening they were walking along the sands to St Dwynwen's Well and Gwil told Gwen that if she called the name of her lover into the well at midnight on midsummer's eve, she would hear the name of her one true love repeated back to her three times. A shiver passed down her spine, while a twinkle flashed through Gwil's eye.

June came, and on midsummer's eve Gwen crept to the well. She held a lantern over the low stone wall and shyly called out, 'Gwilym'. From the depths of the well she heard, 'Gwilym, Gwilym, Gwilym'. Her heart thumped, she peered down into the darkness and saw two bright shining eyes staring back at her. Terrified, she dropped the lantern into the well, and ran.

Gwilym stared upwards as the lantern fell towards him and hit him on the head. He lost his grip on the vertical stone wall that he was clinging to, fell through the darkness and landed in the cold dank water at the bottom of the well. He called out Gwen's name, three times, and begged her to throw him a rope, but she had already run home. He tried to climb the walls, but lost his grip on the moss and fell back into the slimy waters, time and again. No one knows how long he was there or how he got out, but young Gwilym never went philandering again.

St Melangell

Brochfael, Lord of Powys, was hunting a hare through the steep oak woods of the Tanat Valley, hounds whirling around his feet and his goshawk swirling about his head, when he saw a woman sitting amongst the wild garlic. The hare ran towards her and hid beneath her skirt. Brochfael called his hounds and they formed a circle around her, but none would touch her. She stared the dogs in their eyes. A few whimpered.

Brochfael demanded she hand over the hare. She lifted her head and stared into his soul. He shivered, and asked who she was, and she said, 'I am Melangell, daughter of Ireland'. He told her he was the Lord of Powys and he owned this forest and everything in it, including that hare, and he ordered her to hand over what was beneath her skirt. She held the hare tightly, and said, 'You do not own this forest. This forest owns you, and it will own another like you long after you are dead.'

He asked what brought her to Powys and she said she had fled an arranged marriage in Ireland. Brochfael took her by the shoulders and told her he would marry her, if only she would give him that hare. She told him she was already married, to the trees.

He launched his goshawk into the air and it circled above her head. Melangell closed her eyes, placed her hands together and moved her lips

in silent prayer. Brochfael was so overcome with the quiet dignity that
confronted him that he rode away, leaving her unmolested.

She lived in hollow yews in the forest and cared for the trees and
hares for the remainder of her days. In AD 604 she founded a monas-
tery on the spot where she had hidden the hare. She is buried beneath
the floor of the little church at Pennant Melangell and, she was right, the
forest was not owned by Brochfael. It now owns another wealthy family,
the Rothschilds.

Melangell

St Eilian's Cursing Well

St Eilian never knew of the devilry he inadvertently released one day
while walking near Llandrillo-yn-Rhos. He was feeling thirsty when a
spring bubbled up at his feet, so he drank and blessed the water. By the
early 1700s a well was built over the spring and soon the waters developed a reputation for curative powers. Thomas Pennant described
the well as a sixteen-foot square enclosure with a bread-stone at each
corner, and a locked gate in the middle that led to the spring. To gain
access, people were expected to pay the well-keeper and undergo a ritual.

An old farmer with a bad temper and the smell of the cowshed lived at Llaneilian-yn-Rhos. One morning his favourite cow fell sick and he blamed it on the fiery tongue and sour temper of his neighbour, Megan Cilgwyn Mawr. They had a storming argument which caused the sheep to tremble on the Great Orme. Megan went to the cursing well at Ffynnon Eilian, paid the well-keeper and cursed the old farmer. Later that day, the farmer went to the well, paid a few coins, threw some old nails into the water and cursed the old hag. They wished misery and unhappiness on each other for the rest of their days, and their wishes came true, for a few years later they were married.

A woman suspected her husband was unfaithful, so she made a figure of him out of marl and stuck pins through its heart. She paid the well-keeper at Ffynnon Eilian, wrote her husband's name in the book, and lowered the figure on a piece of string into the well. Her husband began to have heart pains. A week later she raised the figure from the well and stuck the pins in its head and her husband had headaches. This went on until he admitted his philandering and begged forgiveness. And that's when his pain really started.

One well-keeper was Margaret Holland, the estranged wife of the local vicar, who lived in the cottage adjoining the well. She charged admittance, wrote the names of the cursed in a book, then wrote their initials on a small piece of parchment, rolled it up, placed it inside a piece of lead and dangled it from a string over the well while she recited a prayer. Meanwhile, the conjurer John Edwards of Northop sold cures and charms to those who had been cursed. He took groups to the well, where they paid Mrs Holland to recite a prayer to lift the curses that she had previously been paid to cast. Edwards ended up in court accused of deception and was sentenced to a year's hard labour for obtaining money under false pretences.

In 1829, following a campaign by the Methodists, the well was demolished and filled in. However, if they thought this was the end of the old cursing well, they were mistaken. John Evans had built a Tŷ Unnos, a one-night house, on common land close to the well. One day, a man was rooting around in the ruins and he asked John if he was the well-keeper. John thought he ought to say 'yes' and, to his surprise, the man offered him money in exchange for a drink of water. This gave him an idea. He piped water from the well into his garden, where he built several wells joined by attractive cobbled walks and pretty flowerbeds. He charged admittance, and became known as Jac Ffynnon Eilian.

Jac learned the art of charming and cursing from conjurers like Dic Aberdaron, and the tricks of sorcery from Doctor Bennion of Oswestry, who showed him how to raise the Devil with enough authority to persuade people to believe him. In 1831, Jac was charged at Denbigh Assizes with fraudulently using sorcery and conjuration to demand money. His defence was that he never advertised the properties of the water, and if anyone came to the house and offered him money, it would be rude to refuse them. He was sentenced to six months, and on his release he carried on pretty much as before.

Twenty-five years later, Jac repented, and gave a series of interviews to the bookseller and minister, William Aubrey of Llanerch-y-medd, acknowledging that he was a fraud. His cottage was knocked down, and to this day there is no sign of him at Llandrillo-yn-Rhos, except in our memories.

GIANTS, BEARDS AND CANNIBALS

Cynog and the Cewri

A poor widow with a flock of small children lived on the edge of a wood in Merthyr Cynog. One night, her neighbours were attacked and their houses destroyed, and fingers were pointed at the giants who lived in the woods. The Cewri were indigenous people who lived there long before anyone could remember, and they were feared as robbers and cannibals. The woman was afraid the Cewri would eat her children, so she called on the one man who could help: St Cynog, who had a reputation for fighting cannibal giants, having skewered one in Caerwedros, after it bit a piece from his thigh.

That night Cynog sat outside her front door and prayed. The giants emerged from the woods and surrounded him. They were big, with shaggy red hair and braided moustaches, armed with clubs and axes. He realised prayer was of little use, then remembered he was a pacifist – with emphasis on the fist. He threw his torch at the biggest giant and hit him such a blow that his bowels that had devoured so much innocent blood burst open. The Cewri had never

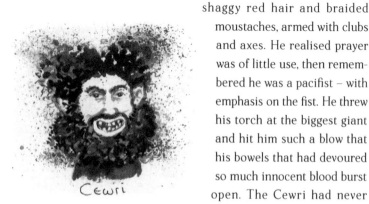

Cewri

seen their own guts. They gagged at the sight of the offal, held their stomachs and ran away. From that day the children of Merthyr Cynog were never eaten again, all thanks to St Cynog the Pacifist.

The Man with Green Weeds in His Hair

Idris was a giant, a poet and an astronomer, who stargazed from a stone observatory on the top of the mountain in Meirionnydd that was named after him, Cadair Idris. He may have been the source of the belief that if you spend a night on Cadair, you will wake up in the morning either mad, dead or a poet. Some locals add the extra option of 'an Englishman'.

One evening two farmers were walking home to Llanegryn from Dolgellau Fair, passing Llyn Gwernan at the foot of Cadair Idris, when they saw a giant man with green water weeds twined in his hair. He was wailing, in Welsh, 'The hour is come but the man is not, from ten at night to five in the morning'.

Next day the body of an Englishman was found bloated in the lake. It transpired he had spent the night in Idris' observatory, causing much discussion amongst the locals, who concluded he must have been a mad English poet before he spent the night on the mountain, so death was his only option.

The King of the Beards

There were two kings, Nynio and Peibio, who agreed on nothing. Nynio said the sky was his meadow, Peibio claimed the stars were his sheep and the moon his shepherdess. One evening, Nynio accused Peibio's sheep of grazing in his meadow, so they declared war on each other, raised armies and there was a most terrible slaughter.

Now, Rhita the Giant King of Wales heard about these two madmen fighting over sheep and stars, so he too raised an army, defeated Nynio

and Peibio, and shaved off their beards, which he wore on a belt round his waist. When the other twenty-eight Kings of Brython heard about this, they declared war on Rhita and marched to Gwynedd, but Rhita defeated them all and shaved off their beards. Now he had enough beards to make into a cloak, which he wore around his shoulders.

However, Rhita was not satisfied. There was one king whose beard he didn't have. One king who had never challenged him. A powerful king. Arthur, King of all the Brythons. Out of respect, Rhita wrote politely to Arthur inviting him to shave off his own beard and send it to him, to avoid unnecessary bloodshed, other than nicking himself with a razor. Arthur refused, leaving Rhita with little choice other than to declare war, the winner to own the cloak of beards.

He knew this was a war he was doomed to lose, and he was right. Arthur marched into Gwynedd, a great battle was fought on Bwlch y Groes, and the giant Rhita was split in two. Arthur buried him on top of the highest mountain, Gwyddfa Rhita, now known as Snowdon. Though another story says he was buried in a trench on Rhiw y Barfau, Beard Hill, near Tywyn. Or maybe Arthur threw him into Afon Twrch. Well, all this happened a long time ago and memory fades, and there we are.

The One-Eyed Giant of Rhymney

In Llancaeach, next to the Pandy, was a mill owned by a giant who had one eye in the middle of his forehead, through which he could see into the Otherworld. He ground his flour from children's bones, for they made such sweet bread. And he could control the wind and rain, which caused floods. And in case anyone thought he was nice deep down, he liked to tear up trees by their roots for fun. He was best avoided.

The giant employed a boy called Siôn to clean the mill and oil the mill wheel, in exchange for not being eaten. One day, the fair came to town and Siôn wanted to go, for there might be girls there, and he liked girls, although he'd never met one because he never left the mill. On the one occasion a girl came to the mill, the giant ate her.

Siôn had an idea. He made a mountainous roast dinner and placed it in front of the giant who stuffed his belly until he was grunting and snoring. Siôn climbed onto the table, took a knife and plunged it into the giant's eye. The giant awoke, looked bemused, plucked the knife out of his eye and threw it at Siôn, but missed. Now blind, he spread himself across the doorway to stop Siôn escaping, so the boy picked up the giant's dog, wrapped it around his shoulders and walked towards the door. When the giant reached down, his hand stroked the dog, who whimpered. The giant thought the dog needed to go outside, so he opened the door and Siôn ran.

One Eyed Giant

When Siôn reached the fair he told everyone what had happened but no one was brave enough to go to the mill to see for themselves. So it was, the blind one-eyed giant of Rhymney carried on grinding bones and making bread until he ran out of children and starved to death.

MINERS, COAL AND A RAT

The Coal Giant

There was a giant in Gilfach Bargoed who carried a huge cudgel with a snake coiled around it, with which he clubbed and ate anyone who came near him. One lad, whose mother and father had been eaten by the giant, decided something had to be done. He was a wild boy who spoke the language of the birds, so he asked the advice of a wise old owl who lived in an oak at Pencoed Fawr, Bedwellty. The owl hatched a cunning plan.

The owl knew that the giant courted a witch beneath an apple tree, so she called on all the birds of Rhymney to build a bow and arrow. Then they hid in the apple tree and waited. That night, the giant came looking for his lover the witch. The birds took aim and fired the arrow and shot the giant stone dead. When the witch found the giant with

Coal Giant

an arrow through his heart, she cursed the apple tree for helping the birds, and the fruit of all wild apples has been sour ever since. She buried the giant beneath the tree, and as time passed his body turned to black crystal and spread through the ground. The people dug it up, took it home, discovered it burned well, and they called it 'coal'.

Dic Penderyn

In the early 1800s, young Dic Lewis left rural Aberafan with his family so his father could find work in the coal mines of industrial Merthyr. When he was old enough, Dic followed his father underground and found himself in a world where miners lost their jobs at the whims of employers, were expected to work long hours for little money, families lived in fear of the workhouse, poor housing and sanitation caused typhus and scarlet fever, and water was so polluted it was thought safer to drink beer.

In 1831, he was twenty-three, married and living at Penderyn, near Hirwaun, when Merthyr exploded. Up to ten thousand miners and ironworkers marched and took control of the town for a week. He watched as a Highland Regiment was called in, colliers were rounded up outside the Castle Inn, there was gunfire, bloodshed, hundreds injured and arrested, and many were killed. Dic found himself charged with riotous assembly and stabbing Donald Black of the 93rd Highlanders in the leg with a bayonet, and he was sent for trial. Black told the court he could not identify Dic as his attacker, but two shopkeepers did, and the death sentence was passed. Of all those arrested, he was the only one sentenced to be hanged.

Merthyr people were convinced of Dic's innocence, and over ten thousand petitioned the Home Secretary, Lord Melbourne, who reluctantly ordered a stay of execution for two weeks. But the government and coal owners wanted a scapegoat, and the death warrant was finally signed. As the noose was placed round Dic's neck at Cardiff Gaol on Friday, 13 August, he said, 'O Arglwydd, dyma gamwedd [Oh Lord, here is injustice]'. Thousands marched with him to St Mary's Church in Aberafan, where they gathered outside the churchyard walls to hear his brother-in-law, the Methodist minister Morgan Howells, speak of an innocent man who had left a world of cruel injustice.

Forty years later, Ianto Parker confessed on his deathbed that he was the man who had stabbed Donald Black, then fled to America and never returned. Yet it is not Parker, nor the mine owners, nor politicians, nor shopkeepers who are celebrated to this day in songs, stories and malt whisky, it is the man they martyred, Dic Penderyn.

The Treorchy Leadbelly

The Texan songhunter Alan Lomax was on an epic ethnographic journey around the world collecting folk songs for the Library of Congress in Washington DC. In 1953 he visited Padstow in Cornwall where the locals thought he was trying to steal their 'Obby Oss' song and put it on the hit parade, like he did with 'Leadbelly'. In August he arrived at the Miner's Club in Treorchy and interviewed singer and storyteller, Tom Thomas, small, bald, rosy and seventy-six. Tom told Lomax this tale:

'Lewis and Sam were miners and they were on strike and, oh, their bellies were rumblin' with hunger. Lewis was comin' down the road and Sam was comin' up the road, and Lewis says, "How you, bwt?"

'Sam says, "Oh be quiet. I haven't had a bite or a sup for three days and my belly's grumblin.'"

'"Oh I've had a lovely feed," says Lewis, "it'll keep me goin' for three days. See that house, with the green grass in front, and the monkey puzzle tree? I was nibblin' the grass there this mornin' and the woman comes out and asks what I'm doin', and I tell her I'm so hungry, and she takes me into the parlour and cooks me a roast dinner, roast tatws an' all. Go to that house."

'So Sam went up the road to the house with the monkey puzzle and he drops down onto his knees and starts nibblin' the grass. The woman runs out of the parlour, and says, "What you doin?"

Lewis

Sam

'He says, "Oh, I'm so hungry."

'She says, "Oh, you poor man. Come into the parlour. Then go out the back door, the grass is longer out there."'

The Rat with False Teeth

In 1951, a miner in Merthyr applied to the council for a replacement set of false teeth. He explained that a rat called Fagin had stolen his upper dentures from his jacket pocket while it was hanging up in the colliery workings. Councillor Williams, a former miner, said a rat once ran off with his tin food box, and Councillor Owen said at his colliery a rat had stolen someone's watch. So they agreed to pay half the cost of replacement dentures, while somewhere in the pit, Fagin the Rat was grinning widely.

Siôn y Gof

Siôn Jones the blacksmith, lived in a cottage at Ystumtuen near Ponterwyd with his wife Catherine and their two children. He earned a living shoeing ponies for the local lead miners, but times were hard. In late 1719, Siôn set off alone in search of work at Dylife, a bustling mine where there was work for a hefty blacksmith. The unwritten laws of the mines stated that whenever a man moved on for work, he left his wife and children behind, for she was the property of the mine and they would marry her to another man.

Catherine, poverty stricken and starved of love, wanted none of this. She wanted her husband Siôn, so with her two children in hand, she followed his footsteps to Dylife, only to find him remarried to a maid servant from Llwyn y Gog. Catherine was distressed, their children were growing up without a father or a wage, and surely her heart had a say in this porridge pot of emotion? Siôn told her to go, Catherine refused, there was an argument and Siôn picked up an axe and stove in her head.

In January 1720, three bodies were found at the bottom of a mine-shaft, a woman, a boy and a girl who had tried to feed from her mother's breast. Fingers pointed at Siôn. He ran towards Castle Rock above the River Clywedog and was caught before he jumped, put on trial in Welshpool and sentenced to be hanged. When asked why he did it, he answered, 'Because of some other woman, and the Devil'. He was taken to Pen y Crocbren, Gallows Hill, sat on a horse with the noose round his neck and the horse made to walk. His body was hung out to rot for all to see, wearing an iron gibbet he had forged himself. In death, Siôn had found the work he had been seeking.

Siôn's head and gibbet appeared in 1938 in a chemist's shop window in Machynlleth, before being donated to St Fagan's Folk Museum. His ghost haunts Llyn Siôn y Gof, the pool below Castle Rock, searching for his head, while Catherine haunts the old mine workings at Dylife, searching for her lost husband.

The Hole

An old miner showed a young miner a hole in the ground and told him that there were rich seams at the bottom. Without so much as a thank you, the lad started digging. Down and down he went, getting smaller all the time. Each day, the old man lowered food and drink to him in a bucket on a rope. Another old collier leaned on his shovel and said, 'There's kind of you. You must like him.'

The old miner said, 'No, can't stand the cheeky bugger. Only time I get a bit o' peace is while he's down there.'

The Penrhyn Strike

The very word 'Penrhyn' was anathema in our house. My father refused to go anywhere near Penrhyn Castle and as a child I never understood why. If the subject was mentioned, he would tell the 'other' story, the one the history books never told.

In 1832 Queen Victoria, aged thirteen, visited Bethesda quarry, owned by the second Lord Penrhyn, Edward Douglas-Pennant. She wrote:

> It was very curious to see the men split the slate, and others cut it while others hung suspended by ropes ... others again drove wedges into a piece of rock and in that manner would split off a block. Then little carts about a dozen at a time rolled down a railway by themselves.

That same year, Penrhyn commissioned Henry Hawkins to paint an extraordinary image of the Bethesda slate quarry with men hanging from ropes, bodies swarming like ants. It was Gustave Doré's engraving, 'Dante's Inferno', intended as a celebration, but it screamed.

Much of Lord Penrhyn's money had been inherited from his father, Richard Pennant, MP for Petersfield and owner of six sugar plantations and six hundred slaves in Clarendon, Jamaica. When slavery was abolished, the Pennants received a huge sum from the government as compensation for losing their workforce. Their quarry workers were regarded as little more than slaves themselves. They were paid a pittance, lived in insanitary conditions with no safety measures, and had only Christmas Day off each year.

The history of the quarry was one of conflict. Wirt Sikes, American Consul to Wales and social reformer, reported that the miners refused to work on Ascension Day 1878, as they believed that an accident was about to happen, and by 1896 they were locked out unpaid for eleven months for joining the North Wales Quarrymen's Union.

In 1900, the second Lord Penrhyn, George Douglas-Pennant, Yorkshireman and conservative MP for Caernarfonshire, prosecuted twenty-six of his workforce for refusing to allow contractors to work at the quarry. The three thousand-strong workforce were barred from contributing to the union and told to work or leave. As they walked out, mine owner E.A. Young locked the gates behind them, beginning a strike that lasted three years.

There were inevitable hardships and police violence, yet there were other tales. A firm in Ashton-Under-Lyne, Lancashire, sent the quarry workers two and a half tons of plum pudding for Christmas, giving rise to a children's rhyme:

> Wele cawsom ym Methesda
> Y pwdin gorau gaed erio'd.
> Chlywodd Young nag Arglwydd Penrhyn
> Ddim amdano cyn ei ddod.
> Pwdin yw, du ei liw,
> Y gorau brofodd neb yn fyw.

> We had in Bethesda
> The best pudding there ever was.
> Neither Young nor Lord Penrhyn
> Knew of it before it came.
> It was a black pudding,
> The best any living creature has tasted.

After Christmas, families left Bethesda in search of work. Penrhyn reopened the quarry with a new work-force of four hundred and signs were placed in front windows saying, 'Nid oes bradwr yn y ty hwn [No blacklegs here]'. The Riot Act was read and troops were sent in to

protect the bradwr. But slowly, one by one, people returned to work. Bethesda was desolate, the market closed, fever shut the schools, outside businesses took the work and strikers were sacked.

Lord Penrhyn played the role of fairy-tale villain rather too well. One of his fifteen children, Alice, fell in love with an Italian gardener in her father's employ. Penrhyn forbade her to see him and confined her in her bedroom, where she scratched a message in Italian on the window pane, 'essere amato amando [to be loved while loving]'.

A woman from Menai Bridge told the tollhouse keeper at the suspension bridge that she once saw a girl in a bedroom at Penrhyn Castle who had been locked in there for falling in love with a gardener. The woman sketched the girl. Next time she came to Penrhyn, she showed her sketch to the staff. They showed her a photograph of the family taken in 1894. She pointed to the girl she had seen. It was Alice.

Well, fairy tales are supposed to have happy endings. Alice fled to London where she worked as an artist, became a devout Christian, and remained unmarried. Her father died a few years after the strike ended, and eight years later the unions were admitted.

Even when the National Trust took over Penrhyn Castle, my father refused to go there. Folk memory is long and deep in Bethesda, where the ancient stories live on in the legendary Mabinogi Fish and Chip Shop.

The Wolf

A miner from the Rhondda caught rabbits for the pot and sold the skins for roof tiles to keep the rain out. But rabbits were tiny and it took a lot of them to thatch a roof, so he decided he could save time and make more money if he caught one big animal. He went out into the woods, and met a huge wolf, which ate him up.

HOMES, FARMS AND MICE

The Lady of Ogmore

A Welshman was caught firing an arrow at a stag on the Lord of Ogmore's Hunting Lodge in the Vale of Glamorgan. He was ridiculed and brought before the Norman lord accused of poaching, and was about to be sentenced to be tortured, when the lord's daughter spoke. She reminded her father that the Normans were an occupying force who had taken the land from this man and his ancestors, and in truth, the land could not be owned, bought or sold by anyone, rather shared equally and worked for the common good. As it was her birthday, she asked her father to release the man and allow the Welsh to be free to hunt the land.

The lord was amused by his daughter's impertinence, but he set the man free and said the Welsh could have all the land that she could walk around barefoot before sunset. She stared straight into her father's eyes, kicked off her sandals and began to walk. The thorns and flints tore her feet, but on she walked, following close to the coast, with her father's soldiers armed with tape measures behind her, until the sun set in the sky. The lord kept his word, and the

The Lady of Ogmore

land his daughter walked around is Southerndown Common nature reserve and open to all, thanks to the Lady of Ogmore.

The House with the Front Door at the Back

An old farmer with a stubbly chin lived in a damp lime-washed house at Deunant near Aberdaron. Every evening before he went to bed he took a few steps outside the front door of his house, loosened his braces, dropped his trousers and squatted down. Over the years, he had created a fine muck heap that he used for mulching his potatoes.

One evening he was sat there, trousers round his ankles, when he noticed a little man staring at him. The little man asked, 'What have I done to make you so angry?' The farmer was confused, and then noticed the little man was covered in dung. 'I have lived here all my life and have never meant any harm to anyone. Yet every evening, I sit by my fireside with my wife and baby, when dung pours down my chimney. If you don't believe what I say, step on my foot three times.' The old farmer did as he was told and he saw, next to his front doorstep, a street he had never seen before, with smoke pouring from the chimney of a tiny house which was completely covered in dung. On the front doorstep sat a little woman holding a baby, both of them dripping dung. The little man suggested the farmer might consider using his back door in future.

The old farmer was full of remorse. He took stones and lime mortar and bricked up his front door, so that he would never again drop his dung over the little family. He built a flowerbed and planted sweet-smelling evening primrose and night-scented stock. Then he took a sledgehammer and knocked a hole in his rear wall, so that every evening he could squat outside his back door instead.

And that is the story of the house with the front door at the back.

The Cow on the Roof

Siôn Dafydd from Denbighshire never stopped grumbling about his wife. She never cleaned the house, the babi was always bawling, the chickens lived in the kitchen, she didn't feed the cow or the pig, and when she did make him a meal it was never enough to fill his belly. He wanted better after a hard day weeding the turnips. Eventually she tired of his moaning. She handed him the babi, told him that he could clean the house, make the porridge, clean out the chickens, sweep the yard, milk the cow, feed the slops to the pig and she would weed the turnips. Siôn was a stubborn man, so he agreed.

So there he was, stirring the porridge. The babi was crying. He picked it up, but it wouldn't stop griping, and he needed to stir the porridge before it burned, but every time he put the babi down it cried, so he sang to it which made it cry more. The pig was squealing with hunger, so he dropped the babi, mixed buttermilk with the slops, spilt milk over the floor, ran outside and opened the sty door. The pig ran between his legs, into the kitchen, licked up the buttermilk, knocked over the porridge and licked that up too. He picked up an axe and hit the pig over the head.

The cow started mooing. Siôn ran outside, and found she had eaten all the grass, so he propped a ladder up against the house and pushed the cow up the ladder onto the roof to eat the thatch. He tied a rope round her neck, dropped it down the chimney, ran to the kitchen and tied the other end of the rope round his ankle. He scraped the porridge off the floor, plopped it back in the pan and stirred, while the babi cried.

The cow was enjoying the thatch when it slipped and fell off the roof. Siôn felt the rope tighten round his ankle and found himself being pulled up the chimney. His legs went either side of the pot-hook which stabbed him in the crotch, and there he stuck, whimpering.

His wife came back having been for a nice walk after weeding the turnips, to find the poor cow hanging from the roof. She ran inside and what did she see? A dead pig, chickens everywhere, a bawling babi, milk all over the floor, and her husband hanging upside down with a pot-hook in his crotch and his head in a porridge pot.

Manawydan Hangs a Mouse

The story so far ...

Manawydan, brother of Bendigeidfran the King of the Island of the Mighty, had returned to Arberth alone. His wife Rhiannon and stepson Pryderi had vanished, and a grey mist hung over the land like a curse.

Homes, Farms and Mice

Manawydan farmed the land well. He sowed three fields, the seeds grew through the soil despite the sun being unable to shine through the grey mist and soon his golden corn was ripe. So he decided to harvest his first field the following day. In the morning, all he found were bare stalks. Every ear of corn had been snapped off overnight.

'By my beard, who has done this?' said Manawydan. He looked at the second field, the corn was ripe so he decided to harvest it the following day. In the morning, all he found were bare stalks. Every ear had been snapped off. 'By the hairs of my beard, I have been robbed again,' he said.

He looked at his third field and the corn was ripe. 'Shame on my beard,' he said, 'I will keep watch tonight, for the thief who stole my wheat will surely try to steal this too.'

So Manawydan armed himself, propped his eyes open with sticks, and kept watch. At midnight he heard a great noise. He leapt to his feet, sword in one hand, spear in the other, and prepared to battle with the monster. What he saw filled him with terror. A mighty army was marching towards him. An army of mice. They were swarming all over his field. There wasn't a single stalk without a mouse on it, and they were nibbling the ears of corn. There were so many that Manawydan couldn't keep his eyes on them all. He chased them this way and that, but they were too fast for him. He was about to have a tantrum, when he spotted one mouse so fat it could hardly move. He dived on it, caught it in his glove, tied it with string, and off he went to Pryderi's court, a proud victorious warrior.

He hung the glove by its string on a peg. Pryderi's wife Cigfa asked him, 'What's in there, my Lord?'

'A thief,' replied Manawydan, and told her the story of his battle with the mighty army of mice. He added that he would hang the lot of them as thieves.

Cigfa told him it was a little undignified for a nobleman such as himself to hang a mouse, better to let it go. But Manawydan was a proud man, and he stomped off to build a gallows. Cigfa shook her head, rolled her eyes, and washed her hands of him.

Manawydan sat on a mound at Arberth, placed two sticks into the soil and began to build a small gallows. A scholar rode up, and asked, 'What are you doing?'

He replied, 'Hanging a thief.'

The scholar said, 'Isn't that a little embarrassing, a man of your rank, hanging a mouse?'

Manawydan said the mouse was a thief, and thieves must be hanged. The scholar offered a pound to set the mouse free, Manawydan refused, the scholar shrugged his shoulders and rode on.

Manawydan was placing the crossbeam on the gallows when a priest rode by, and asked, 'What are you doing?'

He replied, 'Hanging a thief.'

The priest said, 'Isn't it rather humiliating, a man of your breeding, hanging a mouse?' and he offered three pounds to set the mouse free. Manawydan refused, the priest shook his head, smiled and rode on.

Manawydan was tying a string noose from the crossbeam when a bishop rode up, and asked, 'What on earth are you doing?'

He replied, 'Hanging a thief.'

The bishop said, 'Don't you feel silly, a fine gentleman like your-

self, hanging a mouse?' and he offered twenty-four pounds to set the mouse free. Manawydan refused, and the bishop said, 'Name your price?'

Manawydan stared him in the eye and said, 'The return of Rhiannon and Pryderi, the removal of the mist from Dyfed, and tell me who the mouse is?'

The bishop replied, 'The mouse is my wife and she is with child.' The bishop explained he was Llwyd ap Cilcoed, and it was he who had transformed himself and his people into mice to eat Manawydan's corn. It was he who had conjured the grey mist over the seven regions of Dyfed, and had enchanted Pryderi and Rhiannon, all to avenge the wrong Pryderi had done to Gwawl ap Clud for playing badger-in-the-bag (which is explained in the First Branch of Y Mabinogi).

Llwyd lifted the mist over Dyfed, and as it melted away Pryderi and Rhiannon appeared, walking towards him along the road. Manawydan released the mouse and it transformed into a most elegant pregnant woman. And they all looked around and smiled, as the sun shone over Dyfed.

And so ends this branch of the Mabinogi.

The Muck Heap

Back in the day, every farm had a muck heap. A pile of horse muck, cow dung and human manure that was left in the farmyard to ferment like a fine wine, before being scattered on the fields as compost. The sweet smell hung in the air and clung to clothes, and falling in the muck heap was all a part of growing up.

At Nant yr Hebog, the old farmer had died and left the business to her son and his wife. One night the son came home and saw, in the fading evening light, an old woman sitting on top of the muck heap. She was wearing a beaver hat tied to her head with a spotted scarf, and looked exactly like his dead mother. He called her name, she turned and vanished. He ran inside to tell his wife that his mother was sat on top of the muck heap. His wife smelled his breath and told him to keep off the cheap beer.

Next night he came home and there was his mother again, on top of the muck heap, kneeling down as if she was planting something. He hurried inside to fetch his wife, and this time they both saw the old woman before she vanished. Next day, they climbed up the muck heap, and found a little ring of hen's feathers. They stared at each other. For this was a sign that there was something under the heap. They started digging with their bare hands, deep down into the muck, till they were smeared from head to foot, and what do you think they found? Yes, gold. The old woman's savings.

So they opened a woollen mill at Dre-fach Felindre and made lots more money, which they kept in the bank. And they say that every financial transaction to this very day still carries the smell of the old Carmarthenshire muck heap.

COURTSHIP, LOVE AND MARRIAGE

The Maid of Cefn Ydfa

In 1902, William Haggar, travelling showman, purveyor of kinemato-graphs and projectionist at the Kosy Kinema in Aberdare, released a short film, shot around Pontarddulais, based on the old folk tale of the Maid of Cefn Ydfa. In 1914, his son Wil Junior reworked the story of the maid into a fifty-minute silent epic starring himself and his wife, Jenny.

Anne Thomas was born in 1704 at Cefn Ydfa, a mansion at Llangynwyd near Maesteg. Her father died when she was two, leaving her in the care of her mother and Anthony Maddocks, a lawyer from Cwmrisca Farm. They agreed that when Anne was of age, she would marry Maddocks' son, also named Anthony.

One spring day in 1722, Anne heard singing. She looked up, expect-ing to see a lark, and there was a dark curly-haired young man thatching the barn roof. She was captivated, and invited him to share food with her. He was Wil Hopcyn, a poor lad who ran a smallholding with his brother and did odd jobs as a roofer, blacksmith and plasterer. Wil considered himself a poet, so naturally he fell in love with the maid.

Mrs Thomas disapproved of her daughter cavorting with an impoverished poet, so Anne was confined to her room. She wrote passionate letters to Wil, which her maid servant left in a hollow sycamore tree for him to collect. The maid flew between the lovers with messages of desire, until Mrs Thomas discovered their secret and Anne was ordered to marry Anthony Maddocks immediately. In desperation, she wrote to Wil in her own blood on a sycamore leaf, but it never reached him. She married in 1725, Wil's heart broke and he took to wandering the roads as an itinerant musician.

One summer's day, he was watching wheat ripening in a meadow, musing on how a seed so carefully planted by one hand could be harvested by another, when he wrote one of the most famous of Welsh folk songs, 'Bugeilio'r Gwenith Gwyn'. Two years later, word reached Wil in Bristol that Anne's marriage was loveless and she was wasting away. He returned to Llangynwyd, only for her to die in his arms aged twenty-three. She was laid to rest in the chancel at Llangynwyd churchyard, where many years later Wil joined her, buried beneath an ancient yew tree.

None of Wil's poems have survived, and few people left memories of him, apart from Iolo Morganwg, so it was left to William Haggar to seal Wil's immortality in flickering celluloid.

Rhys and Meinir

At a 'Horse Wedding' the groom's party would ride to the bride's house at full speed, serenade her as only young Welshmen can, and invite her to accompany them to the church. The bride's family sang back, explaining she was perfectly happy without a daft man. So the boys entered the house and searched for the bride, who was either hiding or disguised. If she had escaped on horseback, they chased her, and if caught, she was forced to drink a pint of beer before being led to the church. Some brides rode away and were never seen again, others fell from their horses and died, and the custom lost its popularity.

There were only three farms at Nant Gwrtheyrn on Pen Llŷn, where Rhys Maredydd of Tŷ Uchaf was engaged to his cousin Meinir of Tŷ Hen. The wedding was set for the second Sunday in June at St Bueno's Church in Clynnog, and as was the custom, Meinir ran and hid. The wedding party gave chase, Rhys searched for her, but she could not be found. All that day, all week, for months he searched, his dog by his side, through rain and storm.

One evening, a bolt of lightning struck a hollow oak tree on the slopes of Yr Eifl. The tree split open to reveal a calcified skeleton picked clean by the birds, dressed in a frayed Haversham-white wedding gown. Rhys's heart broke and he was buried at St Bueno's, though his soul had died long before. Meinir was to be buried with him, but the horse and cart carrying her coffin slipped over the edge of the cliff into the sea and the lovers were parted forever. Since then, a couple have been seen walking arm in arm along the beach, he with a long white beard and she in a frayed white wedding dress.

You see, the Nant was cursed. Centuries earlier, three monks from Clynnog wanted to build a church there, but the locals threw stones at them and chased them away. The monks cast three curses: that no cousins from Nant could ever marry; the ground would be forever unconsecrated; and the village would slowly die and be reborn.

In the 1950s, the Nant Quarries closed and the villagers left to search for work elsewhere. The empty cottages became a playground for Llithfaen children, a few wanderers slept there in frayed sleeping bags, and the quarry road turned into a popular suicide leap and car dump.

But this fairytale has a happy ending, just as the curse prophesied. The houses were renovated and the Nant was reborn as a Welsh Language Centre, which is now a favourite venue for weddings, where couples can be photographed next to a sculpture of Meinir's oak.

The Odd Couple

Let's be honest, Gruffydd was a miserable old boy. He had few redeeming features. If you greeted him in the street he would grunt like a pig, swear to your face, and tell you to 'Go to Tregaron'. And he smelled. He kept an old pig in a neglected orchard, but it wasn't that. He just smelled. Some of the hippy ladies who moved into the village in the 1970s said that every soul had inner beauty and that Gruffydd was waiting for someone to love him, but it seemed he was just a miserable, smelly, foul-mouthed old man who liked a fight.

So it was something of a surprise that Gruffydd had a wife. And they had been married for almost fifty years. And she was a dark Mediterranean beauty that nearly half a century of living

The Odd Couple

with Gruffydd had not dimmed. There was smouldering passion in her eyes that grey cardigans and print frocks could not hide. Yet he treated her with disdain, and she always walked three paces behind him in the street.

They had a smallholding, Tan y Castell, just a few sheep, chickens, a goat and an ugly pig. The house was spare and clean, for the chickens weren't allowed in the kitchen. There was a lace tablecloth, lace across the mantlepiece, lace doilies for hot mugs of tea and a lace holder for the toilet roll. An empty wooden crib stood by the hearth with a notch carved in it, a sign there had been a death.

She cooked handmade pasta with goat's cheese and spinach, and Gruffydd grumbled before eating it. No one in the village understood what she saw in the old stoat. Surely she could have had the pick of men when she was an olive-eyed girl who combed her shining black hair a hundred and one times each morning. She was held in such esteem that she was showered with offers of help making the funeral sandwiches on the day he died.

He'd been in the pub, grumbling about the beer, and was walking out of the door when he dropped down dead. One of the tin butterflies that was nailed to the porch fell off and landed on his head. And that was that. No one rushed to help him. Nobody important had died, there was nothing to laugh at. Mrs Gruffydd never shed a tear. She left the funeral arrangements with Mr Pritchard, Garage Mechanic and Coffin Maker, the flowers would be supplied by the chapel, and the reception tea by the ladies of the Merched y Wawr. No one blamed her for not crying.

The village was excited with a funeral to look forward to. Bara brith was baked, ham sandwiches were decrusted and several crates of beer were donated by the landlord. They were interested to see if Mrs Gruffydd would cry, whether she had any family, and whether the preacher could find anything kind to say about the old misery in the coffin.

They gathered outside the chapel early. A car pulled up, long and gleaming white, with the words Ferrari FF emblazoned on it. A man leapt out of the passenger seat and peered around. He had slick black hair, greying at the temples, an Armani suit and Gucci shoes. It was clearly

Marlon Brando. Another man, a young Leonardo DiCaprio, leapt out of the driver's seat, opened the back door, and held out a hand, which was taken by a black lace glove, followed by an elegant lady in a black sleeveless gown, her face concealed behind dark shades and a veiled wide-brimmed hat. It was Audrey Hepburn, fresh from Tiffany's. With her arms linked to a man in black on either side, the woman swung her hips through the chapel gates and into the vestry without a word. At the graveside, she watched quietly before returning to the limousine. And she was gone.

Next day, she walked into the village shop, black hair flowing behind her, a loose-fitting grey cardigan over a print frock with a plunging neckline. The two men were with her, in casual wear now. She bought three bags of pasta that the shop stocked specially for Mrs Gruffydd, and left with a beaming smile on her face.

For this extra from a Fellini film was Mrs Gruffydd herself, looking twenty years younger. She continued to live in the farmhouse with the two young men, and elegant visitors called, all white flashing smiles and dripping with gold. Lamborghinis parked on the driveway. She never offered an explanation. But there was talk. Oh, there was talk. Some said she was in a ménage-a-trois with her toy-boys. Others said these were her sons from a previous marriage, who had never visited their mother because they couldn't bear Gruffydd. The truth was that there were darker forces at work.

Gruff met her when she was seventeen, wooed her away from her family who ran an Italian cafe in Cardiff, having fled poverty in Sicily. The family came after her, but she refused to return, preferring this dark young Welshman with sloe-black eyes and a rich Burton voice. Her family disowned her, and as they grew older, she alone understood that Gruff's anger was borne of the frustration of never being able to satisfy her in the way he wished. She would never stop loving him, no matter what, because she saw only that quiet, strong young man who rescued her from an arranged marriage with the Cardiff Mafia.

The Wish

On a farm in Llangadog lived an old couple whose hair had turned to snow. The old man stared at his wrinkled old wife and wished she was as beautiful as the day he first met her. On his way home from market in Llandeilo he stopped by the ruins of Castell Carreg Cennan and followed the underground passage to the wishing well. He prised a rusty old nail from an oak beam, dropped it into the dark water and made a wish.

He arrived home to find a beautiful raven-haired young woman waiting on the doorstep for him. He blinked his eyes and realised this was his wife, on the day he had fallen in love with her. He gazed at her all evening, although rheumatism and arthritis prevented him from doing what he longed to do. After a winter of this, she grew tired of his dog-eared old face, and ran off with a handsome young artist she met at the fair in Carmarthen.

FIDDLERS, HARPERS AND PIPERS

The Gypsy Fiddler

An old Romani folk tale tells of a girl named Mara, who made a deal with the Devil to exchange her family for a handsome man she desired. The Devil made a box from her father, a bow from her mother, and four strings from her brothers, and gave the fiddle to Mara. As she played, her lover began to dance, round and round, till the Devil carried them both away, leaving the fiddle lying on the ground. One day, the Gypsy King passed by and picked it up.

Abram Wood, the Gypsy King, was said to have brought the first fiddle into Wales in the mid-1700s, when he walked here with his family and a few possessions strapped to donkeys. Abram was a fine fiddler and storyteller, tall and middling thin, with a dark complexion, rosy cheeks and a face as round as an apple. He wore a three-cocked hat, an embroidered waistcoat with shillings for buttons, a silk coat with half crowns for buttons, white stockings tied with silk ribbons, silver buckles to his shoes and two gold rings on his fingers. When he died in a cowshed at the foot of his beloved Cadair Idris, he left behind a huge family of fiddlers and storytellers.

Gypsy Fiddler

Ffarwel Ned Puw

A fox had been pursued by a pack of hounds through the Ceiriog Valley and up Llanymynech Hill, and had almost reached the safety of a cave when it stopped, stared into the darkness, turned round and ran straight towards the dogs. The pack parted and allowed old Reynard to pass through unharmed, for his coat had turned snow white.

The itinerant fiddler Iolo ap Hugh, known as Ned Puw, was having a beer at the Lion Inn at Llanymynech, when he found himself embroiled in a discussion with the local choir. Ned told the choir that their singing was weak and feeble, and even his little fiddle could drown them out. He made a bet that if he stood on top of Llanymynech Hill on Sunday morning, the congregation in the church would hear him louder than the choir. Ned's challenge was accepted, although they told him it would not be wise to go near the mouth of the old cave on the Sabbath.

By Sunday morning Ned had sobered up, and he set off up the hill, taking with him bread and cheese, a bottle of home-distilled gin and seven pounds of candles. He settled himself down in the mouth of the cave, took a swig from the bottle, belched with pleasure and took out his fiddle. As he began to play, he heard a voice. He turned and thought he saw someone inside the cave. He stood up and peered into the inky blackness.

Ned was never seen again. They said he had gone to Annwn, where he exchanged his fiddle for a bugle and played for Gwyn ap Nudd's Spectral Hunt. Others said he'd gone to the Devil where he belonged, while a few searched the hedgerows, ditches and ponds, where old itinerant fiddlers were often found curled up frozen.

Then, one night a shepherd saw him dancing in the mouth of the cave, playing his fiddle like a man possessed, face white, eyes staring, head hanging loosely from his shoulders. He vanished into the cave like smoke up a chimney.

Late one cold December evening, the choir were in church singing plygain when they were drowned out by the sound of a solitary fiddle.

The shepherd recognised the tune as the one Ned was playing that night in the cave. The parson quickly transcribed it, and they called it 'Ffarwel Ned Puw'.

And they say if you stand in the mouth of that cave on 29 February you'll see Ned playing his tune, cavorting in a courtly dance of death with other lost musical souls, like Dic y Pibydd and Twm Bach y Corner, who vanished into the Black Cave at Criccieth, yet whose tunes live on.

Dic the Fiddler

Dic lived at Llwybr Scriw Riw near Llanidloes. He was very poor and had a hungry family to feed, and only his fiddle to earn him a penny or two. He busked in the streets, collected money in his cap, and then spent it all at Big Betty Brunt's Public House. When he rolled home in the evening, he told his long-suffering wife he had been dancing with the fairies, and oh how they quarrelled!

One evening after playing at Darowen Fair, Dic was walking along the Green Lane above Cefn y Cloddiau when he had a feeling he was being watched. Thinking it could only be the fairies, he played a weird tune, 'Aden Ddu'r Fran [The Crow's Black Wing]', hoping it would scare them away. When he finished, he heard something rattling inside his fiddle.

He fell asleep on the hill till dawn and when he arrived home he told his wife he had been playing music with the fairies. Well, she played music of a different kind. She called him a fool, a drunkard, an idler, and she was about to break his fiddle in two when she heard a rattling, and out of the sound holes fell some coins. She kissed her husband, placed most of the money in her purse for food, kept a little for a new hat, and gave some to Dic for being a clever boy and told him to go to Richard Evans' drapers shop in Llanidloes, buy a few yards of flannel, and she would make him some new shirts to keep him warm while he was busking.

Dic bought the flannel and found he had enough money left over for a pint of cwrw at Big Betty's. It was here that Evans Draper found him. With a face like thunder, Evans grabbed hold of Dic's lapels and demanded to know where that crown had come from. Dic told him he had found it in his fiddle. Evans said, 'It's fairy money, it's not real', and produced a dried cow pat from his pocket and flung it on the table in front of Dic. 'There's your money.' Evans was a conjurer and knew the ways of the Otherworld. He picked up the flannel, stared Dic in the eye and said, 'The fairies only give money to those who have not long left to live.' Dic said he knew very well he was about to die, because if Evans didn't kill him, his wife would, and he ran out of the inn before Big Betty Brunt realised he'd paid her in cow shit.

Morgan the Harper

Morgan sat in his stick chair in the chimbley corner of his crumbling cottage near Castell y Bere, comforting himself in the warmth of the fire with a cwrw da. The beer had softened his soul, he was singing loudly, something about Myfanwy, when there was a knock on the door. Too tipsy to stand up, he shouted, 'Dewch i mewn. Come in, and mind you wipe your feet!'

Three weary travellers, dressed in red, entered and asked for a bite to eat. Morgan, feeling unusually warm and benevolent, told them to help themselves to the bread and cheese on the table. The travellers filled their bellies, and in return for his kindness they offered Morgan a wish. He thought they were having a joke, so he told them he had always wanted a harp that would play lively tunes and make people dance, no misery or melancholy for him, oh no. Morgan took another drink, and noticed the travellers had vanished, the bread and cheese were still on the table, and there stood a handsome triple-harp.

Morgan started to play, and felt a fine tune beneath his fingers. His wife came home and immediately began to dance. The music attracted the neighbours and they joined in the dance, even the lame and the crippled found a use for their limbs. Soon the house was full of dancers, and after a while they asked Morgan to slow down. But his fingers

wouldn't stop, and the more he played the more the dancers danced, round and round the flagstone floor until their legs buckled and they collapsed in a tangled heap on the flagstone floor. Morgan fell back in his chair, snoring loudly.

Whenever old Morgan played his harp, people were forced to dance till their bones broke, and soon he was the most unpopular man in Meirionnydd. And there's an end to it.

The Harpers of Bala

The giant Tegid Foel lived by the walled spring at Bala, with his wife, the enchantress Ceridwen, mother of Taliesin. Tegid thought of himself as a mighty warrior, a roaring lion and a raging bear, although everyone else saw him as a bit thick in the head and a cruel man who persecuted his own people.

On the birth of his first grandson, he prepared a feast. He ordered all the harpers in Meirionnydd to play for him, though most of them ran away or said they were washing their hair. The only one left was an old blind harper who lived in a hut in the mountains, who cared little for money and had no fear of the indulgences of Tegid's rich friends.

During the celebrations, he played all the tunes he knew, then sat on the steps outside and took solace in a sip from his hip-flask, for medicinal purposes only. Midnight came and went, and a bit worse for wear he found himself listening to a little bird singing, over and over, 'Dial a ddaw [Vengeance is coming]'. The bird flew towards the woods and the harper was entranced, so he followed until the bird landed in a tree and stopped singing. The harper lay down beneath the tree and fell asleep, and the last thought he had was that he had left his harp in the castle.

That night the rain fell and the storms raged, yet the harper slept on, dry beneath the tree. In the morning he shook the last drops from his hip-flask, and walked back towards Tegid's castle to retrieve his harp. But the castle had vanished. The walled spring had burst overnight and a great lake had flooded the whole valley, and his harp was floating serenely across the water towards him. He played a tune to thank the little bird who had saved his life, and all the while Ceridwen smiled.

Many years later, a young harper was wandering home to Yspyty Ifan after playing for a dance, and he was near the Big Bog of Bala when he walked into a mist, tripped over and fell through the moss into the mire. He was sucked down into the peat and was about to give up the struggle when a hand reached out towards him. He grabbed hold of it, and it pulled him out of the oozing slime. The hand was attached to

an arm which belonged to a small sparrow-of-a-girl, with black hair pulled back in a bun. She gave him the kiss of life, his body lit up like a candle, and he fell head over heels in love, as harpers often do. She took him to Tŷ Hafod where her mother and father lived, and he played his harp and there was singing and dancing and he was so happy he would have married the little bird-girl there and then. At the end of the evening he held her round the waist, stared into her eyes, puckered up his lips, moved closer, and found himself lying in the moss by the Big Bog, clothes and hair caked with mud, harp half-sunk in the peat with the sheepdog from Plas Drain licking his lips to wake him up.

And Ceridwen smiled.

ROMANI, DANCERS AND CINDER-GIRL

I hailed the birds in Gypsy speech, the birds in Gypsy speech replied.

Black Ellen

'*Chioya!*' ('Boots!') the Welsh Gypsy storyteller Ellen Wood of Gogerddan shouted at her audience while puffing on her clay pipe, pointing it in the air for emphasis. She expected the reply, '*xolova*' (socks), 'boots and socks', vital to the traveller's life. If the audience didn't reply quickly enough, she asked them what she had just said, and if they couldn't answer, she stormed out and told them to come back the following evening to hear the rest of the tale. She knew three hundred stories, many of such a length they could not be told in one night.

Black Ellen

Ellen was the granddaughter of Abram Wood, King of the Gypsies. A small handsome woman, with jet black hair and a mouth full of pearly white teeth, she had lured many a man away from his wife. She was said to be a witch who was paid to curse enemies, bewitch animals, tell fortunes and make love potions. She passed on her tales to her grandson, Matthew Wood, fiddler and storyteller, who told them at the family gatherings in the foothills of his beloved Craig yr Aderyn near Abergynolwyn. Matthew cut a romantic figure with mystical deep-set eyes, aquiline nose, sensitive mouth and long black curls reaching to his shoulders, often so carried away by the drama and emotion of the story, he identified himself as the hero as the words tumbled from his lips.

John Sampson

John Sampson, librarian at Liverpool University, met Matthew in 1896 and began to transcribe Ellen's fairy tales from Romani to English for the Gypsy Lore Society. Matthew considered Sampson a 'rai', a gent, and at his funeral in 1931, harpers and fiddlers from all the Romani tribes played while Augustus John delivered the oration.

This is the tale of Cinderella as told to John Sampson. 'Chioya!' ...

Cinder-Girl

A small house, three sisters. The two older sisters thought themselves grand ladies, but they were ashamed of their grimy youngest sister, so they hid her amongst the cinders in the coal-hole where no one could see her. If anyone came to call they said, 'Hide yourself, little slut'.

One Sunday, the two sisters came home from church all a-flutter about a handsome prince they had seen. Cinder-girl asked if she might be allowed to go to church and see the prince? 'No, grimy little pig,' they said, 'go and hide with the coal.'

Next Sunday, the two sisters went to church, leaving Cinder-girl alone. An old beggar-woman came to the door. Cinder-girl invited her in and gave her tea and cake. The old woman took the grimy girl by the hand and led her outside. She gave her a white pebble and said, 'Throw it against that rock, you will see a door, go inside, there will be a bed-chamber, take off your grimy clothes, put on a fine dress and a pair of golden slippers, go outside, you will see a pony, ride to the church, sit by the door, the prince will see you, then hurry home, put on your grimy clothes, and say nothing.' And the old beggar-woman disappeared, as they do in fairy tales.

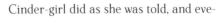

Cinder-girl did as she was told, and everything happened the way the old woman said. Later that morning a fine lady in golden slippers entered the church, the prince asked who she was, but no one knew her. This went on for three weeks. On the third Sunday, the beggar-woman came again and told Cinder-girl, 'This day, leave early, the prince will follow, a slipper will fall from your foot, and he will find it.'

Cinder-girl did as she was told and as she ran home a slipper fell from her foot. The prince followed and found the golden slipper. He held a banquet and invited every maiden in the land to attend. They came, rich and poor, fair and dark, scrubbed and grimy. Each lady tried on the slipper, in they came, out they went, and it fitted none. Eldest sister chopped a piece off her foot and it still didn't fit, and, oh, there was blood and mess. The prince called for the serving maids, until there was only one girl left. Cinder-girl held out her foot. The slipper fitted, the prince wiped away the grime and recognised her. Eldest sister cursed her.

Well, there was a wedding and a feast and they went to bed, and within a year Cinder-girl gave birth to a beautiful baby girl. Eldest sister was so green with envy she stole the newborn baby and left an ugly dog in the bed. When the prince saw his child, he was so embarrassed that he had fathered a dog, he said nothing.

Another year, another child, this time a son. Eldest sister stole the child, left an even uglier dog in the bed, and told the prince that Cinder-girl had given birth again. The prince felt disgraced. Cinder-girl implored him for another chance.

Another year, another son, another ugly dog, and the prince convinced himself he had married a witch. He ordered the servants to drag her out of bed, tie her to a stake and burn her. The beggar-woman appeared, enchanted the servants, freed Cinder-girl, turned her into a grimy pig, and told her to hide in the forest, or else her husband's huntsmen would cut out her liver and hang it by the castle gate.

So Cinder-pig hid in the forest for many years while her three children were raised by her eldest sister. One day, she saw her children playing by the river. She approached them and told them not to cry. She explained that she wasn't a pig, she was their mother, and she was about to be slain by their father's huntsmen, who would hang her liver by the castle gate. She told them not to be squeamish, to go to the castle, take a piece of her liver, make a wish and all would be well. Being children, they were quite happy to follow the advice of a talking pig.

The day dawned when Cinder-pig was chased and slain by the prince's huntsmen, and her liver was hung by the castle gate. Firstborn girl was the bravest. She remembered what her Cinder-pig-mother had told her, and she went alone to the castle gate, reached up on her tiptoes, picked a piece off the slimy red liver and took it to her brothers who were waiting by the river. They made a wish, to live happily together by the river, and in the blink of an eye there stood a cottage full of gold.

The children ran away from eldest sister, and lived in the cottage by the river. One day, a stranger passed by and stopped to light his pipe. He saw three children wearing golden belts, so he knocked on the cottage door and asked for a light for his pipe. The boys invited him in, but the girl said no. He ordered the boys to give him their belts, and as they did, they turned into swans and swam on the lake. Firstborn girl ran into the forest and hid. She remembered what the talking pig had told her.

She crept back to the castle gate, picked a piece of the red liver, returned to the cottage and wished for her family to be together again. The swans turned back into her brothers, the pig liver became her Cinder-girl-mother, and the prince walked in as if he had woken from a dream.

Cinder-girl's family lived a simple life in the cottage by the river, and the brave firstborn girl, when she was old enough, travelled the world and became rich with wisdom.

Well, those are the adventures, there's no more to tell.

'Xolova.'

The Dancing Girl from Prestatyn

Esmeralda was born in 1854, black-haired and dark-eyed, one of four-teen children to Noah and Delia Lock, travellers from North Wales who played fiddles, sold wicker baskets and traded at horse fairs. When Esmeralda was sixteen, she was married to Hubert Smith, a wealthy and persistent fifty-two-year-old solicitor and town clerk from Bridgnorth, who allowed the Locks to camp on his land by the Severn. However, Esmeralda Lock was not a girl to be pinned down. She was a butterfly.

Esmeralda flew away, time after time, only to be chased and returned by her father. Once she escaped by hitting Hubert over the head with a silver candlestick. Then she told him she had been enchanted and had to obtain a charm from a 'gozvalo

Esmeralda

187

gajo', a conjurer. In fact, the gajo was her lover, a romantic young scholar, Francis Hindes Groomes, who was writing a book of Gypsy folk tales and was married to another traveller, Britannia Lee. One evening, Esmeralda told Hubert that she had dreamed that Francis was about to kill himself, and she must go to him to say a final farewell. Hubert made her promise to return within two hours. She never did.

The young lovers fled to Germany, where they lived a bohemian life and Esmeralda earned a living as a dancer and singer. Her divorce from Hubert was both public and scandalous. Francis, too, divorced, much to the disapproval of his father, the Archdeacon of Suffolk, who thought his son was of a temperament unsuitable to holding down a 'proper' job in order to finance himself, and that writing a book of folk tales and running away with a gypsy dancer was the behaviour of a wastrel.

In 1876 the lovers married, and went to live in Edinburgh, where Francis took a job working as an editor on *Chamber's Encyclopaedia*. Esmeralda's uncle, the gypsy harper, John Roberts of Frolic Street in Newtown, wrote to Francis, 'I beg to say that I have read all about what happened and felt sorry for you and Esmeralda; it is to be hoped that you are both happy now.' The old harper remembered Esmeralda's kindness when as a girl she served him plenty of cake and tobacco, and invited him to dance.

Esmeralda's relationship with Francis was rarely less than steamy and stormy, and soon she tired of his book- ish ways. She danced and sang her way through London's thea- tres, where her light shone like the North Star. Dante Gabriel

John Roberts the Harper of Frolic Street

Rossetti painted her as one of his idealised erotic pre-Raphaelite dream-women, and she inspired Victor Hugo to create the gypsy dancer in the *Hunchback of Notre Dame*.

Francis, exhausted, told her, 'We must never meet again on this side of the grave.' He died in 1902, aged fifty, though not till he had published his masterful book of *Gypsy Folk Tales*.

Esmeralda took to the road in her green and yellow caravan, finally settling in 1918 at Pendre Farm on Gronant Road in Prestatyn. She caused the occasional scandal and kept the town on its toes, before she was run over by a bus near the Cross Foxes in 1939. She is buried in Rhyl, an unlikely resting place for Quasimodo's wild gypsy dancer.

'*Chioya!*'

Fallen Snow

An old couple lived in a thatched cottage by a river. One day the old man saw an empty boat on the water. He hauled it ashore, looked inside and found a little baby. He carried the baby home and showed his wife. They decided to raise the girl as their own, and they named her Fallen Snow. She was so fragile, they were loathe to let the wind blow on her.

Fallen Snow lived with the old couple till a cold winter took them and she was left an orphan again. She decided to seek work, anything but remain in the old cottage with its memories. On the day she left, there was a heavy snowstorm. She walked on through the snow until she came to a deep dark wood. She wound her way through the trees until she saw footsteps in the snow. She followed the footsteps until she came to a hollow tree with a red door. She went inside and found herself in a sweet little room full of murderous weapons and walls spattered with blood.

A voice whispered in her head, 'Clean up this mess'. After she had scrubbed away all the blood, she thought the little room looked quite charming. Then she heard voices and footsteps, so she hid inside an old grandfather clock. There were four voices, deep and growling, and one said, 'We must find the person who has done this'.

Just then, she noticed blood on the pendulum, and as she scrubbed it with the hem of her dress the clock chimed. The door opened, and four big men with black beards and ear piercings peered in at her. Like bears, they were. They growled and gnashed their teeth, and she closed her eyes and waited for them to eat her up. But they told her not to be afraid, and one of them held out a beautiful earring, another a necklace, and they invited her to stay and look after their house.

Fallen Snow suspected these men were robbers, which was good, because it meant they would be able to keep her in pretty things. So she agreed to stay. The men liked to play with her golden hair, and soon they asked her to marry them. She agreed, providing they stole plenty of money and jewels. And so it was, she lived there with these four bad men who all loved her.

I know this because I played fiddle at their weddings. There was no beer, only brandy, and I drank so much I don't remember how I got home. But she married all four of them, she did. And they are living there still, happy as Snow White and the Seven Dwarfs.

'Xolova.'

23

SETTLERS, TRAVELLERS AND TOURISTS

Madoc and the Moon-Eyed People

When Owain, King of Gwynedd, died in 1170, a war of succession broke out between his many sons. Madoc, one of Owain's illegitimate children, decided to leave his ravaged country in search of a brave new world. He built the *Gwennan Gorn*, a ship constructed of oak from the forests of Nant Gwynant, held together with stag's horn. He sailed from Rhos-on-Sea and landed in 'Utopia', Mobile Bay, Alabama. Leaving his people to settle, he returned to Wales with a skeleton crew, and told everyone of his plans to build a new Gwynedd, free from civil war. He gathered enough settlers to fill ten ships, and set sail.

Madoc never returned.

Except in folk tales.

Stories were told of a mythical native tribe who had built a stone fort at Devil's Backbone in north-west Georgia, before settling along the Missouri River. They had white skin, blonde hair and blue eyes, and spoke a language not unlike Welsh. The Cherokee called them the 'Moon-eyed people', for they could see better at night. They called themselves 'Mandan'.

Iolo Morganwg heard these stories, and financed an expedition to search for the Mandan, led by John Evans, son of a Methodist preacher from Waunfawr. Evans landed in Baltimore in 1792 with $1.75 in his pocket, and wrote to Iolo saying it was 'the Mabinogion, or Death'. He walked over the Allegheny Mountains to Pittsburgh, then seven hundred miles down the Ohio by boat, along the Mississippi to St Louis, where he was thrown into jail by the Spanish rulers on suspicion of being an English spy. He negotiated his release by volunteering to take the hazardous journey through the Rockies to map the trail to the Pacific for Spain.

In 1795, he set off along the Missouri with thirty men, following the route taken by the lost Welsh. As winter approached, they reached the Omaha territories, aware of the story that Chief Blackbird was said to have killed sixty men who opposed him by poisoning their dog-meat soup. In fact, Blackbird befriended them, and allowed them to build a fort by the river and hunt buffalo on the freezing plains. When spring came, Evans and a handful of men rode north. After three hundred miles, they were attacked by the Sioux and fled back to the safety of the Omaha. Evans was told that a Frenchman had made contact with a white-skinned tribe who lived in houses and grew crops, so he set off again, this time following the Missouri.

Having walked and ridden one thousand eight hundred miles, and travelled five thousand miles from Waunfawr, John Evans found the Mandan. He knew, because a Union Jack was flying over their village, hoisted there by a Canadian fur trader, Rene Jessaume. Evans removed the offending object and raised the Spanish flag. The Mandan chiefs, Big White Man and Black Cat, welcomed him and invited him to stay. He spent a winter with them, examining their skin for whiteness and studying their speech for linguistic traces of Welsh. Counting from one to five in Welsh is 'un, dau, tri, pedwar, pump'. In Mandan it is 'maxana, nunp, namini, toop, kixo'. In the spring, Evans's health had deteriorated, and when Jessaume returned and threatened to kill him he decided it was time to leave the Welsh tribe forever.

When he returned to St Louis, Evans wrote to Iolo, 'There is no such people as the Welsh Indians'. He took to the bottle, his house flooded, and he died in New Orleans aged twenty-nine. The Mandan lived a little longer. They caught smallpox from the white settlers and by the 1830s there were only one hundred and fifty left. The few survivors married into neighbouring tribes, and the last 'pure' Mandan, Mattie Grinnell, died in 1975.

The Mandan told the story of Lone Man, who travelled the world from swamp to swamp, and when the corn was ripe he sang, 'Who am I? Where do I come from?' The earth told him, 'I am your mother. I grow herbs for you. Boil them up for food and medicine. Go into the world and heal your brothers.' So Lone Man travelled. He met a brother, and they argued over who was the oldest, then they smoked tobacco together, and decided to take Mother Earth's herbs and make a world. They created hills and lakes, trees and plains, woodpeckers and buffalo, and the animals multiplied. Old Grandmother Frog complained that they were making too many animals and needed to be rid of some. So they hit Frog with a hot stone and she became the first creature to die. Frog came back and told them Death wasn't such a good idea after all, but they said it was too late, Death was here to stay.

Having created his world, Lone Man had nothing left to do. He was bored. So he became Coyote the Trickster. Coyote came to a village where everyone was thin, despite there being so much food. The people said that whenever they hunted, a raven appeared. It had the head of a bald man and the body of a long-necked bird. When it squawked 'gi-ba, gi-ba', the food turned sour. Coyote tasted it, he chewed and he chewed and spat it out. So he called for friend Spider. They made a fire of dung and sticks, sat and smoked their pipes, and considered how to stop Raven. They knew he lived in a hole in a hollow tree, so Spider spun a web across the hole and when Raven emerged, he flew into the web. Coyote caught him and threw him into the fire. As he burned, his feathers flew into the air like small ravens. Coyote crushed the unburned bones, and out flew a White Raven, as white as Branwen in the old story. As it flew away, White Raven sang, 'Only when the world ends will I return'.

Wil Cefn Goch

Saturday 28 November 1868 was Election Day in Ceredigion, and Tory candidate Edward Vaughan of Trawscoed was defending his seat. There was change in the air. Vaughan had evicted families from their cottages, the windows of his election office in Aberystwyth had been smashed, and a hundred special constables were on the streets armed with staves. Labouring men had the vote for the first time and declared themselves for the Liberals.

Vaughan lost his seat that day, and returned to his mansion to be told his gamekeeper Joseph Butler had been shot dead by three poachers. One of them, Morgan Jones, had been captured. His fourteen-year-old brother gave himself up the following morning. The third, the man who fired the shot, William Richards of Llangwyryfon, was on the run. Vaughan offered one hundred pounds reward for information leading to Wil's arrest, wealth beyond dreams to the poor folk of Ceredigion. And so the hunt began for Wil Cefn Goch.

Wil was described as being:

About 28 years of age, 5ft 9" or 10" high, slight figure, long thin legs, with stooping gait, light hair slightly curled, thin sandy whiskers, long thin face, lower teeth overlapping upper teeth, long nose rather Roman, full grey eyes, speaks very little English, is supposed to be dressed in a dark home-made coarse coat, corduroy breeches and leggings, striped check shirt, and lace-up boots, clumsy feet, and has been operated upon for a bruise in the testicle.

The police searched barns and cottages, but there was no sign of Wil. His girlfriend Elizabeth Morgan of Pontrhydfendigaid refused to talk, for she knew the folk of Ceredigion were hiding him in hayricks, outhouses, pigsties, trees and up chimneys. The police entered a house where a woman had just given birth, and interviewed her as she lay in bed holding her bawling baby, although they failed to spot Wil, who was lying beneath her. He hid behind a revolving mill wheel, and when the police asked the miller to stop the wheel, he said he would if they paid him compensation for loss of production. Being good Cardi boys, they refused.

Months passed, roads were blocked and ports watched. Wil was moved from house to house, protected by Dafydd Thomas Joseph, clock maker from Trefenter, and John Jones, the radical grocer of Aberystwyth. They decided to send him to Ohio where Ceredigion migrants would look after him. They avoided roadblocks by walking the mountain tracks to Liverpool, where Dafydd bought him a ticket for the New World. The police swarmed round the docks but failed to spot Wil, who was disguised as a plausible woman, albeit with a bruised testicle. Vaughan sent a detective to Ohio, but received a letter implying that there were plenty of trees in America to hang a private detective from.

In Ohio, Wil was no folk hero. He worked as an itinerant farm worker, drank too much, and tried to stab an Irish maid who taunted him for his lack of English, but the butcher's knife stuck in a cupboard and before he could pull it out, she escaped. No proceedings were taken as the maid was considered as bad as he was.

He found a job as an iron worker and changed his name to David D. Evans. Elizabeth, his girlfriend from Pontrhydfendigaid, saved up enough money to sail out to join him, and within a year they were married. They bought a farm, adopted a son and she settled him down to a life around the chapel. He lived for fifty-one years in Ohio and is buried in Oak Hill Cemetery, close to the chapel which is now a Welsh museum. The museum staff were unaware of him, perhaps understandably preferring spinning wheels and harps to an unattractive folk 'hero'.

Malacara

In May 1865 the clipper ship *Mimosa* was chartered to take over a hundred and fifty settlers to Patagonia, to create a new colony based around the Welsh language and culture. On board with his father, mother and sister, was three-year-old John Daniel Evans from Mountain Ash. They settled in the lower Chubut Valley where they built farms on land given by the local Tehuelche people, though the soil was stony and difficult to plough. By the time young Evans was twenty-one, he had become a fine farmer and horseman, with an instinctive knowledge of the Pampas and the indigenous people.

In 1883, Evans was chosen to lead an expedition to search for more fertile fields, minerals and possibly gold, further along the river towards the Andes. He set off with his creole pony, Malacara, and a company of young Welshmen.

This was the time of the 'Conquest of the Desert', when Argentina and Chile were fighting for control of Patagonia and the indigenous people were being slaughtered or incarcerated. Evans and his men passed soldiers with Tehuelche prisoners. In fear, the men turned back, all except for three: Davies, Hughes and Parry. They rode for four hundred miles into the High Sierra, tied into their saddles with exhaustion, heads bowed in sleep, horses' hooves splintering on the sharp stones.

A group of Mapuche accused them of being spies for the Argentinians. They realised they could go no further so they decided to return to the Welsh settlement, but as they retreated, Evans heard hooves behind him, turned round to see Hughes and Parry on the ground, and Davies limp in the saddle. All three men were speared. A party of Mapuche were on his tail. Malacara galloped on until they came to a precipice, when the pony leapt over a twenty foot wide ravine, scrambled down a scree slope and began the two hundred-mile journey home.

Two days later, Evans rode into the Welsh colony. The settlers could not understand why the indigenous people would attack them. A party of forty men rode to the valley and found the bodies of Hughes, Parry and Davies. They had been picked at by vultures, their hearts and bones cut out, and their genitals placed in their mouths. It seemed that Evans and his men had been mistaken for an Argentinian patrol. The bodies were buried and a memorial was erected.

Two years later, John Daniel Evans and Malacara again followed the river to the Andes, and this time he arrived in a valley he christened Cwm Hyfryd, where he built a town, Trevelin. He worked as a miller and farmer, helped build the railway, supported the chapel, brought up six children after his wife Elizabeth died, owned the first car in Trevelin, and once returned to Wales to search for the wife of Richard Davies, one of his three companions who had been killed that day. When Malacara died in 1909, John Evans erected a monument to the heroism of his brave horse, without whom he would not have lived till he was eighty-one.

Malacara

And the Tehuelche? They had lived in Patagonia for fourteen thousand years, as hunter-gatherers and nomads, before their hunting grounds were turned into sheep pasture by settlers. They voluntarily changed their traditional way of life in order to live peacefully with their neighbours, but were killed by European diseases and persecution. By the 1960s the native language had died out, though a few thousand people with Tehuelche ancestry still live in Patagonia and Argentina, and a handful are learning the old language – alongside over five thousand Patagonians who speak Welsh.

The Texan Cattle Farmer

A cattle rancher from Texas was on holiday in Crymych when he met an old farmer. 'Howdy,' said the Texan, 'fine little black cattle you got there?'

'Indeed,' said the old boy, 'You're a farmer yourself?'

'Cattleman myself,' replied the Texan, 'Thousand head of pure-breeds. Takes me three days to drive round my land.'

'Duw, there we are,' said the old boy, 'I have a car like that.'

TRAINS, TRAMPS AND ROADS

The Old Man of Pencader

In 1188 Gerald of Wales, Giraldus Cambrensis, priest and chronicler from Manorbier, embarked on a two-month journey around Wales to raise money for the Third Crusade, in the company of the Archbishop of Canterbury.

Gerald had both Welsh and Norman ancestry – a man of two worlds; a born observer who told of the first recorded encounter with the fairies when a boy called Elidyr ran away from home and met two little men who took him to the Otherworld. He lived happily between

Gerald

the two worlds until he stole a golden ball from the Otherworld for his mother and was banished forever. Instead, he became a priest in Neath.

Gerald also told this iconic tale:

In 1162, amidst Welsh uprisings, King Henry II was travelling to Cardigan Castle to meet Lord Rhys. An old man was standing by the roadside in Pencader, so Henry asked his opinion of the future of Wales under English rule. The old man replied, 'This nation may now be harassed, weakened and decimated by your soldiery, as it has so

often been by others in former times; but it will never be totally destroyed by the wrath of man, unless at the same time it is punished by the wrath of God ... I do not think that on the Day of Direct Judgement any race other than the Welsh, or any other language, will give answer to the Supreme Judge for this small corner of the earth.'

The Old Man's words are engraved in Welsh on a Plaid Cymru plaque near the fish and chip cafe. I recently asked for a day return to Pencader on the bus and the driver said, 'We don't do returns to Pencader. Why would anyone want to leave?'

The Tales of Thomas Phillips, Stationmaster

In 1926, Thomas Phillips, stationmaster at Carmarthen, published a collection of tales about the curiosities of life on the Welsh railways, entitled *Railroad Humours: Humours of the Iron Road, or Stories from the Train*.

Pencader Tunnel had a reputation. It was long and dark enough for young men and women to flirt. A young couple were travelling from

Newcastle Emlyn, and the lad had a plaster on his nose when he entered the tunnel but when he came out the other end the plaster was on the cheek of the girl.

Two visiting gentlemen and three local ladies were in a compartment travelling on the 2.20 p.m. to Llanrhystud Road when the train ground to a halt in the tunnel. One gentleman put out his pipe, leaving the compartment in complete darkness. The other gent asked why he did not smoke in the tunnel, and he replied there was no pleasure in smoking in the dark. They heard the sound of giggling, followed by rustling, and a loud sniffing. The gent asked what pleasure the ladies got from taking snuff in the dark and they sang:

> There was a young lady who took snuff,
> she said it was easy enough,
> for she sneezed when she pleased,
> and was pleased when she sneezed,
> and that was pleasure enough.

A little barefoot urchin crept into the train on a cold, wet day, entered an apartment containing a lady and a gentleman, climbed onto the corner window seat and fell asleep. The gentleman rustled his newspaper and grumbled about this scruffy little creature being allowed into his carriage with his dirty feet. The lady arose, removed her expensive

muff, placed it gently under the child's head and kissed him. The gentleman hid behind his newspaper and said no more.

A wicker basket was left on the platform at Carmarthen Station, addressed to a vicar in Cardigan. Tied to it was a label that said, 'Containing live dog'. Two young porters liked dogs so they untied the string, opened the basket and peeped in. A large black Labrador leapt out and disappeared down the platform into the night, pursued by the two porters, a ticket collector and the tea lady. The porters knew there would be hell to pay when the stationmaster found out, so they hatched a plan. The station dog, Tipper, was a messy mongrel with an eye patch, who caught rats in exchange for a meal. The porters tied a pink ribbon around Tipper's neck, placed him in the basket, tied it up, loaded it on the next train for Cardigan and crossed their fingers that the vicar wouldn't notice. The days passed, but nothing was heard of Tipper again. And that's why there were no church mice in Cardigan, while Carmarthen railway station was overrun with rats.

The Wily Old Welshman

A fine gentleman was sitting in the waiting room of a small railway station in the Afan Valley when the door opened, bringing with it a blast of cold air and a small terrified Welshman with a muffler round his neck. 'Which way did she go? Is she following me?' said the little man, eyes almost popping out of his head. The gentleman did as gentlemen do, and pretended nothing untoward was happening. The little man was undeterred, 'She's chasing me, the old witch. Same every night.' And he sat down by the gentleman, looked both ways, took him by the lapels and stared into his eyes. 'She's haunting me, you see. The only thing that frightens her away is when the train comes.'

The gentleman prised the little man's fingers off his camel hair coat, brushed himself down, and stood up with a 'hrmph!' In the nick of time, he heard the whistle of the approaching train and made for the door.

The little man grabbed hold of his coat-tails and begged not to be left alone with the witch of Afan. The gentleman walked hastily down the platform, opened a carriage door, found a quiet compartment and settled himself down. The train pulled out of the station and he breathed a sigh of relief to be out of that madhouse.

The ticket inspector opened the compartment door. The gentleman felt in his pocket. Now, where had he put his ticket? It was in his wallet. He tried every pocket. His gold watch and chain were missing too. Then he realised. Out there was a wily old Welshman enjoying a drink at his expense, probably with the witch of Afan.

Many folk remembered the cunning little man who used to rob rich passengers and although the railway line is now closed they still hear the sound of steam engines and whistles. Though no one remembers there ever being a witch in Afan.

Dic Aberdaron

Richard Robert Jones was born in 1780 at Cae'r Eos near Aberdaron. Dic disliked formal education, refused to go to school, and had no interest in following his father's professions of fisherman and ship-builder. So he left home and walked the old Welsh tramping roads, grimy-faced and barefoot, dressed in a blue poacher's coat crammed with pockets full of books, ram's horn round his neck, harp on his back and a cat on his shoulder. He busked on the streets of Liverpool, where he sang the songs of Homer to the accompaniment of harp.

He learned thirty languages, though spoke only half of them fluently, and he compiled a Greek/Hebrew/Welsh dictionary which never raised enough subscribers to finance publication. He wrote a little poetry, inspired artists to paint his portrait, and his fellow bards wrote odes about him, though at least one of them was somewhat sarcastic. He was also a conjurer, with a 'Book of Spells' from which he could summon pig-demons called 'Cornelius' Cats', which he once invoked to help his friends who were cutting hay in a field near Aberdaron.

Despite his atheism, he was buried in St Asaph churchyard where his lost dictionary is also reputed to rest.

There we are. Dic lived his life, never achieved very much, was considered eccentric by some, and remembered fondly by others, while far more important men are long forgotten. A true folk hero, Dic Aberdaron.

Sarn Elen

Macsen Wledig, the Emperor Maximus, was hunting in the woods near Rome when he felt drowsy. He ordered his men to raise their shields to protect him from the sun, he lay down and began to dream. He was following a river over mountains as high as the sky, across a level plain towards a walled city by the sea. He walked over a bridge of whalebone onto a fleet of ships and sailed to an island where he entered a golden-roofed castle at the mouth of a wide river.

He walked past two auburn-haired lads dressed in black brocade who were playing 'gwyddbwyll' on a silver board with pieces of red gold, and a grey-haired man sat in a chair made from elephant ivory, who was carving the 'gwyddbwyll' pieces. Next to him in a chair of red gold, was a maiden in a white silk dress held at the shoulders with gold pins. She stood up, embraced him, and as their cheeks touched, the dogs pulled on their leashes, shields clashed, spears touched and Maximus awoke.

All the Emperor could think about was the maiden in the white dress. For three years he sent messengers to search for her. Then the Gypsy

King told him to stand in the forest where he was dreaming, and he would know which way to go. He realised he had travelled west, so he sent thirteen messengers who followed rivers and marched over mountains until they came to the Isle of Britain, on to the mountains of Eryri, past the Isle of Môn, to the land of Arfon, where they saw a castle at the mouth of the wide river. Two boys were playing 'gwyddbwyll', a grey-haired man was carving pieces from gold, and there was a maiden dressed in robes of white silk. They informed her that their Emperor had met her in a dream and wished her to be Empress of Rome. She told them that if the Emperor was truly in love, he should leave his dreamworld and come and tell her in person.

The Emperor set off with a great army, took the island of Brython by force and drove the people into the sea. He came to the castle in Arfon, took the maiden and found she was a virgin, so he offered her a maiden's fee. She asked for the island of Britain for her father, old Eudaf, and three forts for herself at Caernarfon, Caerllion and Caerfyrddin. And she asked to be allowed to build roads between them, for she enjoyed travelling. Maximus agreed, and she set to work, straightening and metalling the old Celtic tracks, and the great road south from Arfon was named after her, Sarn Elen.

Elen Luyddog was born to a fourth-century Christian family,

the daughter of Eudaf Hen, the Roman ruler Octavius. She travelled with her husband and her five sons, and accompanied them to Rome in 388. As she was walking along Sarn Elen through Snowdonia, her favourite son was killed by an arrow fired by the giant Cidwm. She wailed, 'Croes awr!', and the village that grew there became known as Croesawr, in memory of her grief. She became known as St Helen of Caernarfon, protector of travellers and roadbuilders.

25

STONES, CAVES AND FERNS

The Giantess's Apron-Full

A smelly giantess and her stinky husband were walking north towards Ynys Môn. Her apron was full of small stones, while he carried two large rocks, one under each arm, with which they planned to build a bridge over the Menai Straits. On the way they met a cobbler from Ynys Môn who was carrying a large bag of old shoes that he was taking home to mend. The giants asked how far they still had to walk. The cobbler could smell the giants. They stank of rotting fish in an open sewer mixed with the perfume of a dead skunk, and the cobbler realised that if these two smellies ever reached Ynys Môn, the people would have to leave. So he tipped out the contents of his bag and told them it was a very, very long way to Ynys Môn, so far that he had worn out all these shoes.

Smelly Giant

On hearing this, the giants dropped all their stones, turned round and walked home.

The rocks and stones are now the mountains and hills of Snowdonia. And Ynys Môn smells sweetly to this day, thanks to the clever cobbler.

The Stonewaller

On the road from Tre-Ysgawen to Capel Coch, part of a stone wall had collapsed following heavy rain. Huw Williams was sorting the fallen stones into piles according to size and shape. He was building two parallel walls, filling the gap between them with rubble, and topping with large coping stones on a bed of cement. He had been working all morning when his wife Ann brought his dinner, and they sat together on a stone eating bread and eggs, when an old woman called Mair Clogs hobbled by, leaning heavily on a stick.

Huw greeted her cheerily, with a wide grin on his face. Mair disliked Huw, for when he was a boy he teased her for having an evil eye and acid tongue. All the village boys were just as bad, but Huw was a particularly cheeky lad who wiped his muddy boots on Mair's stone doorstep and posted cow pats through her letterbox, and the old woman had a long memory. She pointed her stick at him and stared at Ann, 'He'll never finish rebuilding that wall', and she shuffled on. Huw screwed his fore-finger against his head, and settled down to finish his eggs.

As the afternoon passed, Huw built up the two walls and was bending down to fill the gap with rubble when a heavy capstone that was over-hanging the gap in the wall fell and landed on his head, cracking it like an eggshell. Ann found him later that evening after he failed to come home for his dinner. At his funeral the mourners heard the tip-tapping of his hammer. No one volunteered to finish repairing the wall. They filled the gap with barbed wire instead.

Huw was seen many times sitting by the gap in the fence, dressed in a collarless flannel shirt, sacking tied round his knees, trousers held up by braces. Whenever anyone approached him he disappeared, head fading first, then down his body until only his muddy boots remained.

The Scarecrow

Siôn Dafydd lived alone in an old shack in the hills above Rhandirmwyn. All he owned was a mattress stuffed with straw and a few sheepskins. Old Siôn tramped the roads in a shabby coat, a muffler and a peaked cap. He rebuilt dry stone walls, took pride in his work, and spent his money in the Royal Oak where he sang bawdy songs and told rude stories. In the winter he'd be spotted carrying a sheep back to his hut, followed by the smell of roast mutton.

Old Siôn

One winter, a shepherd was looking for a lost sheep, when he found old Siôn frozen to death beneath a hedge. He had no relatives, no one to pay the undertaker, so he was buried in a pauper's grave. His hut fell into ruins, and the neighbours shared his few belongings between them. His old shabby coat, muffler and cap were used by a farmer to make a scarecrow, and some said it looked more like Siôn than Siôn himself.

In the spring a couple of lads were walking home one night when they saw the scarecrow standing in a field. It was singing a bawdy song, and they were convinced old Siôn was back. They ran home as fast as their legs would carry them, and hid beneath the bed sheets.

Owain Lawgoch

On top of Craig-y-Ddinas is an old gnarled hazel tree, but when you look closer, the tree vanishes. This is why.

A shepherd-lad was weary of life, so he decided to leave and seek his fortune. He wrapped his few belongings in a red spotted handkerchief, cut a hazel stick from the tree on Craig-y-Ddinas, and set off along the old Welsh tramping road. A stranger joined him, and said, 'That's a fine stick. Where did you cut it from?' The lad explained and the stranger's eyes shone, 'If you take me to that tree, we will both find our fortunes.' The lad's eyes lit up.

So the stranger followed the lad to the old gnarled hazel tree on the top of Craig-y-Ddinas, handed him a shovel and told him to dig. Soon he heard the clang of spade on stone. He lifted the stone and saw a flight of steps. The stranger gave him a candle, and told him, 'Climb down the steps, and you will come to a vaulted corridor with a rope leading along the wall. Take hold of the rope and follow it to a cave where you will find gold. But be careful to hold the rope gently, as it is attached to a bell, which will wake the armed warriors who are guarding the gold.' The lad only heard the word 'gold', and not the words 'armed warriors'.

He climbed down the steps, gently took hold of the rope, followed it along the corridor, and found himself in a dark cavern dripping with stagnant water. A great oak table stood in the middle, with warriors seated all around, swords and shields by their sides, heads resting on their arms, all snoring, with a smell of sweat in the air. On the table was a pile of gold coins printed with the image of the French King, and next to them was a bell. At the end of the table, sat bolt upright, was a huge man with red plaited hair and a red birthmark on his right hand. This was Owain Lawgoch, listening for the ringing of the bell to waken him to lead his country to freedom.

Owain Lawgoch

The lad filled his pockets with more coins than he needed, so many that he brushed against the bell and there was a clang. The warriors awoke, shook them- selves free of sleep and dust, drew their rusting iron swords and surrounded the lad. Lawgoch's great red hand reached out and grabbed the lad, and he boomed, 'A ydyw hi 'n ddydd [Is it the day]?'

The lad, with commendable calmness, said, 'Nagyw, cysgwych eto [No, go back to sleep].'

The warriors sat down, Lawgoch closed his eyes, and the lad returned to the stranger and emptied his pockets.

There was more money than either of them could ever wish for, so the stranger suggested they split what they had and go their ways. Or, the lad could go back to the cave and bring more gold?

Such is the greed of man, the lad needed no persuasion. But when he climbed down the steps, there was no rope, no corridor, no cave, no bell and no warriors. He climbed back up the steps, but the stranger had also vanished, along with the gold. He looked around and the gnarled old tree disappeared before his eyes. He stood on a bare hillside with a few sheep laughing at him.

Owain Lawgoch, Owain of the Red Hand, was Owain ap Thomas ap Rhodri, the great nephew of the last true born Prince of Wales, Llewelyn ap Gruffudd. He was born in Tarfield, Surrey, but fled to France, where he was known as Yevain de Galles, Owain of Wales. To the Welsh, he was a heroic rebel who would return to free his land from occupation. To the English, he was a murderous outlaw who skulked in caves after his lands were confiscated. In 1372 Owain led a fleet of warships towards Wales, but only reached as far as Guernsey. Seven years later, he had become such a nuisance he was assassinated and buried in Saint-Léger, where he awaits the ringing of the bell.

Aladdin's Cave, Aberystwyth

One evening in July 1940 three men wrapped in greatcoats entered a cave just off Llanbadarn Road, Aberystwyth. The cave was not dank and dark as caves usually are in fairy tales, but dry and ventilated, and at the end of it they found treasure beyond the dreams of Aladdin. There were Leonardo da Vinci's drawings, Shakespeare's manuscripts, Rembrandt's paintings, Turner's sketches, the Magna Carta, the Anglo-Saxon Chronicles, and the journals of Scott of the Antarctic. The three men might have thought about filling their pockets, had they been the cheeky Jacks of fairytale, but they were the deputy librarian of the National Library of Wales, a curator from the British Museum, and a policeman.

In 1933, Mr W.A. Ormsby-Gore, Commissioner of Works, was given the job of finding safe places to store the nation's most valuable cultural artefacts in the event of falling bombs and invading armies. So in July 1939, at the outbreak of war, the nation's treasures were moved by train to a specially constructed cave beneath the National Library of Wales in Aberystwyth.

Ormsby-Gore could not have found a safer place. The writer Caradoc Evans noted in his diaries, 'Mary Tycannol tells me that Hitler was in college in Aberystwyth. This much is certain. Miss Arnold corroborates. Oh yes, everyone knows that Hitler was in college in Aberystwyth. He liked the old town so much that he gave special orders that, "though London be razed, Aberystwyth must be saved".

The Ferny Man

It was midsummer, between midnight and one, when the fern seed ripens and turns to dust. A man was walking home over the Garth Mountain after a night out with the boys in Cardiff. The fern seed covered his coat and boots and formed a shimmering film in his hair. When he reached home, his mother and sisters had gone to bed. So not to disturb them, he curled up on the old oak settle.

In the morning, he awoke to find the women were treating him as if he wasn't there. He thought they must be pretending, angry with him for being a dirty stop-out. He said, 'Sorry my lovelies, I won't be so late again, no indeed.'

Ferny Man

Well, his mother and sisters stopped in their tracks and looked around. He said, 'What's wrong? You look like you've seen a ghost.' This time they screamed, and ran out the door. You see, fern seed turns you invisible.

DENTISTS, COCKLE WOMEN AND ONION MEN

Don't Buy a Woodcock by its Beak

Back in the day, long before prop-forwards were heroes, the village boys in Cefn Meiriadog near Bodelwyddan worshipped mountain fighters, bando boys and foot racers. They could tell you about Griffith Morgan, known as Guto Nyth-Brân, a Rhondda farmer, who ran so fast he could round up sheep, slept in manure to loosen his joints, and died aged thirty-seven when a fan slapped him on the back too hard after he won a race. They knew John Davies, Y Cyw Cloff (the Lame Chick), from Bryncethin near Bridgend, who kept the inn at Upper Boat near Pontypridd and beat Tom Maxfield, the North Star from Windsor, to become the fastest man in Britain. And they knew all about the mountain fighters, Bendigo Caunt, Tipton Slasher, Welsh Jim and Twm Cynah.

Dan and Wil were waiting for the stagecoach in St Asaph to take them to a fight in Denbigh. They had saved all their pennies and were dressed in their finest velvet waistcoats and striped breeches, and kept looking at their turnip watches to show off the silver chains. When the coach arrived, they climbed up onto the box by the driver so they could listen to tales of his prize-fighting days. Next to the driver sat a man in a shabby grey greatcoat, so they told him to move over so they could squeeze in.

The driver was a big ox-of-a-man with a flashing red nose, and he told the boys all about his many victories. Then he offered his opinion on the two Mold fighters, Welsh Jim and Twm Cynah. Jim was a fine fighter, but that Twm, well, he could be taken down a peg or two. Dan and Wil agreed, and soon they were mocking Twm Cynah, along with everyone they passed on the roadside and the man in the shabby coat, and by the time the coach pulled into the courtyard of the Crown in Denbigh, the driver was the finest fighter in the whole of Wales, in the world, even. They tipped him well.

The driver held out his hand to the man in the shabby coat, who rummaged in his pocket and handed over tuppence and some fluff. The driver was incensed, and said for tuppence he'd give him a beating if he weren't such a bag-o'-bones. Shabby took off his coat and put up his fists. The driver was over the moon at the chance to give this scrawny cheapskate a beating.

'C'mon,' he said, and stood there, beckoning. So Shabby hit him. Again and again, until the driver was spinning and fell flat on his face. The audience were open-mouthed. Shabby picked up his coat and walked towards the Crown, saying, 'If you wish to know my name, it is Twm Cynah, from Maesydref, Mold.'

Wil and Dan followed Twm into the inn and offered to buy their new hero a pint, but he refused saying he didn't drink. He told the boys never to mock anyone because of their appearance, especially the old. And if they ever heard anyone singing their own praises, consider them idiots. He said, 'Nid wrth ei big y mae prynu cyfflog [You don't buy a woodcock by its beak].'

Twm Cynah

Wil the Mill

Wil was born in 1878 and worked at Parkmill on Gower as blacksmith, miller, churchman, shepherd, ploughman and undertaker. Now in those days, blacksmiths were also dentists. They pulled teeth with the big iron tongs they used to hold the hot metal over the fire. But Wil had a better method. He tied a rope round the tooth, tied the other end round the anvil, and engaged the customer in conversation. 'Nice weather, how's the garden, what's that over there?' Then he knocked the anvil onto the floor and the tooth was pulled.

A bit of a thug from Penclawdd came to the forge with toothache. Wil tied a rope from the bad tooth to the anvil, chatted away and knocked over the anvil, but it didn't fall to the ground. It just dangled there, with the rope held tight between the big thug's teeth. He roared, knocked Will out with one punch, and ran off towards the river, carrying the anvil in his arms. When Wil came round, he gathered the boys from the mill, they caught the big thug by the ford, dropped him into the river, held him down, took the tongs and pulled his tooth.

As the water turned red with blood, Wil told him, 'You come to the mill to get your teeth pulled, you get your teeth pulled!'

Wil the Mill

216

The Penclawdd Cockle Women

A strange story was told about the cockle pickers of Penclawdd on the Burry Inlet early in the 1800s. The women were well-known characters on Gower. Every Saturday morning they walked barefoot with baskets of cockles balanced on their hats, to sell their week's catch at Swansea Market. They wore their finest clothes – red and black-striped frocks, black and white-check aprons, plaid shawls and bonnets – and before they arrived, they washed their feet and put on boots, to look respectable.

One day, they had loaded their donkey carts full of cockles from Whitford Sands and were walking back to Penclawdd when they heard the sound of galloping hooves coming from Broughton Bay. An enormous woolly rhino-like creature with a large horn on its nose was charging towards them. It upturned the carts, gored the laden donkeys till they lay twitching in the tide and chased the women, who ran for their lives. Over the following months the creature appeared on Llanrhidian Sands and Whitford Marsh, but no one knew where it came from. Soon, not a soul dared venture onto the sands.

Cockle Woman of Penclawdd

The women asked the help of a gwiddanes from Cheriton. That evening the old woman walked through Whitford Burrows to the beach, drew a large circle in the sand with a ram's horn, and made a geometric pattern with dead-man's fingers and laverbread. As she muttered an incantation, the moon shone brightly and the sound of hooves was heard. The woolly creature appeared, scratched at the sand and charged. As it entered the circle it stopped in front of the old woman, snorting and stamping. She ordered it to be gone, never to return to Llanrhidian Marsh or Whitford Sands until a hundred thousand tides had ebbed and flowed. The creature calmed and vanished, the sound of its hooves melted into the mist, and it has never returned.

Although, a hundred thousand tides have ebbed and flowed across the marshes since then, so it would be wise to keep your wits about you next time you climb over the fences onto the National Trust land at Whitford Burrows.

Sioni Onions

The Breton Onion Man laid his bike against the pebbledash wall of the old lifeboat house in Morfa Nefyn, unwrapped a string of onions from the handlebars, and knocked on my mother's back door. She ushered him in and sat him down at the kitchen table, made him a mug of tea and presented him with a selection of out-of-date cakes she had bought for a penny each at the Gwalia in Pwllheli the day before. He spoke a little Welsh and English, and she repeated eve-rything to me, in case I couldn't understand his Breton accent. She bought a string of onions which he hung in the cupboard under the stairs for her. He waved good-bye and pushed his bike along the road towards Edern. His name was Sioni, or Johnny. I had no idea there were hundreds of Sionis, all selling onions throughout Wales.

The first Sioni sailed to Britain in 1828. He was Henri Olivier from Santec, near Roscoff, a fer-

Sioni Onions

tile land packed with poor farmers, just like Pen Llŷn. By 1900, over a thousand Sionis spent their winters in Wales selling onions. The Welsh Sionis formed themselves into small companies, each with their own sales territory, and they learned rudimentary Welsh.

One woman from Pontrhdygroes told a story about her grandmother who had come from Cornwall with her husband and had found work in the lead mines. When Sioni called, the old woman spoke Cornish, her daughter Welsh and the onion man Breton, and they understood each other perfectly well.

Shortly before midnight on 18 November 1905, the GWR Steamship *Hilda* set sail from Southampton bound for St Malo with around a hundred and thirty on board. At midnight there was a snowstorm, the captain lost visibility, the Grand Jardin lighthouse was shrouded in white, and the ship was torn in two on the rocks just outside the port. As the hull of the ship sank, the passengers and crew were sleeping in their cabins. In the morning only five people were left alive, clinging to the frozen mast. One was a crewman, the other four were Onion Men. In all, almost eighty Sionis drowned that day, all from Finisterre, forty-four from the same commune of Cléder, and two companies lost their entire workforce.

The Onion Men continued to trade with Wales. Claude Deridan, born in 1904 on the east side of Roscoff, took over his father's company in Porthmadog, learned Welsh, marched with the veterans on Armistice Day and became a well-loved character in the town. Claude brought his men over from Roscoff each year and they set off with neatly strung onions draped over their bikes, always pushing, never riding. It was one of Claude's men who visited my mother every year. We never knew his real name. He was, and always will be, Sioni.

The Hangman Who Hanged Himself

A hangman used to travel from Chester to Ruthin Assizes and stayed the night at the Duke of York in Buckley. The locals were intrigued by the stranger, but he refused to reveal his occupation. They pestered him and interrogated him until on his last visit he drank a little too much and told them he was the local hangman. There was silence. Someone asked him to prove it, so he stood on a table, hung a rope over the beam and showed them how to tie the knots to make a noose. Someone asked how it worked, so he placed the noose round his neck and tightened the knot. What next, they asked? He explained that the table would be removed and within a minute the poor man would be dead and his soul released to Hell. So they pulled the table away and the hangman hanged himself.

The Hangman

SEA, SMUGGLERS AND SEVENTH WAVES

The Ring in the Fish

Nest, wife of Maelgwyn, Lord of Gwynedd, lost her wedding ring while bathing in a pool on the River Elwy. Her bad-tempered husband was furious with her. That evening they were invited to dine with the Bishop of St Asaph. They were served fresh trout caught in the river, and as Maelgwyn sliced into his fish's belly, his wife's ring fell out.

In Penmachno around 1870, a story was told of a woman who was gathering shells on the beach, when her ring slipped off her finger and fell into the sand, just as a seventh wave washed over it. When the wave flowed back the ring had vanished. She went home in melancholy. The next day a man came round selling fresh herring, so she bought some to fry for dinner. She cut open the belly of one of the fish and what do you think she found? The ring? No, guts.

Jemima Fawr and the Black Legion

On 22 February 1797 the French Government had sent a marauding force of mercenaries and ex-prisoners called the Black Legion to capture Bristol, but the fleet of four ships had been blown off course, and they found themselves sailing into Fishguard Harbour. They heard the town cannon being fired to warn the locals of invasion and thought they were under attack, so they turned round and anchored off Carreg

Wastad Point. Fourteen hundred men rowed ashore and spread out into the countryside. They set up a command headquarters at Trehowel Farm and sent out reconnaissance groups, many of whom deserted, went pillaging, or drank the cargo of brandy from a beached Portuguese ship. One troop broke into Llanwnda Church and warmed themselves round a bonfire made of Bibles and pews, so the story goes.

All the while, the Fishguard and Newport Volunteer Infantry had been called in to help repel the invaders. They were a ramshackle troop of a couple of hundred local men under the leadership of a landowner's twenty-eight-year-old son who had no military combat experience. They gathered in Fishguard and prepared to defend their town, supported by hundreds of locals armed with bullets made from lead stolen from the roof of St David's Cathedral. Late on the 23rd they decided to attack the French, and set off up the hill pulling three cannons behind them, only to retreat due to failing light and exhaustion.

At this point, Jemima Nicholas, known as Big Jemima, the six-foot tall, nineteen-stone wife of a Fishguard cobbler, took things into her own hands. Armed with a pitchfork and a reputation for breaking up bar fights, she marched out into the fields, rounded up twelve drunken French soldiers and locked them in St Mary's Church. The French were in disarray, and were beginning to think they were outnumbered by the Welsh. The final straw came when they saw a line of redcoat soldiers marching over the hill above Goodwick Sands with rifles over their shoulders. The Black Legion surrendered, thinking they were outnumbered by an inexhaustible army. The army turned out to be Jemima and the women of Fishguard marching round and round the hill carrying pitch forks and wearing red shawls and petticoats.

Big Jemima

Jemima is buried in Fishguard Churchyard, where her tombstone reads, 'The Welsh Heroine who boldly marched to meet the French invaders who landed on our shores in February 1797. She died in Main Street July 1832 aged 82 years.' Since then, Wales has never been invaded, thanks to the legacy of tales of how the French were defeated by 'the General of the Red Army'.

Walter and the Wreckers

Walter Vaughan, Lord of Dunraven, had watched many ships wrecked on the coast near his home. He had written to the government offering his thoughts on how to improve safety at sea, but his ideas were continually rejected. He became embittered, his wife died of a broken heart, his eldest son left for a new life abroad but his ship went missing, and his other three sons all drowned, two caught in a storm when fishing, while the other fell into a vat of whey.

Walter turned to the dark side. A cargo ship was wrecked off Dunraven, and this time he plundered the ship for himself and paid off his debts. He went into partnership with the leader of the local wreckers, Mat of the Iron Hand. Years before, Mat earned a living placing lights along the coast to help lure ships onto the rocks. When he was arrested, he was brought before the local magistrate, who just happened to be Walter Vaughan. Mat and Walter recognised they were kindred spirits, each tormented by their own souls, and soon they made their fortunes from ships wrecked on the Glamorganshire rocks.

One night during a storm the two wreckers were watching a ship tear itself apart when one man swam ashore. The custom was that no survivor of a wreck be allowed to live, so Mat walked down to the shore and as the man dragged himself onto the beach, Mat snapped his neck and cut off his ring hand. He showed the hand to Walter, and in that moment the Lord of Dunraven's torment was complete. The rings on the fingers belonged to his eldest son who had left Dunraven years before to make his fortune and escape his father's bitterness.

Potato Jones

At the height of the Spanish Civil War in 1937, General Franco blockaded Bilbao in an attempt to starve out the Basques. 'It makes me sick,' thundered Davey Jones, captain of the *Marie Llewellyn*, a Swansea tramp steamer. 'Has our Navy lost its guts?' So, in partnership with local landlady, Edith Scott, he set sail for Bilbao with a fleet of three tramp steamers and a cargo full of spuds to feed the hungry Basques, earning himself the nickname 'Potato' Jones.

Potato Jones

He was born in Swansea in 1871, and as a boy he cycled to Mumbles Head to watch ships from all over the world sail in and out of the docks. His party trick was to dive under a moored ship, and while the crew looked over the side for him, he swam beneath the ship, climbed up the other side and scrambled like a monkey up the rigging to the top of the mast, before passing a hat round for halfpennies. By the time he was fifteen, he had rounded Cape Horn. It was a dangerous life for a merchant seaman, for commercial ships leaked so badly they were referred to as floating coffins, and diseases like yellow fever were so rife that a graveyard in Santiago was nicknamed Swansea Cemetery.

Jones was sixty-seven when he set sail for Bilbao with his three ships and a cargo of a thousand tons of potatoes. The captains of the other two ships were nicknamed 'Ham and Egg' Jones and 'Corn Cob' Jones. The Royal Navy refused to protect them, declaring them too foolish and alleging that they were smuggling guns and ammunition to the Republicans, which they were. A Spanish battleship was ordered to sink them on sight. Jones found himself without communications in a storm that lasted four nights.

Newspaper headlines asked, 'Where is Potato Jones?' Some thought he had joined the hundred and seventy-four Welshmen killed in the Spanish Civil War. In fact, the weather had forced him to return to Alicante and dump his cargo, leaving him in a right old grump.

Later in the war, Jones rescued eight hundred refugees who were fleeing Franco's fascists, and took them safely to France – the act of a true folk hero.

The Kings of Bardsey

Ynys Enlli is an island of twenty thousand saints, ten thousand Manx shearwaters, three hundred and fifty species of lichen, over one hundred grey seals, a handful of houses, a few fishermen, farmers, artists, poets, birdwatchers and Merlin, who is fast asleep in a glass tomb underground. It is a mythical mix of the sacred and the secular, where pirates built their houses with stones stolen from the ruins of the sixth-century St Mary's Abbey.

On a trip over to Bardsey in the late 1800s, Thomas Pennant said the boatmen stopped in the middle of the Sound, and stared, 'tinctured by the piety of the place', as they prayed for safe passage through the whirlpools.

Bardsey Islanders were fiercely independent. They had their own moral code, their children swam with seals and they were the descendants of pirates who lived there under the protection of the Lords of Pen Llŷn. In 1820, they elected a King, who wore extra ribbons in his hat to signify his authority. In 1826, the second monarch was twenty-seven-year-old John Williams, who farmed twelve acres at Cristin Uchaf. At his inauguration he stood on a chair in the presence of the lighthouseman while Lord Newborough presented him with a tin crown for dignity, a silver snuff box for wealth and a wooden soldier for an army. Fifteen years later, King John drowned trying to cross Bardsey Sound alone. The following day his son was born, and thirty-four years later he succeeded his father.

King John II developed a reputation as a gloomy drunkard who spent too much money at the Ship in Aberdaron. After thirty-six years on the throne, he was advised to abdicate. When he refused, the people of Enlli staged a very Welsh revolution. The King was plied with beer, rowed to Aberdaron and dumped on the beach for the mainlanders to deal with.

His successor was Love Pritchard, farmer and fisherman from Tŷ Pellaf, who inherited the crown with the words, 'I am the oldest, I am going to be King now'. In 1914 Love offered to fight for the King of England, but was politely rejected on the grounds that seventy-one was a little too old. Love was offended and declared Bardsey neutral during the war. Some said he secretly supported the Kaiser.

In 1925, at the height of discontent in the land, he led an exodus from the island. He died the following year and the monarchy passed with him, despite his wish that at eighty-three he still hoped to find a Queen and father a son.

The island was resettled in 1931 and became a home for naturalists, artists, writers, farmers and fishermen, inspired by the solitude and the wildlife, the lack of mains electricity and the thought of being stranded when the wind blows. There are never enough hours in the day, and when you leave the island a thousand and one fairy tales go with you to guide you safely back to the Otherworld.

When I was little, I was standing on the beach at Aberdaron with a bucket full of eels from the river. My mother had banned me from the kitchen because the eels had learned how to escape from the bucket.

King Love of Bardsey

226

I was watching the Bardsey boys load the old wooden boat with provisions when they picked me up and dropped me amongst the tin cans, coal bags and tractor parts. They gave me a fishing line to dangle in the Sound and told me stories about the creatures that lived beneath the whirlpools. I caught a skate, which from nose to tail was as tall as I was. They said it was a mermaid, and I had no reason to disbelieve them, for dried skates were often exhibited in jars at freak shows as mermaids. Later that day, they returned me to the beach. My mother never knew I'd caught a mermaid.

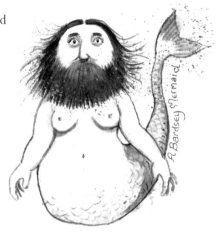

A Bardsey Mermaid

Since then, I always carry a bucket.

28

ROGUES, TRICKSTERS AND FOLK HEROES

Myra, Rebecca and the Mari Lwyd

On 2 January 1886, Myra Evans and her mother had locked themselves in the front bedroom of their house on Park Street, New Quay. Myra, a talkative child, was ordered to be quiet or she would be put to bed in the back room where she would see nothing. Her green eyes peered out of the window from beneath a black fringe. She was waiting for the Mari Lwyd (Grey Mare).

And there it was, outside Bristol House in the ice and snow, a horse's skull decorated with ribbons and roses of yellow and red, carried by a man hidden beneath a white sheet with legs protruding. Mother whispered that inside the horse was William Evans, the cobbler. Following behind were men dressed in animal skins, boys in squirrel tail hats, ugly masks and chanting rhymes, asking people to put their hands in their pockets:

Mae Mari Lwyd lawen yn dyfod i'ch trigfan,
O, peidiwch â bod yn sych ac anniddan.
O, peidiwch yn wir, mae'r amser yn wan,
Rhowch law yn eich poced a gwnewch eich rhan.

The Mari Lwyd is coming to your home,
Don't be mean or miserly.
Truly don't, for the times are hard,
Put your hands in your pockets and give us a share.

They turned into Tin Pan Alley and sang outside Manchester House, asking to be let in and warning the owner not to be stingy with the beer:

> Wel dyma ni'n dwad, gyfeillion diniwad,
> I mofyn am gennad i ganu.
> O tapwch y faril, gollyngwch y rhigil,
> Na fyddwch yn gynnil i'r Fari.

> Here we are, kind friends,
> To ask for permission to sing.
> Oh tap the barrel, release the bung,
> Don't be stingy to the Mari.

Then they were outside Myra's house. Her mother sang sweetly to them, then she went downstairs, opened the door, invited them in and gave them cake, beer and plum and rhubarb wine:

> Rhowch glywed, wŷr doethion,
> Faint ydych o ddynion,
> A pheth yn wych union
> Yw'ch enwau!

> Give me a hearing, wise men,
> What sort of men are you,
> And what is more to the point
> Are your names?

They ate and drank, wished her 'Blwyddyn Newydd Dda' (Happy New Year) and left.

Once they went to the house of Tom Lloyd, the schoolmaster in Maenygroes, a miserly old soul who locked himself in the parlour with his money and refused to open the door. The Mari boys broke in, ate everything they could find, scraped the ashes from the hearth into the middle of the room and trashed the place. They didn't get his cash, though.

The Mari Lwyd was often seen around Twelfth Night in Wales a hundred years ago. In English-speaking South Gower, the custom was called Old Horse or the Horse's Head. At Kimley Moor Farm near Rhossili, the farmer Mr Beynon took the horse round the pubs and farmhouses on Twelfth Night, and then buried the head in a field till the following year. The tradition only ended when he woke up one morning after and couldn't remember where he'd buried the skull.

The Mari is undergoing something of a revival, with at least twenty going out across Wales around Christmas. A festival of horses is held in Chepstow each January, and schoolchildren are learning about the tradition through flat-pack cardboard Maris.

Myra also witnessed the Ceffyl Pren (Wooden Horse) – Welsh vigilante folk-law, designed to disgrace offenders in the community long before tabloid newspapers thought of the idea.

A New Quay man went to sea leaving his three children with their stepmother. One night the children escaped from an upstairs window and ran to their grandmother's house. Public opinion pointed the fickle finger at the stepmother, who was considered too harsh. Y Ceffyl Pren was built on Picton Terrace, a donkey-sized horse made of straw, perched on top of a pile of wooden boxes, with an effigy of the stepmother sat on its back. Men wearing ugly masks paraded to her house, swearing, firing guns, carrying oil lamps, banging on the windows, shouting 'llysfam gas [wicked stepmother]!' There they set fire to the Ceffyl. The stepmother was so terrified that she and her husband fled to sea, but their ship never arrived at its destination. Myra's mother explained that the children and grandmother were at least as much to blame as the stepmother. Life is rarely pure and never simple.

Myra told of her grandfather Rhys, a big strong man who looked like the Duke of Wellington. One evening, his son Thomas (Myra's father), saw him standing in front of the hearth wearing his wife's frock, which was far too small for him. This was too much for little Thomas, who began to giggle uncontrollably, but Rhys told him to hush for this was no laughing matter. It was the late 1840s, when men dressed in women's clothes not to perform on the stage, but to carry out acts of insurrection and subversion. Each man called himself 'Rebecca' to avoid recognition by the authorities. Rhys was the 'Beca Mawr', about to lead an attack on the toll house in Aberaeron to protest at unfair road charges. Capture would mean certain jail, or even death. It was the world turned upside down.

Twm Siôn Cati

Robin Hood is renowned in Wales as the English Twm Siôn Cati. Twm was born to Cati Jones in Tregaron around 1530. He was an everyman, an outlaw, poet, thief, scholar, highwayman, trickster, robber and folk hero, whose adventures have been told in countless books, films, animations and, most importantly, by word of mouth.

Twm was riding to Welshpool when he met a man who said, 'That's a fine horse you have there'. Twm told the man it was a magical flying horse that could perform tricks and illusions. The man was impressed, so he bought the horse and asked Twm to show him a trick. Twm told the man to close his eyes and the horse would magically disappear. The man closed his eyes, Twm climbed into the saddle and galloped away with both horse and money before the man appreciated the trick.

A gentleman was watching a servant carrying a sheep along the road to market when Twm appeared and wagered that he could steal the sheep without the servant knowing. The gentleman took the bet. Twm took off his shoe, dropped it in the road and ran off. The servant found the shoe, but as there was no pair, he left it for the tramps. Further down the road he found the second shoe, so he tied his sheep to a tree and ran back to collect the first shoe. He picked it up but when he returned, the second shoe had gone, and so had the sheep. The servant threw the first shoe away in anger and stomped off. Twm picked up his shoes, showed the sheep to the gentleman, and won the wager. Later, Twm saw the servant carrying another sheep to market. The servant heard a bleating. Thinking it may be the sheep he lost earlier, he tied the second sheep to a tree and went looking for the bleating sheep. And Twm walked off with two sheep and a fat wager.

Twm, disguised in a highwayman's black cloak and a hawk mask, stopped a coach on the road from Llandovery to Llanwrtyd Wells. He robbed the occupants of the coach, a rich man and his daughter, but the girl was so beautiful he returned her necklace and ring, and rode away.

The rich man was Sir John Price of Ystrad Ffin, and the girl was his daughter, Joan. When Sir John returned to Llandovery, he was so infuriated at the cheek of the highwayman that he set the law on him. Twm took refuge in a cave on Dinas Hill, where he thought of little else but

Twm Sion Cati

Joan Price. When the heat died down, he turned up one evening outside her window. He called to her, kissed her hand, took his knife, drew blood from her wrist and threatened to sever her hand if she did not marry him. Despite his unusual courting technique, she agreed and they were secretly wed. On the death of old Sir John, the young couple inherited Ystrad Ffin, and Twm settled down to a reasonably respectable life as a poet and justice of the peace.

Twm's cave is at the RSPB Dinas Hill Reserve and can be visited on a walk with 'Twm's Treks' while Dafydd Wyn Morgan tells the tales of the legendary Tregaron Trickster.

The Red Bandits of Dinas Mawddwy

In the mountains above Dinas Mawddwy lived the Gwylliaid Cochion, bandits and thieves with flowing red hair who stole cattle, robbed travellers and raided farmhouses, while the cottagers kept sharp scythes hidden up their chimneys to protect themselves. They were said to have been leftover soldiers from the Wars of the Roses.

On Christmas Eve 1554, Lewis ap Owen, the Sheriff of Meirionnydd, captured around eighty of the bandits. Two of them were the young sons of Lowri ferch Gruffydd Llwyd, and she pleaded with Sheriff Lewis to have mercy on her boys. When he refused, she bared her neck and said, 'These yellow breasts have given suck to those who shall wash their hands in your blood'. Nonetheless, eighty bandits were executed at Collfryn (the Hill of Loss), and buried at Rhos Goch near Mallwyd.

In October the following year, Lowri's curse came gruesomely true. Sheriff Lewis was found on the road near Dugoed Mawddwy with thirty arrows in his body, fired by John Goch ap Gruffydd. Every male between eight and eighty was rounded up and either hanged for murder or transported. Even Lowri was charged at the court in Bala, though she was saved from the gallows through being with child.

In 1936, the locals acted the parts of the bandits in a film made by the Reverend H.E. Hughes, and two years later they participated in the first colour film shot in Wales, *Gwylliaid Cochion Mawddwy*. To this day, any child born with red hair is told they are descended from the bandits, and there are still said to be a few scythes hidden up chimneys, just in case.

Murray the Hump

In the 1890s, with work scarce and times hard, Bryan Humphreys and Ann Wigley left their farm in Carno and family in Llandinam, and found themselves on the streets of Chicago. Their older children were sent out to work to raise money to support their father's drinking and gambling habits. The third child, Llewelyn Morris Humphreys, dropped out of school, sold newspapers on street corners, took to petty theft and jewel heists, and by sixteen was in jail. However, the judge was so impressed by the boy's intelligence, he persuaded him to study the law.

On his release, Llewelyn set up his own business enterprise in a room above a launderette offering legal advice to the criminal underworld, so inventing the term 'money laundering'. He diversified into dealing in bootleg liquor and petty larceny, and so came to the attention of the Mob, where he became known as Murray the Hump. He carried out killings, though his preference was to use a gun only as a last resort. He specialised in the corruptibility of authority, particularly judges, a skill which came in useful when Al Capone was sent for trial. It was the Hump who used his legal expertise and contacts to reduce the charge to tax avoidance. He coined the phrase 'Vote early and vote often', organised the Mob takeover of the Chicago Labor Unions, and co-ordinated the St Valentine's Day Massacre. On Capone's death, the Hump inherited the title 'Public Enemy Number One'.

In 1963 the Hump came home. On a trip around Europe with his half-Cherokee ex-wife and daughter, he flew into Heathrow and took a black cab all the way to Carno. This amiable family man was welcomed, fed bara brith and taken for a cwrw at the Aleppo. He discovered his blood relatives had fallen on hard times, unable to pay their rents and fearful the sale of the Llandinam estate would mean their eviction. Not long after Uncle Llewellyn had returned to his other family in the States, his Welsh family discovered that the estate had been purchased by an unknown American benefactor and their rents had been paid off.

The Hump died in 1965 of a heart attack, or 'unnatural causes'. So passed the Welshman who helped create Las Vegas, controlled much of Hollywood, knew of the election and assassination of President Kennedy before they happened, was an inspiration for *The Godfather*, dined with kings the world over, had a plaque hanging over his fireplace saying, 'Love thy crooked neighbour as you love thy crooked self', frequently donated money and food to his ex-wife's Cherokee tribe, and gave his name to the legendary Welsh indie band Murray the Hump, who at a record label gig were rated by Joe Strummer as being 'better than Coldplay', although it's uncertain whether Joe meant that as a compliment.

The Man Who Never Was

In January 1943, a tramp was found dying near King's Cross Station in London, having eaten rat poison. As he lay on a slab in Hackney Mortuary, no one knew he was to become an unlikely Welsh folk hero.

The British Government, in the shape of corkscrew-minded Flight Lieutenant Charles Cholmondley and Lieutenant Ewen Montagu, had devised a cunning plan called Operation Mincemeat, designed to end the war with Germany by invading Italy. All they needed was a fresh corpse, so the tramp from Hackney Mortuary was volunteered. He was dressed in an ill-fitting Royal Marine uniform, given false papers and a new identity, 'Major William Martin', and launched from a torpedo tube on board HMS *Seraph* towards the coast of Spain. He was found by the

Spanish authorities on the beach at Huelva carrying top secret plans for an Allied invasion of Sardinia and Greece. The plans found their way to Hitler, who ordered troops from Russia to protect Sardinia and Greece, thus allowing the Allies to land at Sicily unopposed and invade Italy. Churchill received a telegram saying, 'Mincemeat swallowed, hook, line and sinker', and 'Major Martin' was buried with full military honours in Huelva Churchyard.

In 1955, under the guidance of Ewen Montagu, this very British story was told in the film *The Man Who Never Was*, although the tramp was not mentioned by name. 'Major Martin' was Glyndwr Michael from Aberbargoed, gardener and labourer, who only moved to London to live on the streets when his parents died and he was left alone. Like all true heroes, he was a hero by mistake.

SWANS, WOLVES AND TRANSFORMATIONS

Cadwaladr and the Goat

In the days before sheep, the farmers of the Snowdonia Mountains kept goats. Cadwaladr loved his goats, particularly one called Jenny, who he loved even more than his wife, for her beard was combed every Friday by the tylwyth teg.

But his love was overpowering, and one day Jenny ran away up the mountain. He climbed up after her, implored her to come home and promised her flowers for her beard, but she looked at him with such an air of superiority, he saw red, threw a stone, knocked her off the mountainside and down she tumbled into the gorge.

Cadwaladr saw what he had done and came to his senses. He clambered down the mountain, picked up Jenny's broken body, cradled her head in his lap and she licked his hand. As the moon rose, he looked down and there was a sweet young woman. She sat up and held out her hand, and spoke to him with such a sweet bleating voice. Her face was so beautiful and her beard was silky smooth. She took his hand in her hoof, and helped him climb out of the gorge. Cadwaladr found himself surrounded

Jenny the Goat

by his herd of goats, all singing and bleating. One big hairy billy rushed at him, butted him in the stomach and knocked him off the top of the mountain. Down and down he tumbled.

When he awoke, he found himself lying at the bottom of the gorge, the birds were singing and the rain was drizzling and there was no sign of Jenny or his goats, only sheep as far as the eye could see.

Swan Ladies

Grassi was the Keeper of the Well at Glasfryn on Pen Llŷn. She opened the door whenever anyone needed water, then closed it again before they took too much. It was a dreary job, so Grassi lost herself in dreams and fairy tales. One day, she was dreaming and forgot to close the door. The waters overflowed and she found herself drowning in a great lake. Her neck began to stretch, her arms sprouted feathers, her nose turned orange, her cheeks black, she hissed and spat and became a swan. For three hundred years Grassi was cursed to swim round and round the lake, and at two o'clock every morning she was heard whooping and weeping, frightening the servants at Glasfryn House. When she died, she regained her human form and haunted the fields around the lake dressed in a spectral white gown.

Swan Lady

A swan landed on a rock on the coast of Gower, removed her white wings and feathers and a girl stepped out and washed herself in the sea. She lay on a rock to dry herself, dressed in her wings and feathers and flew away. Day after day, the swan-girl swam in the sea, and all was well until a young farmer spotted her and became enchanted. Day after day he watched. His head swirled, for her feathers were as white as her skin was dark, and soon he convinced himself he was in love. He waited until she was in the water, and he stole her wings and feathers. She walked out of the water, stared straight into his eyes and told him to return her clothes. He refused, and said he loved her. She told him he knew nothing about her. He took hold of her, she struggled to escape, but without her wings her arms were weak and she could not fly away. She was pinioned to him.

He took her home and locked her wings and feathers in an oak chest beneath his bed. He gave her pretty dresses which were rough against her skin. He fed her fine and rich foods, but all she craved was weed from the pond. He kept her dry, and she dreamed of drowning. Every night he stroked her feathers against his cheek, and every night she watched him while the muscles in her arms wasted away to string. Three years passed, until one night he forgot to lock the chest. She dressed in her clothes and flapped her wings and, oh, how her arms ached, but she threw herself from the window and flew away, crying tears of pleasure and pain. And the young farmer cried too, every day until he pined away and died.

In the early 1800s, a young man from Rhoose and another from Cadoxton were shooting wildfowl at Whitmore Bay on Barry Island when they were cut off by the tide. To while away the time they went to Friars Point where they saw two swans. They crept closer, raised their guns and were about to shoot when the swans removed their wings and feathers to reveal two young women. The men knew the story of the Gower Swan-girl, so they stole the feathers and wings and forced the girls to promise to marry them. They had children with long curved necks who preferred to swim than go to school. One day, the wife of the Cadoxton man was run over by a wagon and killed. She left her human form, turned back into a swan, found the hidden clothes belonging to the wife of the Rhoose man, and they flew away together as swans.

Snake-Women

A Swansea-girl had eyes that shone like diamonds, sometimes blue, sometimes grey, sometimes emerald. A young farmer from Ynys Môn was mesmerised by her, and she had agreed to marry him on the understanding that she was free to leave twice a year for a fortnight, and he was never to ask her where she had gone. He was happy with the arrangement, because he assumed she was visiting her family and he had no wish to leave Ynys Môn for Swansea.

All was well, until his mother became curious, as mothers often do. She suspected her son was being cuckolded, so she persuaded him to follow his wife. When the girl set off for Swansea, the farmer followed her. She walked through the woods and along the river, never looking behind her, until she stopped by a dark pool. He hid behind an elder tree and watched. She removed the girdle from her waist, threw it onto the grass, stood motionless, and slowly vanished. He ran towards the pool, but all he saw was a huge emerald snake which hissed at him and slithered down a hole in the bank. He poked a stick into the hole and wiggled it about, but the snake had gone.

Two weeks later, Swansea-girl returned, and he asked her about the snake. She stood motionless and stared at him with those emerald eyes, and licked her lips with her tongue. For the first time, he doubted his wife.

Six months later, just before she was due to leave, he hid her girdle. She pleaded with him to return it, but he refused and told her it was for her own good. She hissed and spat, frothed at the mouth, her neck arched, and her tongue flicked. Thinking the girdle must be the cause of her fit, he threw it into the fire. She writhed and wriggled and a fever consumed her, and as the girdle incinerated, she turned to ashes. She became known as 'the Snake-Woman of the South'.

There was a shoemaker in the Vale of Taff who had married a widow for her money. One night, a neighbour heard terrible noises followed by a scream, as if he had struck her. Yet in the morning there wasn't a mark on her face. The neighbour asked if she was alright, and she nodded and covered her face with her black hair.

As time passed the shoemaker became pale and emaciated, as if all the blood had drained from his body. Served him right for beating his wife and stealing her money, everyone said. When he died, no one mourned. Until the doctor examined his body and claimed the cause of death was the poisoned bite of a venomous serpent. The neighbour spoke up and said it wasn't a serpent; the shoemaker had been bitten by his own wife.

That evening, the Snake-Woman invited the doctor and the neighbour to celebrate her husband's life. They raised a glass of sweet honey wine and swapped stories and sang hymns when, suddenly, she hissed and spat. Her neck curved and she became a snake from the shoulders up. She opened her mouth to reveal two venomous fangs. She tore at them and drank their blood, and as she bit one of them, the other fought her off, until their strength drained.

They were found the following morning, draped over gravestones in the churchyard, white as ghosts, blood drained from their bodies and barely alive. The shoemaker's wife had vanished, but from that day a great serpent was seen in the churchyard, which no stone or stick could kill. It was known as 'the old Snake-Woman'.

Frog Woman and Toad Man

Miss Sylvester from Presteigne had a frog's head, face, eyes, mouth, legs and feet. She could not walk, so she hopped, and never went out other than to chapel. When her mother was pregnant, she had turned away a beggar-woman, who cursed her saying, 'Get away with your young frogs', and so it was that Miss Sylvester was born half-woman, half-amphibian.

On moonlit nights, a Frog Woman frequented the road between Cardiff and Llandaff. She croaked and hopped like a frog, and was said to have been from a well-off family who had given her to an old woman to raise. One night, she fell into the Taff and drowned, and her

Miss Sylvester

croaks and cries were heard at moonlit midnights for many years after.

A wood turner in Cemaes fell into a fever and complained that toads were eating his fingers and nose. No one saw any toads, but the man grew hysterical. A gwiddanes was sent for, but her herbs made him speak gibberish. A dyn hysbys left a charm, but the man gibbered even more. One night his brother was dabbing the sweat from the wood turner's forehead when he heard a noise. He lifted up the bedsheets and there were the toads, nibbling the wood turner's toes. They walked up his body and ate his fingers and then his nose. He brushed them away but there were too many of them. So he dragged his brother out of bed, carried him into the top branches of a tree and stripped off the bark. But the toads climbed the slippery tree, and gobbled the man up, fingers, nose and all. The Killer Toads of Cemaes left little more than a bag of bones.

Gerald of Wales told of a young man called Cecil Longlegs who, during an illness, was persecuted by toads. No matter how many toads his friends killed, there were always more to take their place. So they hid Cecil up a tree, but the toads climbed up and stripped him to the bone. The place is called Trellyffant, Toad Town.

Killer Toad of Cemaes

242

Werewolves and Wolf-Girl

In the eighteenth century, gangs of robbers in the woods were called Wolfmen. They emerged only at night, prowled around in packs, raided lonely farmsteads, carried children away and conversed with each other by howling.

In 1790, after dusk on a full moon, a stagecoach travelling from Denbigh to Wrexham was attacked on Llandegla Moor and overturned by an enormous black beast which tore apart one of the horses. In the

winter of 1791, the sheep and dogs at Rhys Williams's farm on the moor were slaughtered by a black wolf-like beast that tried to batter down the farm door. To this day, there are tales of the Beast of Bont, a large black cat that walks in the shelter of the hedgerows, slaughters sheep and provides headlines for local newspapers.

A young man who lived in the Bear's Wood near Wenvoe proposed to a girl from Cadoxton. A year later he dumped her to marry another. Unfortunately for the man, the girl's aunt was the Witch of Wenvoe, and she was not pleased at the way her niece had been treated. The witch left a twisted girdle on his doorstep and when he stepped over it, he turned into a werewolf. He ran naked, hairy and howling around Cadoxton, terrifying his new fiancée and amusing his former sweetheart, until the witch threw a lamb's skin over him and he turned back into a man. He married the girl, but he dribbled and slavered and treated her so badly that the witch turned him back into a werewolf. He was known as 'the Wild Man of the Woods' and there was much relief when a poacher shot him.

A wide-eyed girl with a violent temper lived on the borders of Radnorshire. She was married to a gentle young man who loved her well. He soothed her with poetry while they huddled in the warmth of the fireside, and soon her anger abated. But times were hard, there was no living in words, and their bellies rumbled with hunger. They took to foraging, but nettle soup and mint infusions did not satisfy her. She became hollow-cheeked and sunken-eyed, hunched of shoulder and shadows beneath her ribs. Too weak to be angry, she stared at her young man, chewed her black hair and told him she would provide food for them. Before he could reply, she melted out of the door and returned later with a side of meat. That evening they ate greedily.

Each night she brought meat, sometimes lamb and sometimes chicken, and once again she became wide-eyed and angry. He asked her where the meat came from, but she just wiped the grease from her mouth and took another bite. He explained that he was concerned she

Wolf Girl

was stealing. She made him promise not to reveal what she was about to show him, and she took him by the hand and led him to a lonely spot in the woods. She stripped herself of her clothes, wrapped her arms around his neck, her lips twitched, her nose lengthened, fur grew through her skin, her fingers became clawed, she licked his face and ran into the woods. She returned with a dead lamb between her teeth, dropped it in his lap and brushed the blood from her teeth. She promised all would be well, providing he stayed with her to ensure she hurt no one.

One day, they were in the woods when wolf-girl came hurtling through the trees with a lamb dangling from her mouth, pursued by a farmer and his dogs. Her husband shouted, 'Run, my wife!' and the wolf vanished. Wolf-girl lay naked on the ground, curled up like a foetus while the dogs circled her, sniffing the blood on her body. The farmer stared, not knowing where to look, then he raised his gun. The young man stood between the cowering wolf-girl and the farmer, and said he would take the bullet

Welsh Folk Tales

for his wife. The farmer lowered his gun and said that he would skin her alive if she ever stole his sheep again.

The young husband picked up his wife, wrapped her in his coat, and carried her home, took her to bed and kept her warm. He fed her on cat meat and roadkill, and drained his blood into a glass for her to drink. But she grew weaker and paler and thinner.

Marie Trevelyan

He took jobs, working day and night, and bought her sides of lamb and whole chickens. Soon his wife grew stronger, and he locked her in whenever he worked nights. He never wrote another word of poetry, but he never stopped loving his wolf-girl, nor she him. .

This story was told to Emma Thomas of Llantwit Major by 'JR', who requested anonymity out of fear for their family. Emma was born in 1853 in Llantwit Major, daughter of stonemason and antiquarian Illtyd Thomas. She married a French journalist named Louis Paslieu, left him when she discovered he was a bigamist, and raised her daughter Bronwen as a single mother. To earn a living, she worked as a fortune teller, Madame Paslieu, and as a writer under the pen-name Marie Trevelyan. 'Marie' wrote several books in the 1890s, containing rip-roaring Arthurian legends, stirring stories of the sea and a gentle Quaker romance. In 1909 she published a phantasmagoria of folk tales, collected by herself and her father, very different to folk tales featured in books written by scholars and clergymen. Emma's stories are 'chwedlau'.

BLODEUWEDD, FLOWER AND OWL

Math fab Mathonwy, Lord of Gwynedd, held court at Caer Dathyl in Arfon, where he ruled the North with his nephews, Gilfaethwy and Gwydion. When he wasn't engaged in war with Dyfed in the South, Math had a guilty secret. He took pleasure in sitting in his bedchamber with his feet resting in the lap of a virgin, Goewin ferch Pebin.

Now, Gilfaethwy was infatuated with Goewin. The colour had drained from his cheeks, he had wasted away to skin and bone, and he was scared the wind would whisper his secret to Math. Gwydion knew of his brother's pain, so he decided to help. He decided to conjure a war between Gwynedd and Dyfed, so Math would be forced to take up arms and remove his feet from Goewin's lap.

Gwydion told Math that Pryderi fab Pwyll, Lord of Dyfed, had been given a gift of enchanted pigs by Arawn, Lord of the Otherworld. Math said he wanted a gift, too, so Gwydion offered to find some enchanted pigs.

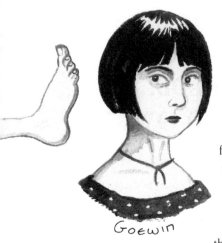

Goewin

So it was that Gwydion, Gilfaethwy and ten men disguised themselves as bards, poets and storytellers and came to Pryderi's court at Rhuddlan Teifi in Dyfed. They were invited in, and that evening Gwydion entranced Pryderi with his words, for Gwydion was the best storyteller in the world. Then he took twelve toad-stools and conjured twelve horses and twelve black hounds with white chests, and he gave their iron collars the appearance of gold. He offered them to Pryderi, who was dazzled by the gold and gave Gwydion his enchanted pigs in exchange. Gwydion and Gilfaethwy fled swiftly towards Gwynedd, knowing Pryderi would awaken from his enchantment and give chase. They stopped that night at a place that became known as Mochdref, Pigtown.

When Pryderi awoke and found his precious pigs had been stolen, he called for armour, gathered an army and marched on Gwynedd. On hearing the battle cry, Math armed his warriors, removed his foot from Goewin's lap and marched to meet Pryderi.

Gwydion and Gilfaethwy slipped back to Caer Dathyl, and while Gwydion distracted the maidservants, Gilfaethwy crept into Math's bedroom, and took Goewin against her will. At dawn the two brothers joined Math and his warriors in Arfon. The men of Gwynedd chased the men of Dyfed to Nantcyll, and there was a terrible slaughter. The men of Dyfed retreated again to Y Felinryhd, where Pryderi sent a mes-sage to Math saying the battle should be between him and Gwydion alone. The two men were armed and fought, and Gwydion enchanted Pryderi and slew him. He was buried in Maentwrog above Y Felinrhyd, while the men of Dyfed chanted lamentations and the men of Gwynedd marched home with songs on their lips.

Blodeuwedd, Flower and Owl

When Math returned to Caer Dathyl, he ordered his bedchamber be made ready to rest his feet in his virgin's lap. Goewin spoke, 'Lord, you will have to find another to take my place.' Math invited her to explain. 'I am no longer a virgin. I was raped, Lord, and I was not silent. Your court heard. Your nephew Gwydion distracted my maids while Gilfaethwy raped me. And in your own bed.' Math swore he would punish his nephews, and offered to marry Goewin himself and give her authority over his kingdom.

Gwydion and Gilfaethwy heard of Math's fury and fled the court in fear, sleeping here and there in barns and trees. Math hunted them down, and struck them with his enchanted stick. He turned Gilfaethwy into a stag, and Gwydion into a hind, and ordered them to live together for a year and a day, with the same desires as wild beasts, and to make passionate love with each other.

In a year and a day, the stag and hind appeared before Math, looking rather sheepish, with a sturdy fawn trailing behind them. Math turned the fawn into a boy and gave him to Goewin, who named him Hyddwn. He took his enchanted stick and turned Gilfaethwy into a wild boar and Gwydion into a sow, and told them to go and make love like wild beasts. In a year and a day they appeared before Math with a sturdy piglet, which he turned into a boy named Hychdwn. Math turned Gilfaethwy into a wolf and Gwydion into a she-wolf, and in a year and a day they appeared with a sturdy cub, who Math turned into a boy named Bleiddwn.

After three years Math had amused himself enough. He turned the wolves into brothers again, told them their punishment was over and their embarrassment complete. He prepared a bath to wash away their hair, and invited them to recommend a new virgin with a comfortable lap on which to rest his feet. Gwydion quickly suggested his own sister, Arianrhod. She was sent for and Math inquired if she was a virgin. She said, 'As far as I remember, my Lord.' So Math invited her to step over his enchanted stick. As she did, she dropped a sturdy yellow-haired baby boy. Arianrhod fled, and as she ran through the door she dropped another baby, little more than a runt. Gwydion picked up the runt, wrapped him in a silk cover and hid him in the chest at the foot of his bed.

Math looked at the sturdy yellow-haired boy and baptised him. As the water touched him, the boy leapt into the sea and swam like a fish. Math named him Dylan ail Ton, Son of the Wave.

Gwydion lifted the runt from his chest and gave him to a wet nurse. After one year he was as tall as a two year old, after two years he walked on his own, and at four there wasn't an eight year old bigger than he. One day Gwydion and the boy walked along the beach to Arianrhod's castle. She asked who this fine young boy was, and Gwydion explained he was her son. She asked his name, and Gwydion said he had no name, so she said she would name him. Gwydion said no, the boy's father would name him, and he called Arianrhod a wicked woman, angry at losing her virginity.

Gwydion played a trick. He disguised himself and the boy as cobblers, conjured leather from seaweed and offered to make Arianrhod a pair of shoes. She came to his boat to have her feet measured, and as she stepped on board the boy threw a stone at a wren, striking it on the leg between tendon and bone. Arianrhod exclaimed, 'Lleu Llaw Gyffes, that fair-haired boy has a skilful hand.' The enchantment lifted, and Arianrhod saw the cobbler was her brother Gwydion, who told her that she had just named her son, Lleu Llaw Gyffes. She knew she had been tricked, and walked away, swearing Lleu would never throw another stone in anger or bear arms against another unless she armed him herself. And she called Gwydion an evil man, frustrated at being unable to love a woman.

One day, two poets from Glamorgan appeared at Caer Arianrhod. She invited them in and fed them and they repaid her kindness in sto-

ries. The older man was a fine storyteller, best in the world. They slept
that night at the castle, and in the morning Arianrhod looked out of
her window and saw a fleet of invading ships approaching and knew
she was in great danger. The poets offered to help, so she gave them
swords, and as she dressed the younger lad in armour the fleet of ships
vanished, and there stood Gwydion and Lleu. She knew she had been
tricked into breaking her vow that her son would never be armed. She
called Gwydion an evil man, he called Arianrhod a wicked woman, and
she cursed Lleu never to have a wife of flesh and blood.

Lleu grew into a handsome youth. He rode wild horses along the
beach at Dinas Dinlle, and soon he was ready to take a wife. So Math
and Gwydion took the flowers of the oak, the broom and the meadowsweet and they conjured a maiden, and named her Blodeuwedd, and
gave her to Lleu as a wife.

As a wedding gift, Math built Lleu and his flower-bride a court at
Mur Castell in the uplands of Ardudwy. One day, Blodeuwedd was at
Mur Castell, when she heard the sound of a horn, and a tired stag ran
past with a huntsman and dogs in pursuit. The huntsman was Gronw
Pebr, Lord of Penllyn, and the moment Blodeuwedd saw him she was
enchanted. She thought it would be impolite not to invite him in, and
all that evening they talked and then passed the night together in
Lleu's bed. And the following night. And soon the lovers were plotting.

Lleu came home late, he spent the next day talking with Blodeuwedd,
and that night they went to bed. She was silent and distant. He asked what
was wrong, and she said she was worried he might die before her, leaving
her all alone. Lleu was touched by her concern and reassured her he could
not be killed by any blow other than from a spear that had been crafted
during Mass each Sunday for one year, nor could he be killed within a
house nor outside, nor on horseback nor on foot. The only way he could
die was if he stood with one foot on the roof of a pig trough and the other
on a billy goat's back. And that was hardly likely to happen, now was it?

Blodeuwedd told Gronw to craft a spear during Mass each Sunday
for a year. She placed a roofed pig trough by the banks of River Cynfael,

hid Gronw in the shadow of Bryn Cyfergyr, and rounded up all the billy goats in the neighbourhood. She persuaded Lleu to bathe in the trough, and when he was washed clean, he pulled on his trousers, stood with one foot on the trough and placed the other on the back of a billy goat in order to step to the ground. Gronw rose up on one knee and cast the poisoned spear. It struck Lleu in the side. The shaft snapped, leaving the point inside. Lleu screeched, flew up into the air as an eagle and vanished. That night, the lovers slept in Lleu's bed, and Gronw ruled both Penllyn and Ardudwy as if they belonged to him.

When news reached Gwydion, he was troubled. He searched for Lleu throughout Gwynedd and Powys, until he came to a pig keeper's house at Maenor Bennardd. The pig man told him he had a sow who disappeared as soon as her sty was opened, and only returned in the evening. Gwydion was intrigued and followed the sow, and found her beneath a tree eating rotten meat and maggots. He looked up into the tree and there sat an eagle, and when it shook itself, maggots and flesh fell to the ground and the sow gobbled them up. Gwydion knew the eagle was Lleu. He sang:

Blodeuwedd, Flower and Owl

Derwen a dyf rhwng dau lyn
Gan dywyllu awyr a glyn.
Os nad wyf fi'n dywedyd gau,
O flodau, Lleu, y mae hyn.

An oak grows between two lakes,
Dark is the sky and the valley.
Unless I am mistaken,
This is because of Lleu's flowers.

And the eagle fell through the tree.

Derwen a dyf ar uchel faes,
Nid glaw a'i gwlych, pydra hi'n y gwres.
Ugain poen a ddioddefes
Ar ei phen, Lleu Llaw Gyffes.

An oak grows on a high plain,
Rain does not wet it, heat no longer rots it,
One is enduring twenty pains,
In its top is Lleu Llaw Gyffes.

And the eagle fell to the lowest branch.

Derwen a dyf ar oriwaered
Arglwydd hardd, dyma'i nodded
Os nad wyf fi'n dywedyd gau,
Fe ddaw ef, Lleu, I f'arffed.

An oak grows on a slope,
The refuge of a handsome prince,
Unless I am mistaken,
Lleu will come to my lap.

And the eagle fell into Gwydion's lap. He struck it with his enchanted stick, and there was Lleu, little more than skin and bone. They returned to Caer Dathyl, physicians were brought to tend to Lleu, and by the end of the year he was recovered enough to tell Math and Gwydion the story of Blodeuwedd and Gronw. Math removed his feet from the lap of his brand new virgin, raised an army, and marched to Ardudwy. When Blodeuwedd heard the battle cry, she gathered her maidens and fled across the River Cynfael towards the mountains. They were so frightened, they ran looking over their shoulders, and so fell into Llyn y Morwynion and drowned. But not Blodeuwedd.

Llech Gronw

Gwydion caught her but did not kill her. He turned her into a bird, and cursed her never to show her face in daylight for fear all the birds would slaughter her. She would fly alone by night, as Owl.

Gronw offered land and gold to Lleu as recompense. Lleu refused, and ordered Gronw to stand on the banks of the Cynfael, in the same spot where he had been pierced by the spear. Gronw pleaded for someone to take the spear for him, then he blamed Blodeuwedd, and held a stone slab to his chest to protect him from the blow. Lleu threw his spear, it pierced the stone and broke Gronw's back, and Gronw Pebr died there on the banks of the River Cynfael in Ardudwy, and to this day there stands a stone with a hole through it, known as Llech Gronw.

And Lleu ruled over his land in peace, as the old story tells. And so ends this branch of Y Mabinogi.

Except that Les Edwards from Borth, bless him, could tell this story and the rest of Y Mabinogi in a couple of minutes by rolling up his sleeve to reveal tattoos of Rhiannon, Branwen and, at the top of his arm, Blodeuwedd.

REFERENCES

This book is a personal selection of folk tales, true tales, tall tales, myths, gossip, legends and memories of people. Some are well known, others from forgotten manuscripts or out-of-print volumes, and some are contemporary oral tales. Some old favourites have been omitted, such as Arthurian legends and ghost stories, as they have books to themselves, while others have been traced back to their earliest printed sources. These stories reflect the diverse tradition of storytelling, and the many meanings of 'chwedlau'.

Chwedlau

Lewis, Saunders, *Crefft y Stori Fer* (Llandysul: Clwb Llyfrau Cymraeg, 1949).

Mimpriss, Rob (trans.), interview with Kate Roberts, from his website: www.robmimpriss.com.

Pontshan, Eirwyn, *Hyfryd Iawn* (Talybont: Y Lolfa, 1973).

Rees, Alwyn D., *Life in a Welsh Countryside* (Cardiff: University of Wales, 1950) 131.

Chapter 1 – Branwen, Red and White Books

Charlotte and *The Mabinogion*

The White Book of Rhydderch is in the National Library of Wales, and *The Red Book of Hergest* in the Bodleian Library, Oxford.

Guest, Lady Charlotte, *The Mabinogion, from the Llyfr Coch o Hergest, and other Ancient Welsh Manuscripts* (London: Longman, 1836–49).

Guest, Revel, and Angela V. John, *Lady Charlotte Guest* (Stroud: Tempus, 2007).

Branwen Ferch Llŷr

Davies, Sioned (trans.), *The Mabinogion* (Oxford University Press, 2007).

Davies, Sioned, 'Storytelling in Medieval Wales', in *Oral Tradition* 7/2, 231–57 (Columbia, 1992).

Jones, Gwyn, and Thomas Jones, *The Mabinogion* (London: J.M. Dent, 1949).

Morus, Gwilym, Welsh Mythology: https://welshmythology.com

Thomas, Gwyn, and Kevin Crossley-Holland, *Tales from* The Mabinogion (London: Victor Gollancz, 1984).

Williams, Ivor (ed.), *Pedeir Keinc y Mabinogi* (Cardiff: University of Wales, 2nd ed. 1951).

Chapter 2 – Ladies, Lakes and Looking Glasses

The Lady of Llyn y Fan Fach

Jones, Gwyn, *Welsh Legends and Folk-Tales* (Oxford University Press, 1955) 208–22.

Owen, Elias, *Welsh Folk-Lore: A Collection of the Folk Tales and Legends of North Wales* (Oswestry: Woodall Minshall & Co, 1896) 16–31.

Parry-Jones, D., *Welsh Legends and Fairy Lore* (London: BT Batsford, 1953).

The Lady of Llyn y Forwyn

Rhys, Sir John, *Celtic Folklore: Welsh and Manx* (Oxford: Henry Frowde, 1891) Vol. 1, 23–29.

The Fairy Cattle of Llyn Barfog

Sikes, Wirt, *British Goblins: The Realm of Faerie* (London: J.R. Osgood & Company, 1880) 36–38.

References

The Red-Headed Lady of Llyn Eiddwen
Oral tale.

Dreams and Memories
Ellis, T.P., *Dreams and Memories* (Newtown: The Welsh Outlook Press, 1936) 66–67.

Chapter 3 – Submerged Cities, Lost Worlds and Utopias

Plant Rhys Ddwfn
Rhys, *Celtic Folklore*, 151–68.

The Ghost Island
Radford, Ken, *Tales of South Wales* (London: Skilton & Shaw, 1979) 94–97.

The Curse of the Verry Volk
'Lyonesse' (George Basil Barham), *Legend Land* (London: Great Western Railway, 4 Vols, 1922), Vol. 2, 36–39.

The Reservoir Builders
Homer, Andrew, *Haunted Hostelries of Shropshire* (Stroud: Amberley Publishing, 2012).
Mysterious Britain: http://www.mysteriousbritain.co.uk/
Powys Digital History Project: http://history.powys.org.uk/

The Lost Land Below Wylfa Nuclear Power Station
Austin, Bunty, *Haunted Anglesey* (Llanrwst: Gwasg Carreg Gwalch, 2005) 99–112.

Chapter 4 – Mermaids, Fishermen and Selkies

Mermaids
Davies, Jonathan Ceredig, *Folk-Lore of West and Mid-Wales* (Aberystwyth: Welsh Gazette, 1911) 143–47.
Owen, *Welsh Folk-Lore*, 142–43.
Rhys, *Celtic Folklore*, 163–64 & 199–204.

The Llanina Mermaid
Davies, *Folk-Lore of West and Mid-Wales*, 144.
Evans, Myra, *Casgliad o Chwedlau Newydd* (Aberystwyth: Cambrian News, 1926) pp.8–9, as 'Chwedl Llanina'.

Another Llanina Mermaid
Evans, *Casgliad o Chwedlau Newydd*, pp.1–3, as 'Chwedl Cantre'r Gwaelod'.

More Llanina Mermaids
Jones, T. Llew, *Tales the Wind Told* (Llandysul: Gomer, 1979) 41–49.
Oral tale.

The Fisherman and the Seal
Medlicott, Mary, *Shemi's Tall Tales* (Llandysul: Pont Books, 2008) 66–70.
Told to Shemi Wâd by Minnie John.

Chapter 5 – Conjurers, Charmers and Cursers

The Dyn Hysbys
Griffiths, Kate Bosse, *Byd y Dyn Hysbys* (Talybont: Y Lolfa, 1977).
Palmer, Roy, *The Folklore of Radnorshire* (Herefordshire: Logaston Press, 2001) 97–113.
Suggett, Richard, *A History of Magic and Witchcraft in Wales* (Stroud: The History Press, 2008) 84–115.

The Conjurer of Cwrt-y-Cadno
'A Book of Incantations' and Harries's papers are in the National Library of Wales.
Davies, *Folk-Lore of West and Mid-Wales*, 252–64.
Phillips, Bethan, *The Lovers' Graves* (Llandysul: Gomer, 2007) 71–94.
Trevelyan, Marie, *Folk-Lore and Folk-Stories of Wales* (London: Elliot Stock, 1909) 215–18.

Silver John the Bonesetter
Gwyndaf, Robin, *Welsh Folk Tales/Chwedlau Gwerin Cymru* (Cardiff: National Museum of Wales, 1989) 74.
Lloyds of Baynham: http://www.lloydsofbaynham.com/Menu.htm

The Cancer Curers of Cardigan
John, Brian, *More Pembrokeshire Folk Tales* (Newport: Greencroft, 1996) 131–34.
Jones T.L., and D.W. Jones, *Cancer Curers – or Quacks?* (Llandysul: Gomer, 1993).

Old Gruff
Oral tales.
Sandys, Oliver, *The Miracle Stone of Wales* (London: Rider & Company, 1957) 27–55.

Chapter 6 – Hags, Hares and Dolls

Witchery
Suggett, *A History of Magic and Witchcraft in Wales*, 27–41.

The Llanddona Witches
Owen, *Welsh Folk-Lore*, 222–23.

References

Radford, Ken, *Tales of North Wales* (London: Skilton & Shaw, 1982) 81–86.

Dark Anna's Doll
Radford, *Tales of North Wales*, 100–101.

Hunting the Hare
Owen, *Welsh Folk-Lore*, 230–32.

The Witch of Death
Trevelyan, *Folk-Lore and Folk-Stories of Wales*, 65–68 & 195–205.

Chapter 7 – Dreams, Memories and the Otherworld

The Story of Guto Bach
Williams, Maria Jane, 'Fairy Legends of Wales', in Croker, Thomas Crofton, *Fairy Legends and Traditions of Southern Ireland* (London: John Murray, 1828) Vol. 2, 207–14.

The Fairies of Pen Llŷn
Evans, Hugh, *Y Tylwyth Teg* (Liverpool: Hugh Evans, 1935).
Oral tales.
Rhys, *Celtic Folklore*, 214–34 & 275.

Gower Power
Radford, *Tales of South Wales*, 87–91.

The Curse of Pantanas
Rhys, *Celtic Folklore*, 176–96.
From the telling of Guto Dafis.

Crossing the Boundary
Told by Ifan Gruffydd to Robin Gwyndaf, tape MWL 1563 at the Welsh Folk Museum.

Chapter 8 – Goblins, Bogeys and Pwcas

The Ellyll
Sikes, *British Goblins*, 15–18.

The Pwca of the Trwyn
Jones, Edmund, *The Appearance of Evil: Apparitions of Spirits in Wales* (Cardiff: University of Wales, 2003) 106–108.
Sikes, *British Goblins*, 21–22 & 117–18.

Red Cap Otter
Jones, *Welsh Legends and Folk-Tales*, 240–41.

259

Sigl-di-gwt

Evans, *Casgliad o Chwedlau Newydd*, 26–29.
Rhys, *Celtic Folklore*, 226–31.

Chapter 9 – Births, Changelings and Eggshells

Taliesin

Llyfr Taliesin is in the National Library of Wales.
Extract of poem from 'Cad Goddeu', in *Llyfr Taliesin*.
Thomas, Gwyn, and Kevin Crossley-Holland, *The Tale of Taliesin* (London: Victor
Gollancz, 1992) 4–22.

The Llanfabon Changeling

Jones, *Welsh Legends and Folk-Tales*, 200–207.
Rhys, *Celtic Folklore*, 257–69. Told by Craigfryn Hughes.

The Eggshell Dinner

Williams, in T. Crofton Croker, *Irish Legends*, 221–23. Told by David Tomos Bowen
in the early 1800s.

The Hiring Fair

Rhys, *Celtic Folklore*, 210–14.

The Baby Farmer

Emerson, P.H., *Welsh Fairy-Tales and other Stories* (London: D. Nutt, 1894) 14, 18.
A combination of two oral stories about 'Kaddy'.

Chapter 10 – Deaths, Sin-Eaters and Vampires

Poor Polly

Williams, in T. Crofton Croker, *Irish Legends*, 287–88. From the oral tradition of
David Shone.

Welsh Wake Amusements

Davies, *Folk-Lore of West and Mid-Wales*, 39–58.
Radford, *Tales of South Wales*, 154–56.

The Fasting Girls

Freeman, Michael, 'Early Tourists in Wales': https://sublimewales.wordpress.com/
Pennant, Thomas, *A Tour in Wales* (H.D. Symonds, 1778–81), 'The Journey to
Snowden', 105–107.
Wade, Stephen, *The Girl Who Lived on Air* (Bridgend: Seren, 2014).

References

Evan Bach Meets Death
Trevelyan, *Folk-Lore and Folk-Stories of Wales*, 287–89.
Popular in Glamorgan in the early part of the nineteenth century and formed part of the repertoire of wandering minstrels.

Modryb Nan
Trevelyan, *Folk-Lore and Folk-Stories of Wales*, 289–90.

Sin-Eaters
Aubrey, John, 'The Sin-Eater', in Hartland, E. Sidney, *Folklore*, Vol. 3, No. 2, 145–57 (London: Taylor & Francis, 1892).
Davies, *Folk-Lore of West and Mid-Wales*, 45–46.
Radford, *Tales of South Wales*, 168–69.

Vampires
Trevelyan, *Folk-Lore and Folk-Stories of Wales*, 54–56.

The Zombie Welshman
Mapp, Walter, *De Nugis Curialium* (Cambridge University Press, 2010).

Chapter 11 – Chapel, Church and Devil

The Devil's Bridge
Lyonesse, *Legend Land*, Vol. 1, 40–43, as 'The Old Woman Who Fooled the Devil'.
Stevenson, Peter, *Ceredigion Folk Tales* (Stroud: History Press, 2014) 112–17.

Huw Llwyd's Pulpit
Owen, *Welsh Folk-Lore*, 226–27 & 252–53.
Trevelyan, *Folk-Lore and Folk-Stories of Wales*, 221–23.
From the telling of Bronwen Hughes.

The Church that was a Mosque
Anglesey History website: http://www.anglesey-history.co.uk/

The Chapel
Oral tale, diolch Lynne Denman.

Chapter 12 – Sheepdogs, Greyhounds and a Giant Cat

As Sorry as the Man Who Killed his Greyhound
Emerson, *Welsh Fairy-Tales*, 19–21.
Freeman, Michael, 'Fabulous Fables'. Paper presented in Aberystwyth, 4 November 2015.
Family tale.

A Fairy Dog
Thomas, W. Jenkyn, *The Welsh Fairy Book* (London: A&C Black, 1938) 231–32.

A Gruesome Tail
Medlicott, *Shemi's Tall Tales*, 51–55.

Cath Palug
Ross, Anne, *Folklore of Wales* (Stroud: Tempus, 2001) 51–52.
Trevelyan, *Folk-Lore and Folk-Stories of Wales*, 73–74.

The Sheepdog
Oral tale.

Chapter 13 – Horses, Fairy Cattle and an Enchanted Pig

The Ychen Bannog
Owen, *Welsh Folk-Lore*, 129–37.
Thorpe, Lewis (trans.), *Gerald of Wales: The Journey Through Wales and the Description of Wales* (London: Penguin, 1978) 227–29.

The Ox of Eynonsford Farm
Radford, *Tales of South Wales*, 78–80.

Ceffyl Dŵr
Owen, *Welsh Folk-Lore*, 138–41.
Trevelyan, *Folk-Lore and Folk-Stories of Wales*, 65–66.

The Horse that Dropped Gold
Sampson, John, 'Welsh Gypsy Folk Tales, No. 26', in *Journal of the Gypsy Lore Society*, Vol. IV (1925), No. 3, 99–103.

The King's Secret
Rhys, *Celtic Folklore*, 231–34.
Stevenson, Peter, 'Retracing Wales', in *Planet* 208, 68–79 (Aberystwyth: Planet, 2012).

The Undertaker's Horse
Oral tale from John Beynon, Kimley Moor Farm, Rhosilli, Gower, heard from Ernest Richards and recorded in Jacob Whittaker's film *From Bard to Verse*.

The Boar Hunt
Thomas, Gwyn, and Kevin Crossley-Holland, *The Quest for Olwen* (Cambridge: Lutterworth Press, 1988) 54–9.
From the telling of Michael Harvey.

Chapter 14 – Eagles, Owls and Seagulls

The King of the Birds
Shepard-Jones, Elisabeth, *Welsh Legendary Tales* (London: Nelson, 1959) 59.

The Ancient Animals
Emerson, *Welsh Fairy-Tales*, 47 (as 'The Long Lived Ancestors').
Williams, Taliesin, *Iolo Manuscripts* (Llandovery: William Rees, 1848) 601.
From the telling of Cath Little.

Shemi Wâd and the Seagulls
Medlicott, *Shemi's Tall Tales*, 'The Stale Currant Bun', 17–27.

Iolo's Fables
Thomas, *The Welsh Fairy Book*, 304.
Williams, *Iolo Manuscripts*, 560, 565, 567 & 568.

Why the Robin's Breast is Red
Oral tale.

Chapter 15 – Dragons, Hairy Things and an Elephant

The Red and White Dragons
'Lludd and Llefelys', in *The Mabinogion* (see Chapter 1).
Trevelyan, *Folk-Lore and Folk-Stories of Wales*, 165–66.

Serpents, Carrogs, Vipers and Gwibers
Trevelyan, *Folk-Lore and Folk-Stories of Wales*, 166–69.

The Welsh Yeti
Radford, *Tales of North Wales*, 50–51.

The Wiston Basilisk
Ross, *Folklore of Wales*, 51.

Shaggy Elephant Tales
Oral tale.
Stevenson, *Ceredigion Folk Tales*, 170–75.

Chapter 16 – Saints, Wishes and Cursing Wells

The Shee Well that Ran Away
Oral tale.

St Dwynwen
Stevens, Catrin, *Santes Dwynwen* (Llandysul: Gomer, 2005).

Dwynwen's Well
Radford, *Tales of North Wales*, 72–73.

St Melangell
Ross, *Folklore of Wales*, 146–47.

St Eilian's Cursing Well
Suggett, *The History of Magic and Witchcraft in Wales*, 116–33.
Trevelyan, *Folk-Lore and Folk-Stories of Wales*, 15–16.

Chapter 17 – Giants, Beards and Cannibals

Cynog and the Cewri
Grooms, Chris, *The Giants of Wales/Cewri Cymru* (Lampeter: Edwin Mellen Press, 1993) 85–87.
Jones, T. Gwyn, *Welsh Folklore & Folk Customs* (London: Methuen, 1930) 77–80.

The Man with Green Weeds in His Hair
Grooms, *Cewri Cymru*, 187–89.
Thomas, *The Welsh Fairy Book*, 210–11.

The King of the Beards
Grooms, *Cewri Cymru*, 214–18.
Jones, *Welsh Legends and Folk-Tales*, 138–45.

The One-Eyed Giant of Rhymney
Gwyndaf, *Welsh Folk Tales/Chwedlau Gwerin Cymru*, 92.

Chapter 18 – Miners, Coal and a Rat

The Coal Giant
Grooms, *Cewri Cymru*, 93–95.

Dic Penderyn
Radford, *Tales of South Wales*, 37–38.

The Treorchy Leadbelly
Lomax, Alan, Cultural Equity Online Archive: http://www.culturalequity.org/

The Rat with False Teeth
'Welsh Coal Mines', from Paul, Neath, 4 April 2013, http://www.welshcoalmines.co.uk/index.html.

Siôn y Gof

Gwyndaf, *Chwedlau Gwerin Cymraeg*, 62.

Stevenson, Peter, and Alison Lochhead, 'The World Turned Inside Out', in *Planet* 213, 22–31 (Aberystwyth: Planet, 2014).

The Hole

Oral tale.

The Penrhyn Strike

Oral version of history, and family tale.

The Wolf

Oral tale.

Chapter 19 – Homes, Farms and Mice

The Lady of Ogmore

Morgan, Alun, *Legends of Porthcawl and the Glamorgan Coast* (Glamorgan: D. Brown, 1974) 28–32.

The House with the Front Door at the Back

Rhys, *Celtic Folklore*. Told by Evan Williams, a smith from Rhoshirwaun.

The Cow on the Roof

Jones, *Welsh Folklore & Folk Custom*, 229–31 ('as told by a Denbighshire teamsman').

Manawydan Hangs a Mouse

Extract from *Third Branch of Y Mabinogi* (see Chapter 1).

The Muck Heap

Told by Kate Davies of Pren-gwyn to Robin Gwyndaf in 1973. National Museum of Wales, tape MWL 3892.

Chapter 20 – Courtship, Love and Marriage

The Maid of Cefn Ydfa

Morgan, *Legends of Porthcawl*, 15.

Morgan, Thomas, *The Cupid* (David Griffiths, 1869).

Rhys and Meinir

Oral tale.

Nant Gwrtheyrn: http://www.nantgwrtheyrn.org/cy

Trevelyan, *Folk-Lore and Folk-Stories of Wales*, 397.

The Odd Couple
Oral tale.

The Wish
Oral tale.

Chapter 21 – Fiddlers, Harpers and Pipers

The Gypsy Fiddler
Jarman, Eldra, and A.O.H. Jarman, *Y Sipsiwn Cymraeg* (Cardiff: University of Wales, 1979).
Roberts, Ernest, *With Harp Fiddle and Folk Tale* (Denbigh: Gee & Son, 1981).

Ffarwel Ned Puw
Sikes, *British Goblins*, 99–100.

Dic the Fiddler
Roberts, Hilda A.E., *Legends and Folk Lore of North Wales* (London: Collins, 1931) 65–67.

Morgan the Harper
Sheppard-Jones, *Welsh Legendary Tales*, 25–28.

The Harpers of Bala
Jones, *Welsh Legends and Folk-Tales*, 231–34.
Rhys, *Celtic Folklore*, 149–50.

Chapter 22 – Romani, Dancers and Cinder-Girl

Black Ellen
Jarman & Jarman, *Y Sipsiwn Cymraeg*.
Roberts, *With Harp Fiddle and Folktale*.
Sampson, John, *XXI Welsh Gypsy Folk-Tales* (Newtown: Gregynog Press, 1933).

Cinder-Girl
Sampson, John, 'Welsh Gypsy Folk-Tales, No. 18 – The Little Slut', in *Journal of Gypsy Lore Society*, Vol. 2, No. 3 (1923) 99–110.

The Dancing Girl from Prestatyn
Romany Valley Stream Project: http://www.valleystream.co.uk/

Fallen Snow
Sampson, John, Welsh Gypsy Folk-Tales, No. 34 – Fallen Snow' in *Journal of Gypsy Lore Society*, Vol. 6, No. 3 (1927), 97–101.

Chapter 23 – Settlers, Travellers and Tourists

Madoc and the Moon-Eyed People
Oral tale in North Carolina, 2015.

Wil Cefn Goch
Phillips, *The Lovers' Graves*, 56–70.

Malacara
Oral tale in Ohio, 2015.

The Texan Cattle Farmer
Oral tale.

Chapter 24 – Trains, Tramps and Roads

The Old Man of Pencader
Gerald, *The Description of Wales*, 274.

The Tales of Thomas Phillips, Stationmaster
Phillips, Thomas, *Railroad Humours, or Stories of Railway Travel* (Carmarthen: W.M. Evans & Son, 1925).

The Wily Old Welshman
Radford, *Tales of South Wales*, 53–55.

Dic Aberdaron
Gwyndaf, *Chwedlau Gwerin Cymru*, 40.
Oral tale.

Sarn Elen
From the telling of Fiona Collins.
'The Dream of Macsen Wledig', in *The Mabinogion* (see Chapter 1).
Jenkins, D.E., *Bedd Gelert, its Facts, Fairies and Folk-lore* (Porthmadog: Llewelyn Jenkins, 1899) 144–46.

Chapter 25 – Stones, Caves and Ferns

The Giantess's Apron-Full
Emerson, *Welsh Fairy-Tales*, 50.

The Stonewaller
Austin, *Haunted Anglesey*, 161–63.

The Scarecrow
Oral tale.

Owain Lawgoch
Trevelyan, *Folk-Lore and Folk-Stories of Wales*, 135–38.
Williams, in T. Crofton Croker, *Irish Legends*, 266–72.

Aladdin's Cave, Aberystwyth
Oral tales.
Sandys, Oliver, *Caradoc Evans* (London: Hurst & Blackett, n.d.).

The Ferny Man
Trevelyan, *Folk-Lore and Folk-Stories of Wales*, 89–90.

Chapter 26 – Dentists, Cockle Women and Onion Men

Don't Buy a Woodcock by its Beak
Owen, Daniel, *Fireside Tales* (Talybont: Brown Cow/Lolfa, 2011).
Translation of *Straeon y Pentan*, 1895.

Wil the Mill
Gwynn, Cyril, *Gower Yarns* (Parkmill: the Author, 1928) 45–46.
Oral tale told by Arwel John, blacksmith at Parkmill Heritage Centre.

The Penclawdd Cockle Women
Jenkins, J. Geraint, *Cockles and Mussels, Aspects of Shellfish-gathering in Wales*
(Cardiff: Welsh Folk Museum, 1984).
Radford, *Tales of South Wales*, 124–27.

Sioni Onions
Griffiths, Gwyn, *The Last of the Onion Men* (Llanrwst: Gwasg Carreg Gwalch, 2002).
Oral tale.

The Hangman who Hanged Himself
Rowe, David, *The A to Z of Curious Flintshire* (Stroud: The History Press, 2015), as told by Buckley 'mon' Jim Bentley.

Chapter 27 – Sea, Smugglers and Seventh Waves

The Ring in the Fish
Jones, *Welsh Folklore and Folk Custom*, 233–34.

Jemima Fawr and the Black Legion
Gwyndaf, *Chwedlau Gwerin Cymru*, 80.

Radford, *Tales of South Wales*, 65–66.

Walter and the Wreckers
Morgan, *Legends of Porthcawl*, 31–34.
Radford, *Tales of South Wales*, 33–36.

Potato Jones
Swansea Pictorial History: http://acs-swansea.no-ip.org/sph/sphloginpage.php

The Kings of Bardsey
Oral tales.
Stevenson, 'Retracing Wales', *Planet* 208, 68–79.

Chapter 28 – Rogues, Tricksters and Folk Heroes

Myra, Rebecca and the Mari Lwyd
Evans, Myra, *Atgofion Ceinewydd* (Aberystwyth: Cwmdeithas Llyfrau Ceredigion Gyf, 1961) 23–26.
Evans, Myra, papers in private collection.
Oral tales.
Stevenson, 'The World Turned Upside Down', in *Planet* 215, 43–55 (Aberystwyth: Planet, 2014).
Trevelyan, *Folk-Lore and Folk-Stories of Wales*, 31–33.

Twm Siôn Cati
From the telling of Dafydd Wyn Morgan.
Isaac, Margaret Rose, *The Tale of Twm Siôn Cati* (Caerleon, Apecs Press, 2005)
Radford, *Tales of South Wales*, 22–26.

The Red Bandits of Dinas Mawddwy
Gwyndaf, *Chwedlau Gwerin Cymru*, 57.

Murray the Hump
From the telling of Phil Okwedy.

The Man Who Never Was
Macintyre, Ben, *Operation Mincemeat* (London: Bloomsbury, 2010).

Chapter 29 – Swans, Wolves and Transformations

Cadwaladr and the Goat
Jones, *Welsh Legends and Folk-Tales*, 242–45.
Sikes, *British Goblins*, 53–55.

Swan Ladies

Trevelyan, *Folk-Lore and Folk-Stories of Wales*, 297–99.

Snake-Women

Trevelyan, *Folk-Lore and Folk-Stories of Wales*, 302–303.

Frog Woman and Toad Man

Gerald, *The Journey Through Wales*, 169–70.

Kilvert, Francis, *Kilvert's Diary* (London: Jonathan Cape, 1938–40) 137.

Trevelyan, *Folk-Lore and Folk-Stories of Wales*, 303–304.

Werewolves and Wolf-Girl

Collins, Fiona, *Wrexham County Folk Tales* (Stroud: History Press, 2014) 90–93.

Trevelyan, *Folk-Lore and Folk-Stories of Wales*, 295–96.

Williams, Nigel, 'Marie Trevelyan, an authoress with three names', in *Llantwit Major: Aspects of its History*, Vol. 8 (Llantwit Major: Local History Society, 2008).

Chapter 30 – Blodeuwedd, Flower and Owl

'Fourth Branch of Y Mabinogi' (see Chapter 1).

The History Press Folk Tales

Collins, Fiona, *Denbighshire Folk Tales* (Stroud: The History Press, 2011).

Collins, Fiona, *Wrexham County Folk Tales* (Stroud: The History Press, 2014).

Maddern, Eric, *Snowdonia Folk Tales* (Stroud: The History Press, 2015).

Stevenson, Peter, *Ceredigion Folk Tales* (Stroud: The History Press, 2014).

Willison, Christine, *Pembrokeshire Folk Tales* (Stroud: The History Press, 2013).

DIOLCH O GALON

Llyfrgell Genedlaethol Cymru / The National Library of Wales.
Amgueddfa Cymru / The National Museum of Wales.
Beyond the Border International Storytelling Festival.
The editors and publishers at The History Press.
Librarians, archivists, and local historians.
Folklorists, antiquarian vicars, and diarists.
Stonewallers, artists, and blacksmiths.
Dreamers, visionaries, and rebels.
Travellers of the Old Welsh Tramping Road.
Fiddlers who find fairy money in their pockets.
Harpers who fall asleep in swamps.
Songbirds who whisper in the ears of lovers.
Elephants who vanish leaving only stories behind.
Those who heard a story yesterday.
And those who will tell a tale tomorrow.

Society *for* **Storytelling**

Since 1993, the Society for Storytelling has championed the art of oral storytelling and the benefits it can provide – such as improving memory more than rote learning, promoting healing by stimulating the release of neuropeptides, or simply great entertainment! Storytellers, enthusiasts and academics support and are supported by this registered charity to ensure the art is nurtured and developed throughout the UK.

Many activities of the Society are available to all, such as locating storytellers on the Society website, taking part in our annual National Storytelling Week at the start of every February, purchasing our quarterly magazine *Storylines*, or attending our Annual Gathering – a chance to revel in engaging performances, inspiring workshops, and the company of like-minded people.

You can also become a member of the Society to support the work we do. In return, you receive free access to *Storylines*, discounted tickets to the Annual Gathering and other story-telling events, the opportunity to join our mentorship scheme for new storytellers, and more. Among our great deals for members is a 30% discount off titles in the *Folk Tales* series from The History Press website.

For more information, including how to join, please visit

www.sfs.org.uk